ANYTHII *VANILLA*

Madelynne Ellis

Mischief
An imprint of HarperCollins*Publishers*
77–85 Fulham Palace Road,
Hammersmith, London W6 8JB

www.mischiefbooks.com

A Paperback Original 2013

First published in Great Britain in ebook format by
HarperCollins*Publishers* 2012

A catalogue record for this book is
available from the British Library

ISBN-13: 978 0 00 753327 5

Automatically produced by Atomik ePublisher from Easypress

CHAPTER ONE

If she'd thought about it, then it might have happened differently. Kara didn't think. She acted. That was why she stood crushed against the railing bordering the canal with her knickers around her ankles. The sweet caress of cool air barely had time to stir against her skin before two warm fingers had replaced it. A thumb swept the line of her slit, driving her up on to toes that were already squashed into ultra-high heels. Hell, that was good. Relief swept through her muscles, replacing the tension there with sweet, sweet bellyache. She needed this. Needed it so much she was hard pressed not to grab hold of his hand and mash the whole lot against her clit. Instead, she writhed against the tease, determined to manipulate his fingers into the exact spot she needed them.

'Eager for this, aren't you?' She felt his smile rather than saw it, as he mouthed along the edge of her jaw. He had an interesting smile, a bit too big and more than a little wolfish. It was that grin that made her pause long enough to accept the drink he offered her, and then to accept being tugged out on to the dance floor, where they'd bumped and ground their way into companionable bliss. When they'd walked

1

outside, it hadn't mattered who led, or that they'd practically spoken in monosyllables all night. Thumping club hits tended to transform anything more eloquent into a series of 'eh?'s and 'what?'s. Body language was key. Body language was all that mattered now.

'Less talk,' Kara barked. There'd been too much talk in her life the last few days. She drove her mouth hard against his lips, ready to worship their generous curves. His perfect cupid's bow moulded to her wide mouth with charming precision. In response, he pressed into her, connecting them from chest to shin save for a little space occupied by his questing hand.

Back and forth, his thumb continued to sweep, until her moisture coated his fingers and turned the motion into a glide. She might be insane for this, but by God he knew how to treat her right. Her clit perked up, hard as a nut, until it was peeping from between the lips of her pussy all desperate for some direct action rather than the elusive pulls on the skin around it.

'Oh, now what have we here?' Mirth flashed from the depths of his eyes as he circled her pearl as though he were drawing a thread around it. 'Could it be I've found something important?'

Oh, lord! He'd found it all right. Damn, it was almost too sweet to tolerate.

Intense arousal flushed Kara's face. Her own need was a metallic taste in her mouth, sharp and bitter like freshly cut lime. Her nipples poked up against the fabric of her dress, desperate for a share of the action.

Jack – was it Jack? She'd never really caught his name over the pounding bass inside the club – cupped one breast. He mouthed the nipple through her dress and bra until all that remained of her was ache and need.

'Enough with the tease.'

His eyes shone with the fact that he was on to a winner. 'What tease would that be?' The devil slid two fingers into her as he spoke, provoking a groan. 'I'm sure you wouldn't want me to be lazy.'

'What I want,' she said smiling back at him, 'is for you to put that pretty mouth of yours to better use.'

'Yeah?' His wing-like eyebrows briefly lifted. The quick flicker of boyish adulation in his eyes was ridiculously endearing.

Kara wrenched aside the materials covering her breast and guided his head into place. His breath tickled her skin first, then the tip of his tongue, before he fell to working the whole nipple. 'Yes, yes, just there. Harder,' she insisted, as she wove her fingers into the back of his hair. With a mouth this good, no way was she letting him escape. She could only imagine how his mobile lips and that tongue would feel against her clit. As it was, a spark stream now connected her nipple to her cunt, where his hand continued to work. Hell, much more of this and he'd bring her off before he ever got anything out of it.

Jack seemed to realise that too. He shook his head to dislodge her grip and shifted his feet so that he could rub up against her hip. She supposed it was quite a subtle move in the scheme of things; there was certainly something enticing about having him writhe against her like that. His erection lay like a sturdy brand behind his fly, already one hundred per cent ready to satisfy. It had to be uncomfortable all caged up like that, which just made her like him all the more for not taking his hands off her to ease his own discomfort.

'Let me,' Kara insisted. She might be many things, fricking

crazy, jobless, homeless as of 7.30 this morning and tipsy as fuck, but to her way of thinking sex was definitely about give and take. Otherwise you might as well cosy up with a vibe and a good book.

Jack made no protest. She grabbed him hard around the arse, grinned in delight as his muscles tightened. He was tall and big-boned, but sleek as a panther beneath his black jeans and equally black top. The sort of man whom you could imagine creeping across the rooftops as a cat burglar or delivering boxes of Milk Tray. Not the sort of rogue that normally wetted her knickers. Fuck, but he tasted more delicious than any chocolate, peppery and citrous, mingled with the sharp tang of salt. It took a moment to release his buckle, less time to open his fly and expose his cock. Kara palmed him through his briefs, teasing him in the way he'd tormented her.

She couldn't keep it up, much as she wanted to make him sweat. She was too antsy and he was already close, that much was evident from the sharp noise he made in the back of his throat when her fist tightened around his shaft. The reflection of the fairy lights strung from the trees lining the quayside glinted in the depths of his eyes. She watched their sparkle a moment, until his eyelids drooped. 'You got something?'

His eyes snapped open immediately. 'Back pocket. Think you can reach it?'

She copped another good feel of his butt as she wrestled the foil from his pocket.

'Want to do the honours?' he asked.

'You betcha.' She was going to go stark raving crazy if she didn't get him inside her soon. Jack – Jack who was showing the first traces of a shadow around his jaw and who was going to feel fucking amazing inside her.

Jack sagged against her shoulder as she split the wrapper. The curve of his lips clove to the pulse point in her neck. He nibbled, began to suck. Damn! Kara bit her lip. It was difficult to concentrate when he was distracting her like that. Still, she took her time dressing him. She liked that he didn't rush her, which meant she got to explore his whole length as she rolled the sheath into place. His cock curved sabre-like towards his body. He was uncut, the skin drawn back like a collar around the silky-smooth tip. A small tattoo of a pentacle occupied the space just below his right hip, the ink dark against the white of his skin. If there was time and somewhere comfortable – if, if, if. She wanted to explore him more thoroughly, get him properly naked. Suddenly it was important to see if the brown thatch of hair around his groin extended upwards. She followed the silky trail to his navel, shoved his ribbed T-shirt out of the way to see the rest. Golden-brown hairs circled his nipples and filled all the space between. Beneath that sign of masculinity he was tautly muscled and every bit as sleek as his outfit suggested. Part of her actually longed to step back and admire him. If she commanded him to stay would he do it? Would he stand exposed against the iron railings, with the dark, mirrored surface of the canal behind him, and let her gorge herself on the visual feast of him? Hairy men turned her on. It didn't matter if was an unruly mass of curls upon a man's head or just thick tawny hairs upon his arms. There was something exciting about a man with some body hair, particularly a good-looking one. So many of them shaved or waxed.

She was so done with Mr Metrosexual.

Jack, perhaps sensing a growing distance between them, shimmied right up close to her, and bent his head so they were looking into one another's eyes on a level. 'Ready?'

Like hell they were, she had no idea how they were going to accomplish anything in this position.

'Hold yourself on the railings.'

Kara grasped the blue-painted metal. She gave a screech and a giggle as Jack hoisted her off her feet and dealt with her knickers. She guessed she was going home bare as they floated away on the canal. She wrapped her legs around him as he lined them up. They were in a public place, but there was nothing coy about his actions. No hesitation and definitely no embarrassment as his cock bucked eagerly at her entrance. That lack made her cheeks colour a little for both of them.

'Tell me.' He held them mere millimetres apart. 'Tell me exactly how you want it.'

Was he a talker, or just making sure he stayed out of trouble? She could hardly cry coercion if she'd begged him for it.

Kara squeezed around his hips with her thighs, dragging them a fraction closer together. 'I want you to fuck me.'

'No – I never would have guessed that.'

Sarky bugger. Shit! He'd probably drop her over the railings into the canal if she admitted any of the stuff in her head, like visions of nipple clamps and chaining him to the railings. Surely the only things that mattered here were that he turned her on and she needed him. The whys and wherefores were irrelevant; the bounty of her inner life more so.

'Nothing more than that to say?' he queried, lifting one of his wing-like brows again. 'You just want me to slide up and fill your cunt.' The way he said cunt made her literally ache with need. 'You're not after anything flashy, just a straight hard fuck.' He delivered as he punctuated the last word, filling her up so completely it took her body a moment to respond to the shock. Heavenly didn't come close to describing it. It just felt right – so goddamned incredibly right. She clamped tight to his body as he drew back to give her what she'd apparently asked for. 'You know, I'm kind of surprised. I never took you to be such a vanilla kind of girl.'

He was right. She so wasn't. What sort of strait-laced girl fucked a stranger up against the backdrop of the murky canal? Why had it taken her so long to admit that to herself, instead of constantly trying to be good?

'So why don't you tell me what really gets you off? Shall I pretend I'm a vampire and sink my teeth in? Do you like a fingertip in your arse?'

'Hold me tighter.' Their position meant they were already pretty much jammed together with no space between. Kara bent her head to his ear. She mouthed around the lobe before breathing the words. 'Come and then I want to lick you clean.'

The muscles in his face tightened into a grin, and then he picked up her and the pace again, pounding into her like it was a race they had to win.

Kara continued to mouth the side of his neck where the skin was thinnest and his pulse raced just below the surface. He was slippery and hard between her thighs. Her clit, already prepped by his earlier teasing, shot out darts of pleasure each time he made a forward thrust. Why wasn't it always this good? Why could she only get this sort of relief with a stranger in a seedy venue? Why hadn't her life worked out, and did that matter when she could get sex this good?

'Ooohh!' The buzz built and suddenly burst. She screamed, panted, scored a few lines across his back. He continued to fill her up the whole while, until the moment passed and she realised he was still hard and hadn't come.

Kara shook herself free of his arms. She knelt down on the

quayside. Took a little risk – what the heck – and closed her mouth over the length of him. She'd said she was going to lick him clean. Well, instead she was going to suck him off.

The plan met with no resistance from Jack. Nah, his knees buckled a bit, but he had some handy railings to cling to, which was good, because she wasn't letting him go. He tasted too nice: part her, part him, the whole ridiculously sexy.

Kara steadied herself, with one palm flat against his inner thigh, the other wrapped around the base of his cock. She liked that he wasn't too long. He was nicely proportioned and she got one hell of a kick out of roving her tongue over the flare of the head and tickling the sweet spot just below the eye. When he started trying to claw at her hair in order to drag her closer, she worked with the roll of his hips.

'You're good at this. Oh, sweetheart.' His knuckles were white against the vivid blue railing.

'Are you going to come?' she asked, grinning up at him in a facetious manner.

'So close.'

They were back to the depth of discourse they'd shared inside the club. 'I want to watch.' Actually, not just watch. She wanted to watch and do. Kara rose and stood beside him with her back to the railing. She cupped his length with one hand and shoved her other hand inside her skirt so that she could rub herself in time with the thrust of his cock through the ring of her fingers. The low-level spark of her previous orgasm rekindled immediately. They almost raced. Who could cross the finish line first? Who could ejaculate the furthest? OK, he won hands down on that one. He was beautiful as he came, his face kind of screwed up and tortured looking, eyes closed, teeth gritted, as if he was doing something painful or hideous. Yet in those few moments he belonged to her totally.

Jack opened his eyes and stared at her. 'You're a dirty minx,' he scoffed as he watched her give in to a minor explosion. The second big O of the day just never lived up to the first. Then he hitched up his jeans and tucked his cock out of sight. 'Got somewhere to go?' he asked. By which he meant: let's continue this somewhere more comfortable.

'Yeah – yeah, I have. I'm good.' She dropped a kiss upon the tip of his nose, backed off, then returned to press another to those delicious lips of his. Then Kara was off, trotting across the tarmac back towards the club. She couldn't face an awkward parting in the morning; better that they went separate ways now. And she definitely wasn't looking for a relationship. No way. Not for a good long time.

'Hey, where are you going?' He moved forward as if he were about to jog after her.

Kara laughed and waved. 'Back to my wedding party.' She hoped he got the emphasis on *my*. The girls were probably scouring the dance floor for her by now. Being tipsy and high on the aftermath of awesome sex meant she could just about tolerate the thought of being found. As far as celebrations went, this one sucked, and sucked in a truly pointless, ridiculous way. It wasn't a hen night, a point on which she'd had to correct several people. It was the fill-in party for what ought to have been her wedding night and an orgy load of sex in a hotel room before jetting off to Hawaii. Only Gavin David 'Tosspot' Covey had gone and ruined that by being a clingy control freak who insisted on knowing her whereabouts 24/7. More importantly, instead of apologising when she'd called the wedding off, he'd gawped at her in horror over the deposits they'd lose. No way was she signing up for a lifetime with him. She hoped the plane carrying him and Gemma – *you are so not my best friend considering how fast you jumped in to console him* – over the Atlantic was hit by lightning and dropped out of the sky. It seemed appropriate punishment somehow, except that she didn't want to hurt anyone else on board so maybe they'd have to accidentally fall out of an open door or something.

Damn! And now her good mood was gone. Time to reinstate it with alcohol. A lone tear trickled down her face as she slipped back into the nightclub via the fire exit. At least she'd just had the most glorious sex she'd had in months, far better than that painting-by-numbers crap she'd been enduring with Gavin.

'Hey, Kara, there you are.' Her sister clamped a hand tight around her arm. 'You've about thirty drinks lined up.'

She hoped that was Karen's usual exaggeration.

'Come and play catch up.'

* * *

Kara woke disoriented in an unfamiliar room. Sunlight so bright she could barely open her eyes flooded in through sheet-glass walls that surrounded her on three sides. Where the hell? For a horrible moment she feared she'd taken up some fool on his offer and ended up in his bed. Only there didn't appear to be anyone beside her. Kara shook her head to try and dislodge the grogginess. Slowly her vision corrected. Karen's place – she was in her sister's conservatory, huddled beneath a throw on the garden swing they'd brought inside for the winter. No wonder nausea bubbled in her stomach like she'd swallowed poison. She'd been swinging in a hammock all night, and she was always travel sick.

The wail of her phone that had woken her compounded the ache in her head. Kara flailed around and eventually wrestled it out from the pile of discarded clothes she must have torn off in the dark. Not Gavin, she prayed, as she unlocked the phone screen. She never wanted to speak to him again. She'd already deleted his number but that was no guarantee that he'd done the same.

Christopher, the caller ID flashed up. 'What do you want, baby brother?' she croaked. Her throat was drier than a carton of crispy fried squid.

'Oh good, you are still alive.'

Kara resisted the urge to tell him to fuck the hell off and opted instead to swallow the water she'd had foresight enough to bring to bed with her last night, but not wits enough left at the time to drink. Didn't he realise she was off limits today, pre-booked for wallowing in a post-my-wedding-didn't-happen party haze?

'I heard a rumour that you and Karen crawled in around dawn.'

Fell, was more accurate. They'd only crawled after they tripped over the doormat. Thinking of which, boy, did her knees ache. Karen really needed to get a rug to put over those tiles. 'What did you want?' While it was entirely possible he'd called merely to be vindictive, even that couldn't explain the hint of excitement in her brother's voice.

'I got the job.' He gave a pause so she could make appropriate noises. 'I'm off to New Zealand for twenty-six weeks to work on that sci-fi flick I've been talking about. Plus, I'm focus puller not clapper loader.'

Kara pulled a cushion over her head and settled down again. The pillow smelled faintly musty, like a caravan that had been locked up for too long. However, it did allow her to open her eyes without being dazzled. The conservatory had already reached temperate and was headed for blistering within another forty minutes or so. 'Does that mean you get to operate the camera rather than just load the film?' she asked. Chris had explained the various camera-related roles dozens of times, but she'd never yet assimilated the facts beyond something to do with angles, trajectories and making the images crisper. 'That's wonderful! Great news.' Faking exuberance only compounded her headache. 'Couldn't you have waited until this evening to tell me?'

'Oh, are you hung over?' he crowed. 'And no, it couldn't wait.' The line crackled and she guessed he was in the car on loudspeaker. 'I've a flight to catch. I'm on my way to the airport now, and you haven't heard the best bit yet.'

An enormous yawn stretched Kara's jaw as she closed her eyes and tried to relax her brain while she waited to make appropriate 'wow' noises over whichever major star he was going to be working with. Unless he was about to offer her a job as chief pamperer to Johnny Depp and throw in a ticket to New Zealand, this absolutely could have waited.

'You know that place I was looking at,' Christopher said instead, which surprised her into jolting upright, and caused the swing to start rocking. Kara bounced against the cushions and dry heaved.

'I didn't get it, but it's OK, because I found somewhere else that's twice as good.'

'That's great,' she said. Somehow she managed to disentangle one foot from the throw and place it on the floor, thus bringing the swing to a tremulous halt. 'So, you've bought a house but you're flying to New Zealand.' Hopeless timing was obviously a genetically wired family trait.

'It's a barn rather than a house, and it's on an island.'

'You mean like Lindisfarne or the Isle of Wight?'

'Nah, smaller. More like St Michael's Mount only with

fewer tourists. It's called Liddell Island. It's less than a mile across.'

'Where's that?'

'It's just off the coast.'

Well, duh, she'd figured that. Where else was it going to be? She couldn't see him moving to the Norfolk Broads.

'Listen, K. I've got all the paperwork done. I just need you to pick up the keys for me. You'll do that, right? You don't mind.'

Of course she did. She'd rather not get out of bed today. Although, considering how much said bed kept moving, rising might not be such a bad plan. 'Yes, I'll do it. Just tell me where.' She gave a sigh.

'Thanks, Kara. Look, it needs a bit of work. I figured you could hang out there and fix it up while I'm away.'

She ought to have known there'd be more to this than just collecting some keys. Chris had a talent for layering things. He'd get you to agree to one thing and next thing you knew you were signed up for a month of hell. She was about to turn him down when he uttered the magic words. 'I'll pay you.' That put an entirely different spin on things. Decorating was hardly her favourite pastime, but ... 'It has to be better than hanging out at Karen's or going back to mum's, right?' Exactly, anything, bar being locked in a room with Gavin, was better than occupying a room in the family home. And since she was homeless – having sold her place to live with Gavin – and jobless – plain old economic downturn – this was likely the best offer coming her way.

'All right. I said I'd do it. Give me some directions and tell me where to get the keys from.' She jotted down some notes on the edge of the TV guide as Chris went through the details.

'You'll need to check the tide timetable before you make the crossing. The causeway floods at high tide for several hours. Once you're on the island, you pick the keys up from Alaric Liddell at the fort.'

'Little of Little Island,' she joked.

'Liddell,' Chris corrected.

'Yeah, I got it.' Kara grimaced at the phone. 'The Liddell king of the castle.'

On the other end of the line, Chris huffed. 'Now you're just being silly. Besides, it's a fort, not a castle. Don't you know the difference? I thought you did history.'

'Evidently I missed the lesson on forts.' Just as he'd missed the lesson on humour. 'Is there anything else I need to know?'

'Not that I can think of. Listen, I'm coming up to the turnoff for the airport. Skype me about the house and what needs doing and I'll transfer you the money. Try and get there without flushing the car away. Talk to you later.'

'Will do. Bye.'

He hung up without muttering a corresponding farewell.

'Was that Chris?' Karen wafted in straight from the shower smelling of lime and carrying two mugs of tea. She passed one over to Kara. 'I had to get up. Mum phoned to nag me about you. She wants you over there later so you can have a talk. She's still pissed off at you about the wedding.'

'Yeah, I got that even though Gavin's the controlling twerp, it's still all my fault that the wedding is off. I think she actually suggested that I didn't look after him right. Like if I baked him apple pie every night and did as I was told there wouldn't be a problem.'

Karen's face wrinkled in sympathy. Her lips made a tight pout. 'I know. You don't have to convince me. I went out with you last night to commiserate, didn't I? That and I've already told you I think you were right to call it off, but you know how mum is. She was all geared up for the big day and now she's disappointed because she doesn't get to don her Donna Karan suit and flaunt it in front of your new in-laws. Give her time and let her have her rant. Deep down I'm sure she knows it was the only choice you had.'

It was bleeding typical of her family that everyone was worried over their mother's disappointment and not the wreckage Gavin had made of her life. Kara scowled into her tea cup. Perhaps Chris had done her more of a favour than she'd initially thought. There was sure to be a downside – where her brother was concerned there always was, like she'd discover his new house was roofless – but anywhere would be an improvement on here.

'Kara, I'm sorry I can't offer you a bed here, but you know there's not space,' Karen started awkwardly. 'Andrew will be back in an hour with the kids. You're going to have to stay at mum's.'

'It's OK. Chris has offered me his place.'

'Isn't Richard there?'

Kara shrugged and let Karen think that she was holing up with their brother's on-off live-in lover at his rented apartment. Doing a disappearing act seemed like a grand plan. Isolating herself on Liddell Island, cut off from the mainland by the tide for hours at a time, suddenly gained magical appeal. No one would know her. She'd be able to wipe the slate clean and begin again. Maybe even have some fun. She'd made that promise to herself last night.

Karen sat hunched in her dressing gown, with her palms curled around her cup. She opened her mouth twice and closed it, before blowing the steam off her tea. 'Where'd you disappear to last night? You were gone ages.'

'Was I?'

'You know you were. Was it that guy you were dancing with?'

Kara shrugged. 'Dunno what you're implying. Who was he?' In God's honest truth she couldn't recall his name. Her memories of him were all of raw sensations, but his appearance she could only recall in the loosest sense – broad brushstrokes forming a rudimentary sketch. She probably ought to regret that, since he'd been a damn good lay.

'Let me have a shower and then I'll be off,' she said, leaving her sister to brood over whatever folly she believed Kara had committed. So she'd had a one-night stand. Big deal! Get over it. She was a single girl and as long as her actions didn't hurt anyone, then what was the problem with her having a little fun? Or even a lot of it.

CHAPTER TWO

The sky had turned indigo and the weather gloomy by the time Kara reached the Devon coastline and saw Liddell Island rising like a Titan's throne from the ocean. A zing of anticipation jigged beneath her skin as she gazed across at its ridge of rocky spires. Karen had once said that their brother had OD'd on Dracula at too young an age and one glance at Liddell Island only confirmed that. It was a little piece of Transylvania stuck out in the ocean.

After two hundred metres of sea spray that necessitated having the windscreen wipers on full, the causeway broadened on to a shingle bay. Kara pulled up and got out of the car. A quick recce showed that the only building was locked up for the night, so she had no choice but to brave the upward trek to the fort. Orange residue stained the looming cliff face as she climbed along a gravel track. To her left a thick rope supported by iron staves formed the only barrier between her and a sheer drop. The situation worsened at the top, where a rope bridge provided the only means of crossing a vast gorge. 'Bloody hell!' She was going to kill Chris the next time she saw him. Kara wobbled across the bridge without looking down, only to be greeted by gargoyles and a nearly sheer flight of steps.

By the time she'd staggered to the top, ducked the port-cullis, found the bell pull and rung it with all her might, she was out of breath and ready for a nice sit down. Hopefully, the owner might take pity. Then again, considering the old-fashioned iron-pinned door she was facing, she half expected Igor to answer.

Instead, the barking of dogs chorused the arrival of the human inhabitant.

'Toby! Horace!' A male voice boomed over the patter of paws on the floor tiles. Kara blinked into the yellow light that shone out of the open door. 'Good evening. Are you lost?' A bare-chested man stood before her.

Kara gave a little croak. OK, Christopher was forgiven. Whatever she'd been expecting – crooked little old man – it wasn't this.

Long blond hair fanned over the top of his shoulders and rested at the top of his tattooed biceps.

'The causeway's crossable now, though I'd recommend a torch,' he remarked without even looking at her. He released one of the huge dogs, whom he had by the collar, in order to plunge his hand into a box of LED keychain lights. He offered one to Kara which she took automatically while warily fending off the freed hound, who danced about her trying to shove its head up her skirt. 'Um, sorry.' He dragged the dog off while the second oversized pooch tried to worm its way between his legs.

'I'm not lost. I'm looking for Alaric Liddell. I'm supposed to pick up some keys,' she said as she clicked the little purple light on and off. 'Do you know where I can find him? I was told the fort.'

The hard lines of his face softened into a tentative smile. He had pale grey-blue eyes, which made a sudden appraising sweep of her body. 'Mrs North? I was told the buyer was a man.'

'Oh no, I'm not married,' Kara hastily explained, not wanting him to think she was off limits, considering the rather pleasant sexual frisson that zapped between them as he took in her windblown appearance. 'He's gay. My brother, I mean. I'm here on his behalf because he's gone abroad. I'm Kara North.' She stuck out a hand, which he declined in favour of grabbing both dogs by the collars and heaving them inside.

'I'm Ric Liddell. Come on in and I'll find you those keys.' He grinned at her showing a few too many lovely white teeth. 'I think they're in the study. Toby. Horace.' He pushed the dogs out of the way to allow her to enter unhindered, then stepped back so that she could walk ahead of him into the hall.

'Thanks.' Kara stepped warily over the threshold. Stranger-danger warnings pushed to the back of her mind in favour of the upswing in her lustometer. Ric Liddell was far too hot to be mouldering away on a fleabitten rock. She prayed he wasn't gay and that Chris hadn't sent her to a heterosexual woman's idea of purgatory.

'Have you come far?'

'Not really. Although it's taken a couple of hours because I had to wait for the tide.' Kara turned to face him again only to be blessed with a glimpse of his back as he bolted the door. Strong shoulders gave way to a trim waist. His black jeans rode low over his hips, held in place by a studded belt, while a huge tattoo of an ankh, entwined within a coil of roses, decorated the length of his spine and shoulder blades.

'Wow!'

He turned his head to look at her, his eyebrows raised in question. Now in the light, with fewer shadows to mask his features, she realised he was slightly older than she'd first assumed, perhaps five or six years her senior. Not old, but no spring lamb either. Somehow that added to his appeal.

'Your back … it's – wow … It must have hurt.'

He shrugged as if to suggest it was no big deal, and then took the lead again, his bare feet making a soft patter on the tiles as he crossed the hall and opened the door on to what she assumed was a study. Two of the walls were lined with books, locked way in old-fashioned wood and glass cabinets. A couple of leather armchairs sat cosily before an open fireplace and a big 38mm camera lay on one of the seats. The two Dalmatians immediately pattered over to slouch before the blaze.

Kara dutifully trooped into the room, in awe of the money that had created this place. His family had probably owned it for generations and ruled over the local populace.

Ric headed over to a bureau on the far side of the fireplace. He rummaged through a few drawers but didn't appear to turn up anything.

'Can I help?' Kara asked, though she was quite enjoying watching his bum wiggle inside those low-slung jeans. Her palms were near itching to cop a good feel of him.

She hadn't thought herself repressed in any way, but the world seemed a whole lot more attractive since her split with Gavin. Maybe that's what being single did to you. Turned you into a compulsive flirt and left you hankering after sex any way you could get it. She'd certainly become ridiculously horny over the last few days. That guy last night – damned if she could remember more about him than how good he felt – and now she was gawping at the arse of a man she'd only just met. Chris would no doubt tell her she was over-compensating for being dumped, only she hadn't been. Quite the opposite: she'd been coddled until she couldn't stand it any more. Although maybe there was something to the notion of her trying to prove that guys still found her attractive.

'No – it's fine. They're around here somewhere.' Ric lifted his head and looked straight at her. For a fleeting moment Kara remained pinned by his gaze while she imagined some indulgent scene of them colliding in a sexual frenzy rather than in any romantic way. His gaze swept over her and then he gave a disarming grin. 'Actually, maybe I left them in the studio.' He swooped past her back into the hall. 'Come on up.'

'Up' was a tightly wound spiral staircase. Kara chased him to the top, where she emerged into a vast white space that she guessed lay over the entryway. Here, blank walls loomed over her, seeming disproportionately high in the absence of decoration. At floor level, all around the perimeter, picture frames leant against the wall in piles. An impressive array of photographic equipment occupied the centre space. Ric stood raking through the pockets of a leather coat that hung on the back of a folding metal chair.

'You're a photographer.'

'Yeah.'

Good one, Kara. Why don't you state the obvious?

'Are you the Liddell family equivalent of Lord Lichfield?' This was some serious set-up he had here, way beyond any kind of hobby studio.

'Nah – I think the only thing I have in common with Patrick Lichfield is that we've both done *Harpers* covers. A-list celebs don't really do it for me.'

So, he didn't like skinny models and glitterati. Probably explained why he chose to live out here on this godforsaken rock of an island. 'No – what do you like?' Kara inched towards him.

'Porn,' he muttered, blowing away her expectation of

coastal landscapes and wildlife photography. She stuck a finger in her ear and wiggled, thinking maybe she'd misheard. Mr blond and sexy couldn't possibly have said anything so crude. Only he had. He most certainly had and, what's more, he didn't even look guilty about it. 'Here, take a look.' He picked up a nearby picture frame and swung it round.

Kara carefully averted her gaze, having no wish to gawp at a naked woman's pussy. Only it was hard not to catch even a teensy glimpse considering the size of the image, plus she didn't want to appear rude, or worse prudish.

As it turned out, the picture was of a man not a woman, and was far too arty to be considered porn, though the black and white image was certainly lewd.

The model looked vaguely familiar too. Not that you could see a lot of his face.

Ric grinned at her and gave a low chuckle. He put the print down and waved her towards the stacks of framed photographs. 'Go ahead. Take a look while I hunt these keys. If you find anything you like we can negotiate a discount, seeing as how we're going to be neighbours. That barn needs something to brighten it up. You've seen it, right?'

'No.'

'OK.'

'OK,' she agreed, her voice a little dry. It felt too intimate to be going through this stuff after such a short acquaintance. That, and it seemed her apprehensions about Christopher's impulse purchase might be on the mark.

The photos weren't all of men. There were women and groups too, but the emphasis was definitely adult, and, more often than not, kinky. They reminded her of the bacchanalian scenes you sometimes found in old houses and castles, painted before Victorian prudery took hold. Back when people were a little more honest about sex, in the way she absolutely intended to be from now on.

The one-night stand she'd had with – Jack? – was the most honest thing she'd done in years. Ever, perhaps.

'Do you sell much?' Kara asked.

'You'd be surprised.'

Maybe not. She could see the appeal of it. It wasn't coy. It was what it was without making a pretence of being anything else, and it was beautiful because of that forthrightness and aggression. Nor did it take much imagining to envisage the response he got from buyers and gallery owners, considering how lovely he was with his strong jaw and Scandinavian pallor.

She understood his honesty in describing it as porn a little better after fanning through the images. Its intended purpose was to arouse, something it was certainly succeeding in doing to her. If Ric's presence had a dynamic effect upon her libido, then his artwork threatened to push that to the max.

Realising that she was growing uncomfortably aroused, Kara squirmed her legs together. 'Here's a good one.' Ric moved up close behind her, so that she could feel his heat even though they weren't touching. His hand shot out to reveal the contents of another frame.

This one featured a very beautiful and liberated young woman, with masses of long hair that flowed over her shoulders and gently caressed the points of her nipples. One man bent before her in a position of submission, one hand reaching out to her beseechingly. His other hand was already clasped firmly behind his back encased in a handcuff held by another man whose erection was angled suggestively towards the submissive man's arse. Another male figure stood behind the woman. His big hands squeezed tight her breasts, as he ploughed her from the rear. It was impossible to look upon the group and not to become caught up in the situation that had created the scene. Kara felt its power deep in her sex. It tugged at that part of her psyche that fantasised about sex with multiple men. She'd never done it. Who had? No one she'd ever spoken to, though among her friends they mostly agreed the idea was hot. Two cocks giving you pleasure instead of one, two erections to play with, so that you could suck upon one while the other satisfied the ache in your cunt.

OK, not all of her friends agreed with her on that. Some of them considered coping with one man hell enough.

Lucky girl, though, whoever the model was. As if Ric sensed he'd hit upon her fantasy, he drew her attention to another image. In this one the same four figures nestled together, their loins and bottoms all perfectly aligned so that they were joined in a lewd chain. 'Are they?' she asked. The men were clearly pleasuring the female model from front and back, while the third man also penetrated the arse of the handcuffed man. Kara gave a low groan. She didn't think she'd ever been so turned on by an image before, but something about it combined with Ric's nearness grabbed her by the guts and rode her for all its erotic worth. This one she'd definitely like to hang over her bed. Sadly, whatever bed there was in the barn, it didn't belong to her, and Christopher didn't share her tastes.

Ric nudged against her as he returned the picture to the floor. For just a moment she swore she felt the ridge of his cock pressing up against the seam of her buttocks. Was he turned on? Did he grow erect looking over his own work? How did he maintain his composure while working? For several seconds she literally ached with the desire to push back against him and discover the truth. If she turned around, would she see the evidence lying trapped behind his fly – would she see it in his eyes? Fleetingly, she wondered if Ric ever photographed himself and, if he did, what parts he bared to the camera.

Arousal thickened between her legs, and a rosy blush began to infuse her skin. What would he do if she pressed back or reached out and touched him? What if she were direct enough to touch his cock? Would they make it as far as the bed, or simply fuck hard and fast amidst the disarray of photographic equipment?

Kara's mouth grew dry. She slowly moistened her lips.

She could picture it so clearly. They'd end up naked, wrapped up in exposed film, surrounded by countless dirty images.

Damn, what was she thinking? Kara risked a surreptitious glance at Ric, who gave away nothing of his thoughts, only a low-level twinkle in his blue eyes hinting at any kind of wickedness in him. What was happening to her? She didn't routinely jump into bed with strangers, at least not since the days before Gavin. Yet here she was craving the affections of a man she'd only just met, whose nearness had rendered her knickers sopping.

It took every ounce of willpower for Kara to remain still. Every single damn ounce, because what she really wanted to do was to wriggle and cosy up against Ric's cock, and to know that he was ready for her.

'About those keys,' he murmured, not quite breaking the spell she'd woven in her head, for his mouth lay just shy of her neck. If she turned now, their lips would almost certainly meet. 'I can't seem to put my hands on them.'

Sod the keys! Having him put his hands on her would be far more gratifying. It took a supreme effort of will to smile at him indulgently instead, like it didn't matter that her only home at present was whatever decrepit barn her brother had bought, which she couldn't get into until Ric produced the keys, or that her nipples were so taut they were poked up against her blouse virtually demanding his touch. It didn't matter that her cunt was wet either, or that it ached for the sensation of something hard to fill it. Or that whatever bed she eventually made it to would be cold and empty.

'I'll keep looking.' He gave her an endearing and rather knowing grin, one that suggested he guessed more of her thoughts than she cared to share, and maybe, just maybe shared one or two of them. 'That said – it is getting a bit late to be trekking over there at this time of night. The visibility sucks and I wouldn't want you stumbling about hurting yourself.'

'Yeah? What are the alternatives?' She leaned a little closer to him.

Ric's tongue briefly wetted his lower lip. 'I've a spare bed.'

'Right. I couldn't – I mean, I don't want to impose.'

Damn it with the social niceties, she definitely wanted to impose. She wanted to jump right into his bed, and have him touch her between her legs, where good girls who had just broken up with their fiancés weren't supposed to ask to be touched. Then again, she'd spent long enough pretending to be the good girl that at heart she wasn't. Time she stopped holding herself to other people's standards and lived a little.

'You won't be.' He reached out and very briefly touched a lock of her hair where it rested against her cheek. 'Besides, it's my fault. I should have been more organised and had those keys set out ready.'

'I could bunk down in my car,' Kara ventured, not really

wanting to. Her poor old VW Golf was only just windproof. Even with the heater turned to max she'd have to shiver to keep warm.

The promise of a hot body versus a crappy heater equalled no choice at all.

Maybe it was time to be bad.

People would forgive her. They'd say the break-up had sent her off the rails.

Oh, yes. She wanted to do wicked things with this man. She had no doubts that Alaric Liddell knew how to make a woman sing. He literally oozed sex appeal, like it was a pheromone, from his shirtless back to his beautiful bare toes. She wanted to do bad things, and she wanted to do them now.

'Don't be ridiculous.' He leaned closer still so that she could smell his aftershave and the musky bass note of his underlying scent. 'It's no problem at all.' Her pussy clenched tight in anticipation. Her folds were already moist and swollen. *Kiss me.* Her entreaty rang in her head. She needed him to touch her. She wanted to come.

Instead, Ric stepped back. She'd missed her cue.

'Come on back down and I'll fix us a drink. I can show you over to the barn in the morning.' His grey-blue eyes glittered with mischief. Then his arm shot out, neatly trapping her in the entrance to the stairwell. His palm lowered from the wall to caress her cheek where a few strands of blond hair clung to her skin. 'Don't worry. I don't ruthlessly adhere to the old ways.'

'Old ways?'

He laughed; the sound seemed to tickle her insides all the way down to her stomach. 'Welcome to Liddell Island.' He leaned in, so that her taut nipples brushed pleasurably against his chest, while his mouth closed over hers.

Kara gasped as his kisses zapped fire all the way down to her cunt. Then he took her by the hand and led her back downstairs to the study.

CHAPTER THREE

Kara stood befuddled by the doorway, a glass of malt whisky clutched tightly within her hand, staring at the black-lettered document that granted the Liddells of the islands certain rights over the island's inhabitants, the primary one being the right to tame any maiden that came to live in their domain.

'This was never upheld, though,' she croaked. The tingle of Ric's kiss still lingered on her lips, while the sight of his still naked torso did nothing to calm her raging libido.

'I assure you it was. There's documentary evidence.' He waved at the shelves of books surrounding them. 'Lists of who and when, and how old they were and where they came from. Even some stuff about whom they went on to marry, although details about the actual main events are pretty scanty.' He edged towards her again as he spoke, having returned the spirits decanter to its home.

'Blessedly so, I'd have thought. Most of them must have been scared out of their wits at being summoned up here to warm the master's bed for the night.' Somehow she doubted many of Ric's ancestors had been quite so beautifully put together. Physically, she got off on the wiry, hard-edged make-up of his physique, and that swathe of flaxen hair. And no way had they smelled as good. His scent, a perfect blend of good old-fashioned male spice and expensive aftershave, reached her at that very moment, sending her senses into another meltdown. He led her across to an armchair, and bent down by its side.

A faint smile played upon his generous lips. 'Don't you care to know how others enjoy sex?'

She cared to know how he enjoyed sex.

Kara blinked at him uncertainly, unsure if he was leading her somewhere or just teasing. He knew she'd enjoyed his welcome kiss, because she hadn't been able to stop herself groaning. 'I've never thought about it.'

'Oh!' He nodded. 'If I revived the practice, I'd make sure to record every aspect.'

'You'd photograph it.' Kara swallowed slowly around the sudden tightness that gripped her whole body including her throat. Heat zipped between them like fireflies.

'Film,' he corrected.

Damn, was he seriously suggesting this? The way he looked her right in the eyes as he spoke rather implied he was. Kara rubbed her fingers over her lips to hide her nervousness. She wasn't camera-shy like some folks she knew, but she'd never before considered allowing herself to be filmed having sex. Was that even what he was really suggesting?

Perhaps sensing her uncertainty, Ric dipped on to one knee before her and removed the whisky tumbler from her grip. 'What do you think? Are you shocked?'

'No, of course …' Damn it, yes, she was. And intrigued, and aroused, and petrified.

Gently, Ric pressed a kiss to her curled fingers, which caused every nerve in Kara's body to light up like sparklers. Oh God! They were going to fuck. No, judging by the look in his eyes and the fact that she had to avert her gaze because her cheeks burned with embarrassment, they were going to do something far less straightforward and far dirtier than that.

Kara's clit perked up immediately. Damn, she didn't want to wait while he set up lights and a camera. She reached a hand out towards him. Made that first contact, but touching him in the centre of his chest.

Ric wasn't hairy in the way her one-night stand had been, but nor was he man-sculpted. A few springy curls skirted the hollow of his navel, and thickened where his stomach flattened out. No doubt if she followed that line, she'd find a crisp thatch above his loins.

'Are you sure about this?' Ric ran his tongue over his canines in a fox-like fashion. 'Are we going to start up the old tradition together?'

She didn't believe for a second she was the first woman he'd done this with. 'Am I expected to just fall into your arms, or make some attempt to fend you off?'

'Do you want to fend me off?'

A tiny cry escaped her throat. He had to know that she didn't. Damn, if he so much as touched her again she'd jump. 'Maybe. I don't know anything about you. I don't even know if those keys are actually missing.'

'Ah.' His eyebrows hitched a fraction. She hadn't meant anything by it but, by God, she'd hit on the truth. He'd known where they were all along. The swift glance he made towards the desk confirmed it.

Despite her desires riding her like a bitch, Kara grew momentarily serious. They hadn't known one another, but he'd made a snap decision earlier. He'd chosen not to be honest within seconds of her crossing his threshold, like she'd tripped some sort of slut alert and he wanted in on that action.

31

Kara pushed up out of her seat. 'If you've hidden them, if you've been playing me ... I'll –'

'You'll what?'

'I'll ...'

'Sorry,' he pleaded before she had a chance to ruin all the lovely tension they'd built up. 'They're not lost. I didn't hide them, if that's what you think. I just haven't handed them over yet.'

'Why?'

'Not that it's a great defence, but I don't get very much company up here. Especially not beautiful company that didn't just knock on the door in order to use the facilities. Besides, you couldn't have trekked over to the barn in the dark with this wind anyway.' Certainly the wind had got up. Even cocooned inside the metre-thick walls of the fort you could hear it howling. 'Forgive me.' His hand settled lightly upon her calf.

Kara froze. Oh, God, it wasn't right that a touch there should have so much power. Her pussy instantly flooded with heat.

'Where are they?' she asked tremulously.

'The keys? Oh, Kara – don't be a spoilsport, not when you're enjoying this just as much as I.' His hand crept a little higher up her leg, and disappeared under the hem of her skirt.

'Give me those keys.'

'I will. As soon as I've made a proper apology.'

Hell, he was pushy, and she really ought to stop him rubbing her inner thigh like that, because it was ridiculously pleasant, and he was a liar, and obviously not to be trusted, and a cad who only wanted her for one thing.

It just happened to be the same thing she wanted him for.

He was on both knees now, his lips closing in on the spot

where his hand lay warming her thigh. 'I'm going to kiss your cunt now. Say yes, please, Kara.'

'Oh, God!'

'I don't think he's any real jurisdiction here, do you? It's far too wild, and far too lonely.' He lifted up her skirt so that every inch of her legs was exposed along with the fabric of her knickers. 'Hm, on or off. Decisions, decisions. I know.' He wriggled his fingers into the seams of her panties and drew them down to her thighs. 'Much better, don't you think?'

'Um ... I don't know.'

'How can you not know –' he laughed, clearly enjoying her discomfort '– whether your knickers are best left on or off? Surely the issue is a simple one. If they're on, I can do this. And you want me to do this, don't you? You want me to make that apology, and if they're off I can't.' The very tip of his tongue ran along the split of her sex. Kara grabbed tight hold of the cabinet at her rear, and then changed her mind and laced her fingers in his hair instead.

Damn, that felt good.

'Off,' she squeaked. 'They're definitely better off.' She squirmed against his tongue, trying to get him exactly where she wanted him.

'Yeah – then why don't you step right out of them?'

Yes, absolutely. Why didn't she? Only they seemed to get snagged around her ankles and he didn't let up with that tongue of his. It tickled every sensitive nerve-ending in her body all at once, and that was before he lashed it softly against her clit.

Kara's fists clenched tight in his hair. She was probably pulling a little too hard, but he didn't object, rather he seemed to thrive on the sheer intensity of the moment. The sweet massage had caused her sex to plump, making it difficult to

33

keep still. She felt dizzy, uncertain. Fire burned in her cheeks and her womb. God help her, if he kept it up, she would come right against his mouth before he received any reward for his efforts besides a glorious stiffy. Then again, maybe that's what he got off on.

'Don't, you're gonna …'

'I'm going to what?' She felt his smile as a rub of his cheek against her thigh. His next move concentrated his efforts on her clitoris. He tickled and petted the stiff little nub until she was totally undone. Her hips rolled of their own volition, pushing the whole of her pussy up against his mouth, wordlessly begging him for more, for him to never ever cease.

'Pull up your top,' he insisted. 'Show me your tits.'

Kara wrenched her clingy top up over her bra. Her breasts were achy, the nipples pronounced against the satin fabric that confined them.

'Touch yourself.'

She wasn't sure what he was getting out of the demand. It wasn't as if he was positioned to enjoy the view, for his attention remained on her pleasure. Kara understood a little better when she nipped one nipple between her thumb and fingertip. A pulse fired between her breast and her cunt, linking the two and making her orgasm ride up fast.

It broke as she squeezed both nipples hard and his tongue completed the circuit, dabbing against her clit. She sobbed into his shoulder when he rose and held her tight.

Ric didn't remain still for long. First his lips swept against hers, bringing a second wave of heat to her insides. The kiss was by far the dirtiest she'd ever shared. The taste of her body clung to his lips, while the scent of her arousal flooded the air. Although shirtless, Ric remained otherwise properly dressed. Kara reached for his belt buckle, only for him to grin and step back. Still, the ridge of his erection showed clearly behind his fly.

'I thought you wanted to know where those keys are.'

'They're not in your pants?'

'No,' he grinned. 'But let's see if you can find them before I get fully into yours.' He led her over to the bureau, not even giving her a moment to straighten out her clothes, and bent her over the polished surface so that her face lay close to the myriad little drawers set into the top. 'They're definitely in one of those. Shall we see if you can find them before I make you come again?'

He already had a head start, for one hand immediately wedged between her thighs, where it confidently stroked her still swollen clit. Kara gave a desperate whimper. She couldn't concentrate while he did that. Nor did she really care to find the keys right now. She wasn't about to sacrifice this for a faceful of biting cold wind and a night in her car wondering what could have been.

Ric's breath tickled her ear. So too did his hair. 'Ready?'

'No, wait. What does the winner get? You're not exactly convincing me that I want these keys.'

'Bedding rights. One time, wherever, whenever.' His breath tickled as it whispered past her ear. 'And I don't make this offer every day. Go.'

Kara reached out and tugged open the first of the drawers. Her current position didn't allow her to see inside, so she had to rely on touch – paperclips, another one of those LED torches he had so many of, but no keys. She yanked open the second drawer without closing the first, just as she heard the slide of his zipper. The crackle of a foil wrapper immediately followed.

Damn, she wanted to crane her head and look at him,

in order to know what his cock was like. She liked visuals, though she was pretty sure he was going to feel damn nice. Ric stood so close behind that even if she did turn she wouldn't have gained a glimpse of him. Hell, if she moved a millimetre they'd be as intimate as it was possible to get.

Kara's mouth fell open in anticipation. The second drawer remained unexplored.

'You're not looking,' he prompted, still stroking her clit. 'That's kind of cheating, you know.' The blunt tip of his thumb found her entrance and dipped inside a way. It came out wet. 'Anywhere, anytime, anyhow, no matter who's watching.'

Maybe, just maybe, she ought to try a little harder to win. God knows what sort of kinky hell he'd subject her to. Only she was way too interested in feeling his cock to focus on finding keys. Kara feigned interest in the drawer contents, waving her hand about inside the little wooden trough, but her attention remained focused on the nudge of his cock up against her sheath.

'You're very wet,' he observed. The smack of his lips followed the comment, and she knew he lifted his thumb in order to taste her.

Suddenly, it was all too much. Kara pushed back against him, unable to keep still with him poised so close any longer. Instead of sliding home, his cock pressed hard against her bottom instead, almost testing her untried hole.

'Steady now. Eagerness will get you everywhere.' He lined them up properly then thrust inside her in one big push that knocked all the air from her lungs. When he drew back, it released her cry.

Sex oughtn't to be allowed to feel this good, especially not the first time with someone. It made her behave like a perfect slut. She jiggled against him, bracing her palms flat against the desk. He seemed to fill her up right to her hopelessly sensitised clit. They rocked together hard, so that their joy was punctuated by the thump of the desk hitting the wall. Kara's pants turned to squeals. She couldn't hold it in. She couldn't keep how good it felt locked inside her.

Ric's teeth grazed the side of her neck and the top of her shoulder, which only encouraged her to push back harder. She strained against him, loving the sensation of her back brushing against his tight abs and his long hair tickling her skin.

They were both coasting close to the edge when he slowed everything down and turned each thrust into a crazily sweet figure of eight. Her cunt clenched around him, desiring the hardness of their previous pace, yet loving how this slower roll seemed to sensitise the whole of her body. For a while they danced in perfect harmony. The graze of Ric's teeth became the sort of deep kiss that marked. He sucked her up into him, possessing her fully. Then just as her body had begun to sink into a liquid and languid state, he switched things up again.

Ric fucked like a perfect madman, his blond hair whipping them both while he filled her with perfect precision. Her heart rate doubled and heat filled Kara's cheeks. The buzz in her clit started out small, just a little fizz that grew until it encompassed the whole of her pussy. She drowned in its power, gasping for air. For the first time ever, her second climax was so much greater than the first. It rolled on and on, pulsing inside of her and making her muscles clench tight around the glory of his cock. Normally, if a lover managed to wring a second orgasm from her, it was a quiet, paltry little tremor. This was huge. It crackled through her synapses and almost knocked her out.

Boneless and dazed, Kara peeled herself up off the surface of the desk. 'Wow!' Even that monosyllable didn't convey the magnificence of the act. She leaned back against Ric in order to seek his kiss. His arms wrapped tight around her as they supped upon one another's breath. He stayed inside her too, his cock rigidly hard. It took a moment for her to realise that he hadn't come, that despite the mind-blowing peak he'd propelled her to, he hadn't found satisfaction of his own. No wonder he lapped up her kisses like a man dying of thirst.

'Keys,' he murmured when they came up for air and all Kara could do was crane her head to look at him. He dropped the bunch square into her palm. They'd been in the second open drawer.

Kara let them fall from her hand on to the carpet, thoughts of promises and prizes cast aside for the moment. 'Do you need me to see to something?' She squeezed tight her muscles around his cock to drop him a clue, though she was planning on planting his arse firmly on the desk before sucking him so that he came like a supernova.

Ric shivered, but held her fast, preventing her from turning. 'Keep on doing that.'

'This?' So he clearly liked the feel of her. He'd love the generosity of her mouth, but as instructed she concentrated hard on fluttering her sheath around his shaft. 'Don't you want to move? I could show you exactly what I can do on my knees.'

'Stay.' He briefly encompassed her breasts, holding them cupped within his big hands before he drew his hold down to her hips. 'I'm going to put my fingers in you.'

'Huh?' Kara barely had time to comprehend his intent before he wriggled a – correction, two fingers inside her

38

alongside his cock. The stretch made her groan. It was a wonder she could accommodate the extra girth, especially when he moved so that he was slowly stroking them both.

'Know where I want to put my thumb?'

Given that he'd somehow managed to bend her over the desk again, so that her bottom was waving in the air and her cunt was full of both his cock and fingers, the answer seemed plain enough. 'Wait up. I ... I don't do, I haven't done ... Fuck!' Kara bit her lip as his thumb rubbed lightly over the whorl of her anus. What was it with her bottom? Mr One-Night Stand from yesterday had suggested sticking a finger up there too.

'Have you never been fucked in the arse?' The hitch in Ric's voice betrayed his surprise. He stared at her intrigued, his gaze switching back and forth between her expression and her exposed rear.

'Well, have you?' she asked, the high pitch of her voice betraying her defensiveness.

Ric graced her with another of his feral grins. 'Yeah, actually.' Nary a hint of colour troubled his cheeks.

'I meant –' Kara interrupted.

'I know what you meant and the answer's yeah, whichever way you intended it. I've both done and been done. You're not going to get all shocked because I've done it with a guy?' Actually, that didn't surprise her one bit, not considering how predatory he was. She didn't think gender made much impact on his choices. Matter of fact, she'd lay money on him having pulled the whole *jus primae noctis* thing even if Chris had picked the keys up in person. Damn, maybe Ric hadn't made a snap decision; maybe he'd been planning this from the moment he'd signed over the barn.

'So, Miss North, are you going to let me slip you a finger

or two?' Given that he was already moving two fingers inside her along with his cock, it seemed something of an odd question.

'That's all. Just fingers.'

'For now.' He laughed, baring his teeth. Damn if she didn't like the way he did that. It suggested just enough aggression to really wet her panties. Not that she had any on any more. 'Remember I won our little trial. So, anytime, anyplace, anyhow.'

'Yeah, I bet you have it all planned out.'

He preened just a little. 'Well, there is a nice little cove down by your barn, with some very convenient rings bolted into the rocks. I find they're just perfect for spreading wayward tenants out and making sure they lie still and take it while I collect any tithes owed.'

'No, you don't.'

'Believe what you like, Kara, but don't short change yourself. Admit you're intrigued by the notion. This is my island. My roots here date back to the eleventh century. Think about how hard you'll come once I've stripped you naked, tied you down and spanked this pretty plump arse of yours until it glows. And then, and only then, will I slip my cock into you and claim my tithe.' His lips briefly nudged her ear. 'Maybe I'll take a few snapshots too.'

True enough, her breath grew heavy in her lungs as he spun out the fantasy. She didn't even know if the cove existed, but the cheeks of her bottom were tingling with anticipation and the lips of her cunt were slick with fresh arousal. Somehow the notion of paying her taxes to him in the form of sexual favours didn't seem all that wrong. At least it would be time well spent.

'So, about that thumb,' he teased, walking his digits over

the curve of her arse. Kara immediately tensed, only for him to crack his hand down hard across one cheek.

'Ouch!' Fire plumed out from the point of impact, making her flesh tender. Ric rubbed a hand over the same point which seemed to emphasise the sting. It was too sensitive to tolerate but too intense a pleasure not to crave. She twitched when his thumb brushed against the tight whorl of muscle he'd made his goal, prompting him to deliver a second sharper smack.

God, it took her breath away. 'Don't' she whimpered. 'I'll hold still. I swear it.'

Ric leaned close. He tickled the shell of her ear again. 'Maybe I don't want you to. Maybe I like the way your muscles clamp down tight.' She hadn't realised it, but her muscles hugged his cock in a death embrace. Kara willed them to relax, which rewarded her with the first real groan she'd heard him make. He lifted his hand again, but he didn't smack. Instead he smoothed his thumb over her puckered entrance. 'You know, I'm still finding it a little hard to believe that you're untried. You're not lying to me, are you? Because you seem the sort to experiment?'

'Yeah, so maybe my partners weren't so adventurous.' She repressed memories of Gavin's cock-centric, stick-it-in-and-wiggle-and-it'll-all-work-out style of loving. He'd never understood the allure of the taboo.

'Then it's a good job you ran into me.' He rubbed again with the super-smooth pad of his thumb. Maybe developer fluid had softened out the grooves. 'Easy, now. Easy. Let me just dip in.'

Goosebumps broke out across Kara's skin. She tried not to tense up again, but the sensation was new and he'd made it into a big thing by discussing it. If he'd just slipped her a finger while they'd been caught up in the act of fucking then it'd have been a turn-on but nothing so mentally intense.

Ric pushed a little but drew back at the resistance. When he tried again it was with one of the fingers he'd just withdrawn from her cunt. It slid in up to the first knuckle. A second soon joined it, and they massaged her inside, causing hasty exhalations. He'd hit on a hidden set of nerves that lit up and tangoed at being caressed.

'That's right. Good girl,' Ric praised. Slowly, his hips began to rock again, the demands of his cock too urgent to ignore any longer. It was sheer bloody amazing he'd managed to hold still the length of time he'd managed already. His shaft moved in time with the stab of his fingers. Kara's body sucked on to both penetrations with equal ardour. No one had ever made her come three times in a row. She'd spent plenty of time trying to accomplish it all by herself, but had reached the conclusion long ago that her body simply wasn't wired up like that. Some women could come over and over, but she wasn't one of them. Mind you, she'd never tried pushing a finger up her arse. Clearly, that was key.

'More,' she groaned.

Ric gave a sharp whistle, but he rose to the challenge. He stretched out his fingers inside her too, so they slid deeper. Then he scissored them apart like he was treading water with his fingers. 'When I set up that shoot for you with two guys, I swear you're going to thank me for this.'

Two guys – yeah, she guessed the possibilities opened out if she was prepared to take one of them in her arse as well as her cunt. She'd reach bliss like the woman in the photograph upstairs.

Kara's neck arched and her legs began to tremble. Ric didn't let up. This time he was going for broke, and he was too caught up in the action to tune it down a notch. His lightning-quick rhythm turned everything into a frantic blur. She knew the moment he came though, even before the bellow he made gave him away, because the pulse of his cock beat hard inside her. He jerked and jerked, hanging on to her as though his life depended upon it. Maybe it did. Her balance was shot to hell. Sandwiched between Ric's hold and the desk she managed to stay upright despite the trembles that magnified and ballooned into a thunderous climax.

When he withdrew, she felt sticky and sore. Ric's wet cock briefly crossed her palm. She made a feeble attempt to capture him. 'Behave,' he chastised. He picked up his whisky tumbler and downed the remainder in one gulp.

Kara straightened up. Her legs wobbled but she managed to rearrange her clothes and hobble over to her former chair. She slumped into the leather embrace, where she sat looking at Ric, wondering what the hell to say. This was the point at which she would expect her instincts to tell her to snatch up the keys from the carpet and get out of here. It had been intense, but nothing that burned this brightly could possibly survive the daybreak. Still, she couldn't make herself leave.

'Spare bedroom's on the first floor,' he said.

Kara's heart plummeted into her gut.

'Right.' She might not be so eager to run, but Ric obviously felt differently. While he wasn't about to turf her out, the party was definitely over. His whole mien had changed. He'd clammed up so tight the strain showed around his eyes. 'Goodnight,' he managed to croak as he left the study.

Kara took a breath but held back the tart retort that sat on her tongue. 'Yeah, right,' she whispered to herself as she climbed the stairs a few moments later. She was so going to sleep well after that mine had just blown up in her face. Alaric Liddell might be a damn good fuck but apparently he also had a chip the size of his blasted island on his shoulders about engaging in post-coital intimacy. Shame, because she'd rather been looking forward to laying her head down next to his on a pillow.

CHAPTER FOUR

Ric lingered on the stairs watching the guest room door. He knew the exact move to make to turn what had been a fabulous evening into an all-night lust fest. It would start with an apology and include room for grovelling and penance. Only one thing stopped him – he'd made this mistake before, rushed in before he'd really judged a character and lived to regret it. A playful smile didn't necessary equate to a great long-term lover. Sometimes, it didn't matter how plain he made it that he was in this for fun and nothing more; as soon as he turned up the heat, women expected emotions to follow.

The idea of exposing himself to that level of intimacy set a shiver racing down his spine. Ric folded his arms before him. He took a deep breath and forced himself along the corridor, head down, absolutely not straining his neck to look back over his shoulder at what could still be, if he simply knocked upon the guest room door.

Don't be a fool. Kara North might be a very welcome addition to Liddell Island; she looked good, smelled better and, boy, did she make a good after-dinner guest, but he absolutely wasn't looking for a permanent fixture in his life.

Still, he only crossed the threshold of his room once he'd

seen her light blink out. Much as the idea of company enticed him, intruding on a person's sleep overstepped certain boundaries, and, if all you were offering was one night of no-strings sex, it moved you firmly into dickhead territory.

Ric stripped off in the dark, leaving his clothes in a heap upon the floor. Sleeping apart was for the best. It meant that come morning they'd part company with no further expectations of one another. It might not constitute the most comfortable arrangement, but at least he hadn't helped to generate any false hopes on her part. She wouldn't be the first lover he'd had that had called him a bastard for laying things out straight. He'd wait and see how she settled down on the island before he even thought of claiming his prize.

Ric grinned as he flopped on to the pillows anticipating that future date. The memory of Kara's long legs and the silk-smooth grip of her pussy still made him feel warm and fuzzy.

Sometimes he liked to imagine he could get by without sex. That he could genuinely lock himself up in this fort and not bother with the world outside. But he'd tried celibacy once. Gone stir crazy in a matter of weeks and then ended up wanking himself stupid, before hitting Torquay as though he meant to shag every inhabitant. Few good memories existed of that weekend. Not so this evening. He'd hardly believed his luck when he opened the door to find her peeping in at him from the gloom like some sort of sea sprite.

She had an earthy sort of beauty: faerie-like angularity set within an oval face, the delicate bone structure combined with a wide, giving mouth. Everything about that mouth said she was a girl who liked to suck. Maybe he should have pressed more to find out. In his mind's eye, he pictured her crouched over him, ready to dip her head and pull him deep.

Not that he was ready to hand over that sort of power. He had issues on that score already.

Ric instantly switched the scenario in his head, imagining her sitting, him standing. He cupped her bounteous breasts together, while he thrust his cock into the soft chasm between them. Every time his shaft peeped from between her breasts Kara dipped her chin and licked the tip of his cock.

Damn – his hand closed around his shaft and began to pump – it'd been too long since he'd met a woman willing to roll with her desires. The last few he'd become embroiled with had been ridiculously coy and swore they wanted nothing but vanilla sex. Not so Kara. It hadn't mattered what he'd suggested, she'd gone with it. She'd let him lead, and trusted him enough to guarantee her pleasure.

Fuck! This was no good. Ric snatched his hands away from his crotch. He clenched his fists by his sides. Now he was randy as a satyr again, with only his palm to relieve him. Well, his palm and a few toys he liked to torture himself with. There were loops of silk cord knotted around the posts of his bed for good reason and they were fuck all to do with being tied up. Ric preferred restrictions to restraints. He preferred to keep his hands away from his cock. Wanking oneself was altogether too easy, too addictive and just didn't relieve any of the strain.

That which is harder to attain is always more rewarding. Saying it didn't help with the cockstand he was facing. Ric splayed his fingers over the eiderdown. He lay breathing in a steady rhythm for several moments, but his erection wasn't going away. Masturbating would be a poor substitute for the gorgeous woman occupying the bed across the hall, but with any luck it might get him to sleep tonight.

You sad bastard.

He stretched sidewards to open the top drawer in the bedside table, only for his phone to buzz just as he closed his hand around a bottle of lube. He kept hold of the lube, and answered the phone with his free hand. 'Yeah,' he drawled into the receiver.

'We need to talk,' the husky voice of his favourite fuck buddy purred into his ear.

Shit! Not now. 'I can't imagine what about.'

A deep sigh reached him from the other end of the phone line. 'Cut the bollocks, Ric. We've known each other too long. Credit me with some brains.'

'Fine. I assume this is why you're not over here now.' They had a semi-regular date. Shagathon Sunday, Zach had once branded it. It would certainly have been that if Kara had arrived in the middle of what they normally got up to. Considering her reaction to that group shot, he didn't think she'd have balked at a threesome with two guys.

Ric flicked open the top of the lube and slathered it over his hungry dick. 'Wouldn't this have been more appropriate face to face?' he asked sweetly.

There was a lip-chewing pause on the other end of the line, before Zach's deep voice rumbled, 'I know what happens when I come near you.'

'You come,' he quipped in return. 'Isn't that the whole point? That's what fuck buddies do.'

'Stop calling me that.'

Ric formed a ring with his fingers and began to work his cock. The silky lube made for an extra-smooth glide that eased his overwrought nerves. Now he had two lovely images in his head. One of Kara's cunt clasping him, and one of Zach's delightfully wicked tongue lighting up an array of very sensitive nerve-endings.

'Shit! Are you with someone?' Zach cursed.

The sounds of his self-loving must have reached Zach's ears, or maybe it was the catch in his breath each time his palm rubbed over his glans. 'Not just at the minute, but the new owner of Beachcomber's Barn has arrived. She's staying in my guest room,' Ric confessed.

'You fucking …' Zach's words trailed off. 'Uh!'

Ric refused to let the frustration in Zach's voice rile him. He hadn't changed in any way. Zach was the one suddenly murmuring about commitment after years of them enjoying a very casual and open relationship. They'd always had other partners. 'Shall I tell you about her?' He deliberately made his voice low and sexy. They often traded sexual encounter stories. Sometimes it really helped to set the mood.

'What else do I need to know, beside the fact that you fucked her?'

'Hey, needs must when your date doesn't arrive. And you're hardly a saint yourself.'

Several moments of uncomfortable silence stretched between them, during which all Ric could hear was the unsteady sound of Zach's breaths. 'You could still come over,' he suggested. His cock pulsed at the idea, giving a little nod of approval.

'Oh, yeah. I'm an idiot like that.' Zach began to laugh. 'You screwed it up, didn't you? Just like normal. What did she tell you that you were – vermin, a bastard, a right fucking wanker? All of which are true, by the way.'

'I did not screw anything up.' Ric bristled. 'I'll have you know that my new tenant is a very amenable lady.'

'You're a fuckwit. And I'll be amazed if she's talking to you in the morning.'

Why was it so hard for people to accept the truth? 'What's

so wrong with being honest?' It was a shame more folks didn't appreciate it. He didn't pretend. He didn't offer anything he wasn't prepared to give. Zach had always understood that – well, until recently. If it had been anyone else bleating on about having a proper relationship, he'd have severed the damn thing on the spot. For some reason he hadn't been able to do that to Zach, perhaps because they'd been together for so long.

Zach understood him, when few others did.

Zach had been there for him.

'The problem isn't with being honest,' his lover patiently explained. 'It's with how you drop the bombshell. For someone with such ace seduction skills, you're fucking awful at letting people down gently.'

Oh hell! They'd moved on from talking about Kara again. This was about to turn into another session of 'Poor old Zach' and how unfair it was that he wasn't valued or appreciated, and how crass Ric was for not wanting something deep and meaningful.

'Go on, call me some more names,' Ric insisted, planning on derailing that line of talk before it started. 'Purr those sexy thoughts into my ear.'

There was a pause, during which Zach clearly held the phone to his chest. The echoes of the snort he made still rumbled down the line. 'I did not phone in order to get you off,' Zach said peevishly, although Ric guessed that the guy was also smiling. 'We need to have a proper talk, and, just so you know, it hurts to hear you're still shagging around.'

'So talk. I'm all ears.' Ric tucked the phone receiver between his shoulder and ear, and then he grasped the silken cord above his head with one hand, while his other continued to provide vital life support to his needy dick. He used his strength to lift himself so that he was doing tiny pull-ups that caused his muscles to burn, and his erection to drum against his stomach each time he strained.

'Tell me how you want it to be, Zach. Do we fuck more or less in your head, once you've wrung a confession of undying love out of me?'

'What would you say if I said yes?'

'I'd say describe it to me. Convince me. Prove to me that a dose of romanticism is going to help me get off.'

'Ric, my sister's in the next room.'

'Then keep your voice low. Come on, Zach, talk to me. You know I like the sound of your voice, especially when it gets all low and husky.' Breathless. That was the word. 'How's love gonna change things?'

It wouldn't, as far as Ric was concerned, at least not in any positive way. It only meant he'd be beholden to someone in a way he didn't wish to be. He'd been there before. The episode hadn't really done a lot for him. He barely registered what Zach was saying. It didn't matter. What was important was that just the suggestion that he was even considering the issue was enough to provoke the response he wanted out of Zach.

When Zach fell silent on the other end of the line, Ric knew it was because he was slowly sliding the teeth of his zip apart.

Ric waited, bating his breath. Prickles spread out with increasing urgency from his loins and crossed his belly and thighs. 'Zach, are you still there?'

'I'm here,' Zach eventually said, in a ridiculously husky purr that fanned up the heat in Ric's groin.

Ric strained against the cord, holding himself still in anticipation of his lover's next words. He formed Zach's image whole in his head. Brown hair falling in a haphazard fashion over his face, his teeth drawn into a pseudo snarl, while, lower down, his thick cock sprang up from its nest of wiry curls. Zach was pretty much hairy all over, but there was something especially appealing about the thatch around his loins.

'I'm picturing us together. Your cock and mine, pressed close, like that time in the shower. Do you remember that time?'

'Yeah.'

Rivulets of water had streamed over their bodies. White condensation had steamed up all the glass. They'd started off soaping one another, and getting hard because of it. Ric had wrapped his palm around both of their cocks and began working them together. In his head, he relived those slow, slow tugs upon his cock. The sensation of Zach's cock rubbing smoothly against his own literally stole his breath away.

'Do you remember what came next?' Zach asked.

God, did he. The memory caused blood to surge into his loins. His balls grew tight as his erection surged.

Mostly, Ric preferred to fuck rather than be fucked, but once in a while, not very often at all, he'd consent to switching things around. That night in the shower had been one of those occasions. Zach had pinned him, face to the wall. His stomach had been pressed tight to the cold tiles, his cock sandwiched between their hardness and the desperate heat of his body. Zach had nuzzled up against the back of his neck. He'd rained kisses there, as he'd directed his cock to the ring of muscle he was desperate to try.

'Remember how it felt. You were so goddamn tight that I could hardly move inside you. And like an inferno.'

Ric gripped the phone more tightly, hanging on to every word. He no longer held the silk cord, but concentrated on the swoop and swish of his palm riding up and down his cock. His hips began to lift. His stomach muscles cramped with each thrust. On the other end of the line, Zach's breathing had become loud and breezy. But not so loud that it masked the sweet sound of his hand rubbing his dick.

'Is that what you want to do? You want to fuck me again?' Ric asked.

'I want to get deep inside you. So deep, that it feels like we're merging. That I'm fucking through you right into your cock. But I'm not going to touch you, not unless you beg. I'm going to take my fill while I hold your wrists so you can't jerk yourself off. Then when you come you'll know it's all because of me fucking you and not because of any damn thing else. Do you understand me, Ric? I'm going to make you come because my cock is in your arse and you're loving it.'

Right now, he was making him come just imagining it. It no longer mattered that it was his palm doing the physical work. The essential spark arose from Zach's words. 'Oh God! I'm almost there.' Ric gave a series of airless gulps. His back arched so that his forehead pressed tight against the headboard as his body fired up to release its gift.

He listened to Zach trying to stifle the same moan he always made the second before he came. Whatever he used as a muffler didn't exactly do a good job. Zach continued to whimper until he was completely spent. 'Shit!' he swore. 'Shit. Shit. Shit.' Muddled up in the stream of expletives, Ric caught the sounds of footsteps and doors banging. 'Rest of the family is back. I need to clean up. Gotta go. We'll finish this later.' He hung up before Ric could say a thing. No matter, he was content to wallow in his post-orgasmic glow, instead of having to deal with the high emotions that were likely to have followed.

Deep down, he did love Zach. He just wasn't about to tell him that. And it absolutely wasn't going to stop him fucking Kara.

Ric roused himself enough to wipe the pool of semen from his stomach. Then he settled back down and thought of his guest. Dependent on how things panned out in the morning, she might make a very nice alternative playmate until Zach pulled his head out of his arse and stopped insisting on exclusivity and a boatload of lovey-dovey stuff. Hell, even after that, maybe they could have fun together.

CHAPTER FIVE

Kara pre-empted any kind of showdown or breakfast weirdness with Ric the next morning by skipping out on him at sunrise. Since the island stood little more than a mile across, she figured it'd be easy enough to spot an unoccupied barn.

Ric's study still reeked of sex, when she went in to retrieve the barn keys. They lay exactly where she'd dropped them the night before. For a moment the memories of their loving made her pause. She didn't blame him for giving her the brush-off. It was only what she'd done to Jack the night before. What irked her about the experience was her own desire to prolong the encounter. She'd genuinely wanted to spend the night with him.

Well, it hadn't happened, and that was that. Kara bustled herself out into the fresh air. Barely dawn: the sky still held the purple edge of night. A bracing wind blew in off the Channel. Instead of taking the path back to the bay, Kara scrambled down the dirt track to the left of the bridge. Several nettle stings later she crossed a stone boundary wall and spied her new home perched on the headland overlooking a sandy cove dotted with enormous rocks. Her thoughts immediately cast back to Ric's promise of anytime, anyplace, I'm so going to strip you naked and fuck you in the cove that sits right on your doorstep. It didn't take a close inspection to know this was the location he'd meant. From the track that skirted the cliff top she could see the iron rings fastened to the rocks. One presumed they were intended to tie boats to but, given Ric's feudal claims about his family's past, she couldn't be sure. Either way, it wasn't something she had time to dwell on right now. Nope, she was not going to think about mister lean, sexy and emotionally stunted, not one itty bit. The ball lay in his court. She had no problem with casual sex.

Chris's purchase proved to be dark and cobwebby. It was also minus electricity and hot or cold running water and empty of food, just when Kara's stomach had woken to the idea of breakfast.

'Shit!' She didn't want to go back to Ric's to ask for help. There had to be someone else living on this accursed rock who could assist. There'd definitely been some sort of shop in the bay where she'd left her car. With any luck, they'd know the relevant numbers to call. She had to head down to the car to pick up her luggage anyway.

Several vehicles occupied the bay when she reached it, including an ice-cream van that already sported a five-deep queue, and an enormous camper van. An assortment of kids in shorts and cagoule-wearing tourists milled around the bay, carrying camping equipment and chasing after balls. One or two were scrambling over the seaweed-strewn rocks in order to fish amongst the rock pools.

Kara made her way to the building she'd spied the night before. THE BUNKER, the sign said. It had a concrete frontage, but clearly made use of a natural fissure in the cliff face. A plaque outside detailed its history as an ammunitions store and a guard-post some time during the nineteenth century. Inside, the windowless structure felt decidedly cave-like. The air had a damp, sea-salty quality to it despite twin dehumidifiers rumbling by the counter. She'd hoped for supplies, but what faced her was a barrage of tat; tinkling wind-chimes, vast arrays of semiprecious stones, buckets, spades and an awful lot of overpriced seaside-themed holiday gifts. There was not one edible item in the whole shop, unless you considered Kendal Mint Cake edible, nor did there appear to be a shopkeeper.

Downcast, Kara mooched over to the ice-cream van and joined the queue there.

'What can I get you?' the serving girl asked her from beneath the brim of a baseball cap.

'A bacon butty,' Kara replied wistfully. Given the way her stomach was imitating a chorus line, she needed to put something inside it, and quick. She supposed she'd have to nip across to the mainland for supplies once she'd found out how to turn her utilities on.

The girl shook her head. 'Sorry, no can do. Hot drinks and ice cream only, and we don't do anything overly fancy, none of those frappe-latte-mocha things.' She raised a hand to point out the blackboard hanging from a bracket secured to the outside of the van.

'Fine, I'll have a ludicrously oversized black coffee and an ice cream then,' Kara replied without giving the board much more than a glance.

'Flavour?'

'Anything but vanilla.' She was already regretting the notion of something quite so sweet for breakfast, but she had no idea how far it was to the nearest supermarket, and her stomach absolutely couldn't wait.

'My kind of girl.'

Kara jerked her chin upwards, half expecting to find Ric, hands in pockets and sporting an enormous grin. Instead a man with much shorter brown hair stood looking at her. It was the guy from the night before last. 'Jack?' She furrowed her brow straining to remember.

'Zach,' he corrected

'Zach, right.' What the hell was he doing here? When she'd left Zach on the quayside, she hadn't expected to cross his path again. Doing so made things awkward. It placed certain expectations on them that she hadn't sought. 'What are you doing here?'

Zach mussed the long top strands of his hair so that they fell over his brows in a messy tumble. 'I was going to ask you the same thing.'

Gah! Talk about awkward. Now he probably thought she'd pursued him here and was looking for a repeat performance. Not that he was a bad choice if she was going to contemplate such actions. His appearance certainly lived up to her memory of him, all big-boned and yet oddly wiry. Zach seemed to have been put together by someone who liked strong features, but had no idea about what they actually wanted to achieve. His brows and especially his mouth seemed over-generous for his narrow features, while his nose seemed almost petite. Nevertheless, the result was certainly arresting.

'Um, my brother just bought Beachcomber's Barn.' The actual house name had been handily carved into the front-door lintel.

'You're the new occupant?' His brown eyes widened a fraction, and a ripple of tension seemed to stiffen his limbs. 'No, I mean that's great. How are you settling in?'

Kara fluttered her fingers at him in response. 'No supplies.

I thought I'd be able to get some things here, but I guess not unless I want a new wind-chime.'

'Flavour?' The girl in the van prompted, thrusting the ice-cream scoop towards Kara. 'Sorry to hurry you, but there's a queue. We have cherry, chocolate, mint choc chip, rum and raisin, pistachio, rhubarb, lemon sorbet, toffee or vanilla.'

'She already said she doesn't do vanilla, and I can vouch for that.' Zach flashed Kara a cheeky grin before looking up at the girl. There was an obvious family resemblance. 'I'm guessing rum and raisin.'

'Lemon,' Kara said decisively. She needed something sharp and palette-clearing at the moment.

'Tart,' Zach remarked.

The serving girl took no notice, but made an efficient job of doling out the ice cream on to a cone, which she handed over along with the coffee. 'That's £4.85.'

'I've got it. It's on the house.' Zach settled a hand upon Kara's arm as she made to delve into her purse, which earned him a look of exasperation from his employee. 'Whatever,' the girl mumbled. She turned to the next customer and began talking over Kara's head.

Kara turned away from the serving window. 'Your van?' she asked Zach.

'Yeah. This and the Bunker.'

She really hadn't pegged him as the owner of a tat cave, or an ice-cream vendor. He wasn't dressed in oversized sweat pants and a three-quid T-shirt, for starters. No, he had on a shirt and a pair of beautifully clingy moleskins that made magic out of his thighs and would no doubt set his butt off to perfection. In short, he looked every bit as scrumptious as he'd been the night before last when she'd wanted to lash him to the canal railings and take lewd snapshots of him.

The thought of draping him over a rock instead and taking said pictures briefly entertained her, but Kara pushed it aside for the moment. Her muscles still ached from the workout Ric had given her.

A sudden thought briefly entertained her. Maybe she could persuade Ric to give her photography lessons, or take her on as an apprentice, and she could start a new career as … as what – a pornographer? Actually, sticking to happy snaps might be a better idea.

Zach offered her a tight smile, so Kara raised the oversized paper cup in a gesture of acknowledgement. 'Well, thanks for this.' She headed to her car in order to eat, feeling just a teeny bit guilty at dismissing him.

Just moments after she'd settled into the front seat with the radio on low, Zach rapped upon her window. Kara wound it down, squirming a little in her seat, then fixed on a smile and endeavoured to be nice. It wasn't as if she'd say no to a repeat performance with the guy. He was smoking hot. It was just a tad awkward, seeing as she'd fucked someone else in between.

'Have you met Ric yet?' he asked, much to her astonishment. Kara gaped at him, knowing it to be a loaded question. Hell, she could see it in Zach's eyes, and the way he scanned her face searching for an answer.

'Last night.'

'Yeah?' His mouth broadened into a slightly uncomfortable grin. 'And how did that go?'

Kara spluttered coffee over the dashboard. What sort of question was that? Did he expect her to relate every sordid detail and then cry on his shoulder about the horrible nasty man? 'It was interesting,' she replied, once she'd wiped the droplets away with her hand.

'Yeah, I'll bet it was.' Explicit knowledge glittered in Zach eyes, which suggested he knew all of Ric's quirks and exactly how x-rated her introduction to island life had been. Evidently, her supposition that Ric Liddell tried it on with all the island's newcomers was right on the mark. Yet, she didn't detect any sort of censure from Zach. In fact, he continued to smile in a genuine way.

'Word of advice, not that I especially think you need it, but just so that you're straight. He's not for keeps. As long as you realise that, I'm sure you'll have a great time living here.'

Somewhat embarrassed, Kara grinned her way through another slurp of coffee. 'Oh, that's subtle,' she muttered against the paper lip. She hadn't particularly intended Zach to hear the remark, but he shook his head slightly, betraying the fact that he had.

'Believe me. Nothing about Ric Liddell is subtle. He's sexy as hell, but if you're after an emotional connection look elsewhere. The guy's heart is at zero Kelvin. You'll get more affection out of a barnacle.' Zach began walking back towards his van.

'Hey, what about you?' She couldn't figure him out. Had that been intended as friendly advice, to warn her off, or to set himself up as a better option? Zach swung around to look at her. 'Me? I go with the flow, Kara. Best way when your life's dictated by the tide.' He jerked a thumb towards the causeway. 'Catch you later.'

'Wait up.' Kara hung out of the car window. 'How did you know? Did Ric do you your first night here?'

Zach's lips split into a brilliant smile, which he backed up with a chuckle. 'I don't live here.'

'Oh!' Now she felt like a fool, and the excitement that had started brewing in her stomach transformed into an odd sort of disappointment. She lowered her gaze to the cobblestones beneath Zach's baseball boots – an odd choice to go with his clothes – only to find him moving towards her again. He bent down once he drew close. 'Round the back of the Bunker in five minutes and I'll show you what he did to me. But only come if you're game. Otherwise –' he tapped the side of her head with his index finger '– I guess you'll just have to imagine the scene. You know, two hot blokes, getting a little bit intimate with one another.' He straightened up, and then shoved both palms into his pockets in order to mooch off back to his business.

Kara watched him go while finishing off her ice cream. What the devil did he intend to show her? All right, fair dos to him, she was intrigued.

* * *

Kara North … Kara North. Zach shook his head. No way was she here. After she'd left him on the quayside with his fly undone he'd hoped they might run into one another again. Actually, he'd fantasised about it. But he hadn't expected it to happen, especially not here and not after Ric had given her the serfdom speech. OK, so it wasn't all that much of a speech. Ric tended to go for the more hands-on approach, not that he couldn't sweet-talk the panties off any bugger he wanted if he set his mind to it. And who could blame him wanting a piece of the delicious morsel that was Kara North, with her pretty blue eyes, quirky smile and absolutely straightforward attitude. Her never-ending legs that disappeared into that tiny skirt didn't hurt either.

The only galling bit was knowing that Ric had had his hands all over her. Sure, they had an open relationship, sure, he'd had Kara too – first in fact – but it still hurt to put a face to one of Ric's passing flings.

Zach had been angry last night when Ric had admitted to shagging someone else; now his vexation was doubled on learning it was Kara. Somehow, even when he tried to tug away from Ric, things ended up turning back in that direction. Why her out of countless women? The one woman he'd like to know better and Ric just happened to have shagged her too. He ought to walk away from both of them and find someone altogether less capricious to pin his dreams on.

That probably made what he was about to do doubly stupid, but he was sick of giving in to Ric. If he couldn't have Ric, then Zach was definitely going to have Kara.

He kept his pace relaxed as he headed back to the Bunker, not wishing to give off any revealing vibes to his blessed pain in the arse of a sister whom he'd been blackmailed into giving a job. Heather worked all right, the problem was that it left him with time on his hands, as there simply wasn't space inside the van for two servers, and crap-all ever happened inside the Bunker. Sure, people came in and had a quick nosey about and picked up bits and bobs, but he did all the sales from out of the ice-cream van. The upside, he supposed, was that no one would bat an eyelid at him taking a mid-morning stroll. 'Going off for a bit,' he called to his sister, before ducking inside the Bunker and going into the storeroom for the necessary supplies.

The wind had dropped over the last hour, and it was gearing up to be a bright, sunny day. Zach followed the rocky coastline that the tide exposed when it went out, and then took a sharp left in order to weave back inland so that he'd end up behind the Bunker. The tourists stuck to the obvious paths and picnic spots, so he could guarantee seclusion back here. In essence the spot was little more than a blanket of ferns wedged between two ravines, but the sun normally managed to find it, whereas the wind didn't.

Zach settled his back against one of the rock faces and rolled up his shirt cuffs. One thing he had learned from Ric was to always be properly prepared, that way you weren't left cleaning up a mess when you ought to be enjoying a nice post-coital flush.

Mere moments later, Kara followed him into the dell. She glanced around, and then came forward with her hands raised, a position he rather liked as it caused her top to ride up and reveal a sliver of her midriff. Zach never quibbled over a show of skin. He wasn't fussy over which bit, just as long as some was showing. He did like women's ankles though, something about their shape, particularly in high heels.

Kara wasn't wearing heels today, just a modest pair of deck shoes. They were the most sensible item on her. God, she was so wonderfully curvy and so totally inappropriately dressed it made him want to weep with joy. He didn't think it had even crossed her mind that a short skirt and a titchy top weren't exactly the best combo for stumbling about a rock in the English Channel.

'OK, tell me. What did Ric Liddell do to you the first time you met?'

He loved that she was all business. It saved on the small talk. Zach pasted on his best butter-wouldn't-melt expression and made an act of coyly nibbling one fingernail. 'Let's see. He cooked me dinner, and got me a wee bit tipsy on his excellent malt whisky.'

'Yeah, and then,' she prompted, edging a little closer to him, not so that they were touching, but close enough to scream intimacy to a casual observer, 'I got my own whisky T-shirt.'

Zach pushed back against the rock, relishing the prospect of becoming trapped. He wasn't a straight-up submissive by any stretch, he just enjoyed the sizzle Kara generated when she got an idea into her head and acted on it. Right now, she was staring at him like she intended to superglue him to the rock and then lick him all over. The prospect was absolutely fine with him. In fact, he'd brought just the thing to really make the experience simmer.

'I'm waiting.'

Zach shot a glance up at her from beneath his brows. He figured it wouldn't hurt to make her wait a teeny bit longer still. Matter of fact, he intended to maximise the anticipation. After all, he wasn't about to share the most staggering story on the planet. In the annals of Liddell Island history, it barely rated as tame. Still, to set the scene, he raised the bottle he'd taken from behind the counter in the Bunker and squeezed a drop of sauce out on to his fingertip. 'And then ... and then, he fed me dessert.'

Kara frowned. 'What is that – tomato sauce?'

'Chocolate.' He sucked off the bead upon his fingertip and squeezed out another. 'Rich as sin, bitter, melt-on-the-tongue, expensive chocolate sauce.'

Despite sweeping her tongue over her lower lip in appreciation, Kara continued to eye him dubiously.

'Think about it.' Zach held out his finger to her, so that she could take the dot of chocolate with her tongue.

'I am.'

The moment her lips closed over his fingertip, lust gripped Zach hard around the groin. He'd known the moment he set eyes upon her, just from the way she moved upon the dance floor, that she was every bit as much of a sensualist as him. Not that sensualist adequately summed it up. It'd be more accurate to say that she was dirty like him. Up for certain things and acts that nice girls didn't always consent to. Kara got off on the idea of taboos – hence them flaunting their arses so they could do it standing up against the canal railings, instead of finding a nice secluded spot inside the club, where they wouldn't have been noticed or remarked upon, or heard.

The way she sucked his finger brought back the sensations of having her curl her tongue around his cock. He'd never had a girl go down on him in a public place like that before.

'Ask me how he fed it to me,' he prompted.

'On his dick,' she blurted.

Oh yeah, she cottoned on fast, but what really undid him was the way she smacked a hand across her mouth the minute she realised that she'd spoken aloud. Doing came easy to her. Talking about it evidently did not.

'He didn't, did he?'

Zach pursed his lips, trying not to allow his smirk to become a full-blown laugh.

'No way. You're pulling my leg.'

'Babe, I hope I'm pulling all of you, not just your leg. And yes way, he most certainly did. Come on, you've met him.' He waggled an eyebrow at her. 'Ric put that stuff on like it was a glaze and had me slowly lick it off.'

'Yeah, but how did he know that you'd go for that? How did he know you …' She paused to choose her words carefully. 'Know that you swung both ways?'

Zach took hold of her hand and lifted it up so that he could squeeze a line of chocolate sauce along her extended index finger. 'Ah, well. The thing you have to understand about Ric is that he … well, he just doesn't give a fuck. He

66

doesn't see boundaries in quite the same way as the rest of us.'

'You mean all the feudal whatnot.'

'Partly that, coupled with the fact that he acknowledges very few sexual boundaries. I don't think it actually occurred to him that I might not be interested in sucking his cock. I hadn't flinched when he stuck his hands down my pants so why should I when he came to me all cream-filled and chocolate-coated?'

'You know –' she ticked a finger against his lower lip '– that sounds just a little bit icky.'

Zach feigned disappointment. 'So I can't tempt you into making a reconstruction?'

She straightened her fingers out to cup the side of his face. 'Seriously? You're asking me to paint you with chocolate sauce and lick it all off you? Isn't that a little presumptuous for a second date?'

'I don't know, seems to me I have a little ground to make up.' Ric had already had his way, which meant that, if he wanted to stay on Kara's radar, he needed to inject some sizzle right now. Candlelit dinners, flowers, that whole shebang would have to wait for later.

'Well, if we're talking about making a good impression, shouldn't it be you doing the licking?' Kara asked. 'I seem to recall you're rather talented with your tongue.'

Zach stuck out that curled appendage, only to inhale sharply as Kara vanquished the last inch of space between them. She crushed her soft breasts up against his chest and taunted him with the nearness of her lips. They only just brushed his, but the resultant tingle charged straight down to his loins.

'Know why I think you gave in to Ric?' Her hands moved upon his chest, slowly, but expertly undoing the buttons of his shirt. 'Because you liked him taking charge. You like having things done to you. Shall I take charge, Zach? Shall I be really demanding?' He'd lay money on the fact that she hadn't pulled this sort of move with Ric. More than likely, this was a reflection of what that hot bastard had done to her. There were certainly Ric-like elements to it.

Nonetheless, Zach gave a low moan of agreement. Some things, like imagining her mouth wrapped around his cock, overrode reservations about their source of origin.

'Yeah? Good.' She reached the end of his shirt and began fiddling with his belt buckle. 'Here's how it works, then. I'm going to unzip your fly and get your cock out. Are you hard for me, Zach?'

You bet he was. The moment she slipped the button of his fly, his zip gave way to the strain of retaining his erection. Kara's hand encompassed his length, and glided swiftly upwards towards the head. 'Then I'm going to make use of this chocolate sauce you kindly brought, exactly as you suggested.' She pried the bottle from his fingers with her free hand, then took a step back to admire the picture of him with his shirt and fly undone and his cock all bucked up and eager. Dear God, she really was like Ric, right down to the way she made a frame with her fingers to view him through.

'My, aren't you pretty. But I think we need a little embellishment.'

Kara angled the sauce bottle so that a thick line of chocolate dribbled down the centre of his torso. She immediately bent to lick it off.

'Yes,' he groaned, his cock bucking towards her in anticipation of being drawn into her moist, willing mouth.

'Ah, but here's the catch. You're not allowed to come, not until I've licked away every last smear of chocolate.' She dribbled another line out now, this one along the length of his cock. 'If you do – not that you will, because you won't disappoint me like that, will you, Zach? – then you forfeit all right to fuck me no matter how hot and horny you get. And ...'

Like they needed an and.

'The next time Ric invites you over to dinner, I get front-row viewing privileges.'

He couldn't resist cocking an eyebrow at that one. Evidently the possibility of seeing him being fucked by Ric appealed to her on some level. He hadn't pegged her as a straight-up voyeur, which suggested a more convoluted reason for the request. 'Sure,' he agreed, already amused by the possibility of having to broach the subject with Ric. The guy was great behind the camera, but he didn't perform pay-per-view. The only people who got to see Ric fuck were the ones he was doing it with at the time. 'Do your worst.'

'Babe,' she laughed as she wove her fingers through the springy curls at his groin. 'I absolutely intend to.'

* * *

Watching Zach's eyes close in pleasure brought a smile of amused satisfaction to Kara's face. Was she making this awkward for herself by engaging in a second seduction with Zach? Yes, perhaps, but she reckoned Zach understood. He certainly wasn't under any illusions about what had gone down between her and Ric, which meant he was unlikely to get any funny ideas about them becoming a couple. Plus, it sounded as if he had a pretty complicated relationship with Ric himself. That particular fact set her alight more than any of Ric's pictures. All she could think of was somehow getting the two men together and wangling herself a ringside seat. Not that she intended just to watch. That would certainly be eye-opening, but not compared to a night of totally amazing blow-out sex where they both worshipped her as Aphrodite.

Well, first she needed to do a little worshipping of her own. Although considering the eagerness with which Zach's cock was standing, rapture couldn't be that far off.

Kara touched the very tip of her finger to his glans by way of hello. He bucked a little more upright in response, though his erection already stood damn near vertical. He made a noise too, right down deep in the back of his throat: a strangled, plaintive, whimper that made her insides clench like a tightly wound coil. Why should her pussy lips plump because he gave a cry? Did the whys even matter? He'd looked scrumptious two nights ago when she'd held him fast against the railings and gone down on him, and if possible he looked even more so now. Zach had such a hint of vulnerability about him, in the way his lips formed a needy pout that just begged for kisses, and in the way his limbs seemed to loosen despite the fact that all his muscles were drawn tight. He had his palms pressed flat against the cliff face. Kara half expected to find an impression of him left behind in the rock when he moved.

She dropped on to her knees. 'Shh!' she soothed, so that her breath whispered over the angry red tip of his shaft. 'It's fine, let me help. I can make it better.'

His cock seemed to agree with the sentiment, for it gave a nod in her direction.

'Now open your eyes.' He needed to see what she was doing to him. No hiding in the dark behind his eyelids in order to tone down his reactions.

Zach obeyed. He looked down at her, his dark eyes shot

with magic and expectation. His lips parted to release his shallow, uneven breaths. All the frown and laughter lines smoothed out of his face as he watched her dribble chocolate sauce on to her finger. Kara daubed a spot on to his glans, which made his eyes close and caused his breath to hiss. Good, he was sensitive there. His eyes snapped open again the moment she withdrew her touch.

Kara unscrewed the top of the bottle and dipped her fingers into the stickiness.

'Oh God!' he moaned, as she finger-painted him all across his stomach and along the length of his cock, paying extra attention to the head. Only when he was coated from base to tip did she screw the top back on the sauce. She licked one finger clean, then fed him the others while she swirled her tongue around his taut nipples.

His suck was surprisingly gentle, given how shaky he seemed to be, but he'd been like that the last time too. A perfect gentleman, waiting on her, not demanding attention or that they hurry things along just because he was aching with need. Zach – yeah, she liked Zach, because he was prepared to wait for his pleasures. He understood that drawing things out led to greater rewards.

The chocolate was both sweet and bitter on her tongue as she kissed her way down his abs to where his cock pointed skywards. Zach crooned the whole time. She cleaned him with slow loving licks, starting with the underside at the base and then working up and round, finishing with the tip, which she popped into her mouth whole.

The muscles in his thighs jumped in response. 'Kara,' he gasped, and jerked himself so hard against the rock she swore he hoped it would eat him.

Well, the cliff wasn't going to eat him, but she definitely

was. 'Easy now. Just remember to breathe.' He seemed to be having a little trouble with that part.

Zach caught his lower lip between his teeth. 'I'm fine.'

'Sure you are.' Absolutely, he was fine. More than fine, in fact. He was quite awesomely delicious. She opened her mouth and relaxed her throat, so that she took almost all his length. Zach, though not enormous, was a big enough boy, especially when he was this turned on. She could feel the pulse of his blood pumping just below the skin upon her tongue and the way in which he relaxed just a fraction as she pulled back. He stiffened up again the moment her head dipped, then relaxed again, until it became part of the rhythm of suck and withdraw.

'Now, remember,' she warned, when his hips started pumping a little too eagerly. 'You won't get your reward if you come too quickly.'

'You said until the chocolate was gone.'

True enough she had, and there wasn't so much as a smear left on him, a matter she rectified at once. The second coating was far less artfully applied. The chocolate had warmed up and become runnier, so that when she squeezed it out, it ran down the length of his shaft in sticky rivulets, which she caught on her tongue.

It brought him a little welcome relief from the assault on his glans, but Zach had gone past the point where he could tolerate being teased, and his body was begging her for proper action with the jerky thrust of his hips. Kara pressed one chocolate-covered hand against his stomach, intending to win even if it did involve a little bit of cheating, and then took his cock into her mouth again. She alternated long pulls with lavishing attention on the cluster of nerves around the tiny eye-slit.

'Frig yourself,' he managed to gasp. It seemed Zach wasn't planning on admitting defeat quite so easily. 'Stick your hand up your skirt and pull aside your knickers.'

'Can't.' She pushed her tongue into her cheek. 'Not wearing any.' She'd mislaid the pair Ric had taken off her, and hadn't yet had the opportunity to pull on any others.

'You're commando in that skirt!' He gaped. 'Show me. Prove it.'

To do that properly, she'd have to stop sucking him, but she didn't think that had been a factor in prompting the demand. Rather, he was genuinely shocked.

Kara rolled backwards off her knees until she landed on her bum amidst the ferns. Then she spread her legs wide before her and rucked up her skirt to her waist.

Zach stared at her pussy like a man starved. Admittedly, she was pink and plumped, glistening in readiness. She hadn't realised her own need was so great until she saw her clit peeping out from inside its hood. Then she had to resist taking a hand off the ground and stroking herself.

Oh, what the hell! She wet her middle finger and ran it right along her slit. Her flesh was still tender from the night before, but that seemed only to prompt her to repeat the process rather than call a halt to things. Inside, the muscles of her cunt clenched tight, at the memory of cock filling her. She hadn't really meant to give it up to Zach, but she really wanted him now.

'You are one beautiful, sexy, dirty, woman.' Zach slowly began to peel himself off the rock face, fingers stretching first, soon followed by his shoulders and then the rest of him. He staggered forward towards her, doing a bad impersonation of Frankenstein's monster as he worked the stiffness out of his joints.

Laughing, Kara shuffled backwards further into the basin of ferns.

The moment he caught her, he pushed her on to her back and planted a lascivious kiss across her mouth. Not stopping there, he followed up by pushing his tongue inside her and making her groan. Zach settled comfortably between her thighs. He bent his head and gave her pussy a very wet lick before testing her willingness with two fingers. Having apparently decided she was still a little tight, he rubbed his thumb up and down over her clit.

With one move he'd managed to turn the tables. Now she was the needy one, writhing so that her hips bobbed up off the ground seeking further stimulus. Zach gave a chuckle. He sucked his fingers clean, and then moved so that he was balanced right over her, with his erection pointed to where she needed to feel it.

'Wait up.' She planted a hand against his chest. 'Unless you've a wrapper, you ain't coming in.'

He cursed briefly. 'You know where I keep them.'

She did – his back pocket. It took a bit of stretching, but she found the foil and had him dressed in record time. Then it took only a teeny bit of wriggling to get them all lined up.

His cock bumped against her pussy lips a few times, before he finally pressed home.

'Yes,' she gasped in welcome as he stretched her. The tenderness she'd felt in her lips didn't extend inside, making the penetration wholly bliss. He slid smoothly, going in deep. 'Hard,' she insisted.

Zach puffed a breath upwards to blow aside the hair that had fallen over his brow. 'Is there any other way?'

Considering what a tight leash he liked to keep himself on during the preliminaries, she guessed in his case probably not. He was like a coiled spring that had been allowed to unwind, and in doing so was gaining momentum. The thing was, the deeper he thrust, and the more he grabbed her bottom and lifted her on to him, the more infectious his excitement became, until her need matched his in strength and they were clawing one another trying to get that fraction closer as they raced towards the end.

Kara both wanted to get there and didn't want it to end. Sex seemed to have become a whole lot more exciting since she'd given the notion of matrimony the hoof. She was shimmying so hard against him by the time her orgasm began to well up that it was beyond her power to even alert him to the fact that she was coming. Maybe he sensed it from the way her pussy began to tighten around his cock.

'Almost there.' Zach's words rasped against her cheek. He kept on thrusting, maintaining the punishing pace even as her climax simmered up and began to overflow. 'Fuck, you're so wet, so silky smooth. I could do you for ever, Kara North.'

It felt exactly as if he were doing that right now. Her orgasm rode her hard and wrung out every bit of pleasure she was capable of feeling. Her muscles continued to twitch around him as Zach also lost himself to the moment. He grunted, trying to keep up some sort of rhythm with his thrusts, but really they were both done for, dripping with sweat and buzzing with shared energy.

He rolled over on to the ferns once they'd finished with a big ol' smile upon his face. 'That was ... Yeah ...' He lapsed into another grin while he recovered his breath.

Kara cuddled up to his side, appreciating the fact that, unlike Ric, he hadn't immediately leapt to his feet and moved on to other business.

'I think we need to make a date for a repeat.'

'My place?' she suggested. The heat of her blush prickled her cheeks and nose. Crazy that they could have wild sex together but she felt nervous about inviting him to her home. If she wasn't careful, he really would get the wrong impression.

'Tonight,' he agreed, looking at her with a smile in his eyes. 'I'll come over after work.'

'Don't expect much,' Kara insisted, suddenly reminded that she had no supplies and no power. 'I don't suppose you know a plumber and an electrician, by any chance?'

Zach helped her stand. 'I won't expect anything. It's just a visit.' He started working her skirt back into place, but paused before accomplishing the task to give her pussy a farewell stroke. 'And I think I might have an idea who to contact over your water and electricity problems.'

* * *

Monday. Mid-morning.
Text message from Zach Blackwater to Ric Liddell:
I met your date. Cute. She'd like some power in her house. Are you going to fix it?

Text message from Ric Liddell to Zach Blackwater:
Already did. Come over tonight and I'll fix you up too.

Text message from Zach Blackwater to Ric Liddell:
F off. Xxx

CHAPTER SIX

Since Zach had promised to make the appropriate phone calls to sort out her utilities, Kara took the opportunity to drive to the mainland in search of supplies. The nearest town was only a few miles along the coast and, as the tide was out, it wasn't long before she pulled back into the parking space she'd left, her boot loaded with shopping. Alas, Zach wasn't on hand to help carry it back to the barn. He was taking a stint inside the ice-cream van, and his queue wound around the edge of the parking lot. She'd have to shoulder as much shopping as she could and then come back for the rest.

'Are you the new Beachcomber resident?'

Kara raised her head to find a plump young woman standing a yard away. Her mass of wildly curly red hair whipped around her heart-shaped face, which was make-up free except for a thick coat of scarlet lipstick that served to emphasise her smiling mouth.

Despite that smile, Kara steeled herself, wondering if this was one of Ric's former conquests come to start a fight. 'I am.'

'Did you know that your skirt is rucked up and that you don't appear to have put any knickers on?'

'Oh God!' Kara immediately dropped the shopping in

order to tidy up her appearance. Her skirt had ridden up her thighs in the car and hadn't fallen back into place when she'd stood up. 'Thanks for telling me.' Her apprehensions melted away, replaced by a sense of gratitude. Really, she ought to have picked up some new panties along with the food, but she rather liked how wicked it made her feel not to wear any. Gavin would have died at the notion of her going commando. He'd have considered it far too whorish. Well, she liked the freedom. What's more she was big enough and bold enough to make that choice for herself. Hell knows why she'd ever let Gavin sap her of her independence. Evidently, love really was blind – during the first bloom at any rate.

The woman was still smiling at her. Kara got her skirt straightened out. 'I'm so sorry. I'm Kara, by the way.'

'Robin. I'm kind of Alaric's go-to girl. And don't be. I often skip wearing them myself. You know how it is. Sometimes you don't do the laundry and run out, and sometimes they get mislaid.' The woman gestured wildly as she spoke and her smile became complicit, so that Kara suspected rumours of her night with Ric were already running rife. 'But don't worry. I won't enquire which of those applies in this instance.'

'Thanks,' Kara mumbled, thinking Robin may as well have said, 'I know where your knickers are, you rampant slut, and I bet I know what he did to you.'

'Is my power sorted out now?' she asked instead.

A tight knot of wrinkles briefly creased the space between Robin's eyebrows. 'Should be. Maybe you oughtn't to have run off so fast after he'd welcomed you.'

Kara blushed furiously. 'I'm not one to impose.'

'Aren't you? Well, more fool you. If he'd just given me the traditional welcome, I'm damn sure I'd have lapped up as much of it as I could get.' Her smile wavered a little. 'I don't live on the island, in case you haven't guessed. I did think about buying your place, but it didn't make financial sense, and it seemed a bit far-fetched to halve my income just to ensure I got Alaric's attention for a night.'

'You ... you considered buying the barn so that Ric would shag you?' Kara stared at her incredulously. That was just crazy. Sure, Ric was striking and charming and a damn fine lay, but in many ways he was also scum. He certainly wasn't the sort of guy you wanted to go losing your heart to.

Robin gave a rather girly shrug.

'Well, thanks for letting me know,' Kara said. She lifted a hand to close the car boot, only for Robin to dart beneath her arm.

'Here, let me help you with those.' She grabbed the remaining shopping bags and took a couple off Kara. 'I can show you a better route to the barn too, one that bypasses that god-awful chasm. You don't like the rope bridge, do you? I wish he'd put a solid one in.'

'Not especially,' Kara agreed. She particularly didn't fancy it while burdened with shopping. And while she wasn't precisely sure she wanted Robin's company, it beat having to traipse back here later in order to schlep more stuff.

'You know, I once saw him chase his naked wife across there,' Robin mused, her mind apparently focused on the bridge, though her feet had started moving in the opposite direction.

Kara stumbled with the shopping. Her heart leapt up her throat. She hadn't made herself many rules post-Gavin, but no married men had definitely been one of them. 'Shit!' she hissed through her teeth, as her fists clenched tight around the carrier bags. Of course, her personal dismay was nothing compared to her re-evaluated opinion of Ric. He performed all that feudal shenanigans stuff despite being married. Surely to God the woman didn't approve of his exploits. If Robin mentioned that he had a child, she was going to be sick.

'Hey, are you all right?' Robin paused to allow her to catch up. 'I suppose you know all about his wife. Everyone does.'

'Yeah – no, actually.'

'Gaw, you can tell you're new around here. She died about five –' Robin screwed up her face as she performed the mental arithmetic '– seven years ago. It was all very *Rebecca*-esque. Boating accident. Very traumatic. Very hush-hush. Shame, she was a lovely lady, a model. Not that they spent much time here. Alaric only became a permanent resident after her death.'

'Is she buried here?' Kara enquired. 'I guess they were close if he wanted to stay here afterwards.'

Robin's neat little brows furrowed again. 'Devoted. They certainly fucked a lot, and she was very beautiful. I don't think he could keep his hands off her. Hey.' Her frown transformed into an impish grin. 'You will share the deets about what he did to you, won't you, because I'm literally dying to hear them.'

Oh, God, thought Kara. *Oh, dear God. I seem to have hooked up with an obsessive.*

* * *

The route Robin took to Beachcomber Barn swept wide of the fort, so that they almost reached the western edge of Liddell Island before doubling back towards the south-facing cove. The barn seemed to have come to life since first thing that morning. With the external shutters drawn back, the penetrating sunlight gave all the interior wood a wonderfully buttery glow. There were still one or two cobwebs lurking in out-of-reach corners, but nothing a broom wouldn't fix. In the kitchen, a large platter of fruit made a wonderful centrepiece for the old-fashioned wooden table. Ric had also left a demijohn of – potent by the smell of it – homebrewed cider and a tray of scones, clotted cream and jam.

Kara stared at the banquet and wondered if it was meant as a peace offering, or if he'd have made the effort regardless.

'I'll put the kettle on.' Robin jumped to the task immediately. While Robin searched the cupboards for cups and began unpacking the shopping, Kara surreptitiously picked up the card that had also been left on the table. It said simply, 'You still owe me. I will collect.' While it wasn't signed, clearly it had come from Ric. Evidently, having a snit over his bedroom arrangements didn't get her off the hook from the sexual deal she'd made with him last night. More surprisingly, she was secretly thrilled. He had threatened to tie her up and roger her mercilessly, the prospect of which warmed her sex. A fact she intended to keep to herself.

She did wonder if the loss of his wife was the reason behind his post-coital coldness. If they'd been very much in love, and he'd been that emotionally bruised, then that could explain why he avoided relationships. It wasn't the sort of thing you could explain to someone you were shagging either. Like 'Oh, by the way, my wife died, so don't expect me to be affectionate.'

Kara tucked the card into her pocket and sat down in time for Robin to thump two steaming mugs down on the pitted table.

'The jam's mine,' Robin explained as they tucked into the scones. 'I make vats of the stuff every year. I pick the berries

81

off the bushes that grow on the island and then sell it at the Bunker. That's the shop in the bay.'

'I know. I've been there.' Kara took a huge bite of her scone that caused jam and cream to splurge everywhere. 'They should sell these there too,' she said, thinking back to her ice-cream breakfast. 'Everyone would come. And they ought to invest in some tables, so that customers could sit down properly and admire the view.' She'd suggest it to Zach when he came by later. It'd breathe some life into the place. Maybe he could even clear out the tat and open up as a café, and consider providing intimate candlelit dinners of an evening.

'Hm, maybe.' Robin seemed less enthralled by the idea of decent dining. Possibly because, judging from the jam, she didn't suffer from Kara's ineptitude in the kitchen. Cupping her pointed chin in the V she formed with her hands, Kara's new friend gazed at her with dreamy expectation. 'About Alaric.'

The scrutiny caused Kara to twitch uncomfortably. While she'd enjoyed Ric's attentions, she'd never been one to talk about her sex life, and sharing such details with a virtual stranger struck her as plain weird. It would be like comparing operation scars, or birthing stories, or making a sordid, guilt-ridden confession to a sex addicts' support class. The very place her mother would be marching her to if she caught so much as a whisper of what she'd been up to since her break-up with Gavin. Besides, it was disquieting enough to know that other island folk, beside her and Ric, knew about the tryst. First Zach, now Robin – had a bulletin gone out that she'd got down and dirty with the local lord?

'How come the house is furnished?' she asked, in order to derail Robin's salacious need for details.

'Huh?' Robin snapped out of her expectant daze. The

resulting jerk made her stool rock, and dipped the ends of her hair into her tea. 'Oh, that's normal for the few properties there are here.' She dried off her hair with the end of the tea towel. 'It's so difficult to get furniture out here, even the flat-packed crap, that everything is included in the sale.'

Presumably Chris had known that when he'd made the purchase. She'd Skype him later and tell him anyway. Let him know everything looked fine, though she'd skip asking him if he'd been aware of the *droit du seigneur* clause in the contract. The thought of talking sex with her baby brother was even ickier than discussing it with Robin.

'More tea?' Robin asked, rising to reheat the kettle.

'Actually, no. If you don't mind, I'd like to make a start on sorting things out. And I could really use a bath.' She wanted a chance to pamper herself a bit before Zach arrived after work.

Robin looked downcast for a moment, only for her pretty smile to reassert itself. 'I could help with that. I can run the water, while you get undressed. I could help with other things too, like ... you know.'

Kara was about to refuse help with her unpacking, when Robin began to gesture downwards with two fingers. When Kara continued to stare at Robin in confusion, the other woman pushed her curled fingers between her thighs to make the offer more obvious.

'Um ...' Kara squeaked in alarm. 'Um, no. Actually, I don't think I need any help with that.' Masturbation had been a mainstay of her relationship when work kept her and Gavin apart. Interestingly, it hadn't been necessary since. Being single had rather pepped up her sex life.

Robin's smile didn't waver. 'I wasn't suggesting you did, but it's not exactly relaxing, is it, rubbing away at oneself?

Why go to the effort when you've a perfectly good offer in hand? Think of it like you would any other chore. You'd totally go for it if I offered to do your ironing, right?'

'It's not really the same,' Kara muttered. Where the hell had this come from? She hadn't picked up any sexual vibes being beamed in her direction.

'Well, believe me, I know my way around girly parts far better than I do an ironing pile. Think about it. You'll be all relaxed and ready for when Alaric comes over.'

'Eh?' Hang on. Kara was about to ask how Robin knew that Zach was coming over, when she realised that Zach hadn't actually been mentioned. 'Ric's not coming over.'

'Duh, honey, didn't you see his card?'

Fabulous! Apparently, even the content of her mail was public knowledge. Not that Ric's message had given any indication about a time or place. Then again, the deal they'd brokered had specified anytime, anyplace – shit! She couldn't have Ric turning up whenever he wanted, because she'd arranged for Zach to be here.

The swell of panic must have shown on her face, because Robin crushed her into an enormous hug. 'I'm going to run you that bath. You look ever so strung out. Here –' she uncorked the homebrew and poured Kara a glass '– get this inside you. It'll help you relax. I'll go rustle up some bubbles and then we can work on your tension.'

Kara dutifully drank the cider, which left her faintly buzzing, then went to the master bedroom to strip off. She couldn't have Ric and Zach both turning up, not even knowing that they'd shared intimacies in the past, because she simply wasn't brazen enough to suggest a threesome, and anything else would be excruciatingly awkward.

Not that she didn't fancy them both, or together. It just

seemed a tad unlikely to happen, even here on Nookie Island. First off, though, she had Robin to get rid of. She'd have to be firm with her.

* * *

When Kara charged into the bathroom, Robin was kneeling by the side of the ancient claw-footed tub. She'd taken off her little bolero jacket and draped it over the doorknob. Both her hands were swishing about in the froth of bubbles on top of the water.

'It's all ready. Bathrobe off and jump in. I can look the other way if you want. We can just chat for a bit.'

Feeling decidedly prudish, Kara still hesitated. She never worried about how men would view her body, but women were always far more critical. They always focused on the bits that weren't as toned as they ought to be, or that waxing had missed. The last time she'd stripped entirely naked before another woman she'd been pre-teen. Her figure was fuller now, curved and soft in some places, a little skinny in others. Guys seemed to appreciate that.

Robin gave her a cheeky, dimpled smile. 'Am I giving you palpitations? That's definitely going in my diary. Come on. Don't be scared.' She lifted one hand free of the water in order to beckon her over. 'I've got the water just right.'

Somewhat exasperated, but at a loss over how to get rid of her new friend, Kara climbed into the high-sided bath, the true dimensions of which she hadn't appreciated until she sank back in the water and the bubbles reached over her shoulders, completely covering her nakedness. Robin had indeed judged the temperature perfectly.

Kara closed her eyes and wallowed. Bubbles tickled the

back of her neck as they burst, and swirling currents rode against her thighs. Slowly, as the heat began to permeate her skin, she realised how tightly some of her muscles were wound. Vigorous sex had given her an intensive workout and her body was feeling the strain. If she kept it up, she'd be sleek as a panther.

Her worry over the chances of both men arriving together diminished too. In actuality, it was quite unlikely. It wasn't as if she'd specified six o'clock sharp to them both. Rather, she'd allowed Robin's obsession with Ric to affect her judgement.

'So, I'm thinking that you're not going to share.'

The sound of Robin's voice cracked through Kara's thoughts. She opened her eyes to find Robin gazing at her with her head cocked to one side.

'I hoped you were a talker, but I can see you're not. Maybe if I talk you can just nod your head and *mmm* if I'm on the right track?'

Kara had almost forgotten that Robin's hands were still in the water until a soap-slicked palm slid up her left leg.

'Where were you? I need to set the scene. Bedroom, his studio, the lounge?'

Something must have flickered through her expression, for Robin settled on the last, though it was more accurately a study than a lounge. Odd that Robin didn't know that. However, the thought bounded away from her as, seconds later, Robin's fingers danced among her pubic curls.

Robin ignored her stiff jerk of surprise. 'Just open your legs a bit,' she insisted, and gave Kara's thighs an encouraging push, until her legs were spread wide enough to comfortably accommodate Robin's questing hand. The tip of one finger stroked against her pussy lips, causing Kara to make a half-choked mewl. She loved the way men explored her cunt with their big blunt-tipped fingers, and how they'd be a fraction too rough in their eagerness to get to the good parts. Robin adopted a far softer approach. She didn't push at all, instead she stuck to gentle caresses that encouraged Kara's body to open up and reveal its secrets.

'Hmm, I think you're a little tender down here. I hear a good fuck can do that, and I know Alaric can get a little vigorous. That's why we need to get you all relaxed again.'

'How do you know?' Kara was tempted to ask. Robin had admitted she had no first-hand experience with Ric, which rather suggested a more suspect method of obtaining that information. Kara had a sudden vision of Robin lying on a cliff-top with a pair of binoculars clamped to her face, or maybe even a camera with a telescopic lens. The thought caused the muscles in her abdomen to cramp. Her nipples stood up too, like crooked towers that crested the surface of the water. Robin unfortunately took that as a sign of arousal.

'Hold still. Let me find the soap.'

Kara started to relax, thinking that Robin meant to spend some time actually bathing her; only her hand remained over Kara's mons as she wrestled the bar of soap out of the water and brought it to her nose to give it a good sniff.

'Excellent,' she pronounced. 'Unscented. This'll do the trick.'

The precise nature of the trick, Kara dared not ask. It became apparent when the firm edge of the soap swept along the seam of her labia. Unlike the sweeps of Robin's fingers, this pressure was more insistent. It caught her clit, causing joy to stab through her pleasure centres, as it stroked back and forth, slicking her folds until she was completely open to the assault.

Kara instinctively rocked her hips.

'That's right, honey. Just there, isn't it? I told you I was good at this. Imagine what Alaric could do with a bar of soap.'

She did. She knew without question that he'd photograph himself soaping her all over. Then he'd shag her on the tiled floor so that they slid about together, hardly able to hold on to one another properly.

'Tell me what you're seeing. Tell me what he did.'

Kara kept her lips sealed. Ric would make her talk, but Robin didn't possess that power, even if she had cajoled her into this.

Just then, the curved end of the bar caught the underside of Kara's clit at such a perfect angle that her hips bucked upwards seeking repetition. Oh, God! It was perfect. Just the right place, the perfect pressure, coupled with that delicious glide. If she ever wanted to come fast, this would be the way to achieve it. Short sharp strokes that lavished attention on her clit and seemed to make that organ swell and form boundless connections with nerves all across her body.

'Kara,' her new friend begged. 'Please. Just tell me how it was between you. I'm not looking for anything else. Did he stroke you like this?' Robin's fingers linked with Kara's. She drew their hands out of the water and then placed Kara's hand upon her bare arm where it rested upon the rim of the bathtub. 'One squeeze for yes and two for no. Let's have a practice. Did he touch you like this with his fingers?'

He hadn't. Not really. Kara squeezed Robin's arm twice.

'OK,' Robin hissed between her teeth. 'With his lips then? Did he lick you?'

Closing her fingers around Robin's arm made the confession easier. She could answer without divulging any real details, which Robin could then interpret as she chose.

Meanwhile, the soap continued to glide in short swift

strokes that focused on Kara's clit, making her back arch against the enamel. A buzz began to build behind her clit, the pleasure radiating outwards, like white noise from a radio. It intensified each time the caress swept the underside of her nub, and caused her inner muscles to clench tight.

Kara squeezed Robin's arm again, not really caring what sort of admission she was making.

'Did he put his cock inside you?' Robin asked. She said it in a way that seemed to amplify the question.

Of course he had. He'd fucked her long and hard and she'd adored it. He'd filled her up in a way that knocked the breath out of her. He'd made her pant and cry out, not to mention beg him for more. Kara didn't divulge any of that, even though she knew it was what Robin really wanted to hear. Robin wouldn't be content until she knew how long Ric had fucked her for and in what positions, and the minutiae of every act. Even then, she still wouldn't be entirely satisfied. Only actually having Ric would ensure that. And after years of frenetic masturbation and imagining, it was likely to result in disappointment.

'Face to face?' Robin asked. She thrust two fingers into Kara's cunt as a substitute cock. 'Oh, man! You're so ready for him, all plump and needy. I bet he stretched you real nice.'

Heaven – it had felt like heaven. Even this felt pretty good. Kara lifted her butt up to meet Robin's thrusts, no longer concerned about whose hand she rode. Only the buzz mattered, that magical rise into oblivion, and the final moment when all existence coalesced before it blew apart again.

Rather than explaining what had happened, Kara rolled over in the water. It meant disengaging briefly, but Robin quickly obliged again. Things became more lewd once Kara rested on all fours. Her rear poked up clear of the water so that her arousal was clearly visible as the engorged pink lips of her slit.

'Oh, yeah. I can totally see him doing this. Lift that bum up a bit, so that I can reach.'

Robin slid three fingers back into Kara's cunt. She worked them like a short stubby cock, perfectly matching Kara's rocking motion. 'Oh, honey, think of him. Remember him for me. I can feel how wet you are. I bet he shafted you long and good. He'll be here with you again later too. He's going to put his long cock into you and fuck you right up to heaven. Do you think you can take another finger?'

Apparently she could. The walls of her sheath clasped tight at the intrusion, milking pleasure out of it, while her clit, which had been neglected a little, became painfully tight.

'Tell me when you need to come, honey. I know what to do. I can satisfy you like he did.'

'Now,' Kara gasped. Enough waiting. She was going to have to frig herself if Robin didn't deal with the ache.

Robin found the soap again and then, moving both her hands in unison, speed gradually increasing, raced Kara towards her climax.

Kara's orgasm flashed like lightning engulfing a hillside. The quake of thunder followed, making her shake and call out. She glowed, heated all over, before sinking back into the still warm water. Her hot cheek pressed against the sloping side of the tub. Eyes closed, she lay still, just breathing.

'Thank you for allowing me to share your time with him like that.' Robin leaned over her, briefly blocking out the light from above. She dropped a chaste kiss upon Kara's lips. 'You're so lucky. He won't even look at me.'

'People don't appreciate what's there for them every day.'

One had to wonder what Ric's object was. Given the 'take me now' vibes Robin had to be giving off, it was a damn miracle he hadn't taken her up on the offer. Maybe he just didn't mix work and pleasure.

'I'll catch you about,' Robin said. Her pretty eyes twinkled in the growing gloom.

When Kara next opened her eyes, her guest had departed. She cleaned herself with shower gel and then rinsed off under the shower. It'd been fun, but she hoped Robin didn't think they were going to make this sort of thing a regular date. She'd spent too long relating the facts of her whereabouts and life to Gavin; she wasn't about to start relaying everything to an obsessive friend instead.

CHAPTER SEVEN

Kara woke to the twilight of her laptop screensaver. She'd spoken to her brother, but that must have been some hours ago. The creaky, tapestry-strewn master bedroom lay in almost total darkness now, with only a trace of moonlight visible through the circular stained-glass window set at knee level in the wall. Someone – oh God, was that Zach? – was banging on the door. Judging by his impatience, he'd already been out there some time.

Kara hopped off the bed. She fastened her bathrobe tight around her waist as she ran for the stairs. Honestly, she ought to give lessons on how to make a poor impression. She'd have to make it clear once she'd invited Zach in that he'd caught her out and that she hadn't dressed this provocatively on purpose.

'Shit – oh, shit! I'm so sorry. I didn't mean to make you wait. I fell asleep, you just woke me.'

Only it wasn't Zach idling on her porch with his feet planted on her doormat and his bum resting against the wall – it was Ric.

His flaxen hair framed his narrow face as he turned to her. His hands were pressed prayer-like to his generous lips.

He'd dressed almost entirely in black, which by moonlight gave his skin a luminous pallor. Kara's heart did a sort of hiccup, while her feet glued themselves to the spot. Speechless, she blinked at him. Heaven help her, but she'd forgotten exactly how striking he truly was. She'd given in to lust last night for a very good reason: he was magnetic. Suddenly, his offhandedness in dismissing her after sex seemed a minor issue. He was here after all, come to claim his prize, and not even twenty-fours had passed.

The outline of the thickly bunched muscles that made up Ric's torso showed briefly through his ribbed cotton top as he shifted slightly on the spot. He hadn't given her an opportunity to explore his body. That had to be rectified immediately. A smile tugged its way across her lips. How glorious he'd look stretched out in her bed with only a sheet to cover him. She was going to spend hours doing just that, stroking him, teasing him, until he was quaking and desperate for release.

'I wasn't expecting you.'

'Evidently not.' His pale gaze swept across over her body, dwelling briefly on the hasty knot she'd made in her belt. Kara returned the look with an equally salacious one of her own. His jeans were low-slung, and pleasantly tight around the thighs. They also fastened with a button fly, perfect for teasing open slowly.

'I'm not interrupting anything, am I?' He straightened up from his slouched position.

Kara swept the horizon behind him, wondering if Zach were about to arrive too and what would happen if he did. God forgive her, but she couldn't help fantasising about an arrangement in which she got to have them both. Zach claimed that he and Ric had been lovers. They both seemed open-minded. A threesome wasn't such an enormous ask, was it? Perhaps it was. So she kept her mouth closed about Zach. What was the point in stirring up trouble unnecessarily?

'You got my note?' Ric asked.

Kara tugged the handwritten card out of her bathrobe pocket. Got it, thought about it and hadn't quite believed in it. 'You were a bit sparing with the details. So, you're here to claim your prize?'

He had a nerve. Boy, did he have a nerve. She didn't hate him for what he'd done, but he did owe her an apology, and he was outright presumptuous turning up like this.

Ric tilted his head so that his hair shadowed his face. His luminous eyes grew dark. 'Actually, I wondered if you fancied coming for a walk.'

'In the dark!' Was he for real? Who the hell invited their neighbours out for an evening stroll any more? The human race had just about forgotten how to walk. Another few years and they'd be zipping about on floating motorised pedestals.

'I often walk in the dark,' he elucidated, evidently prompted to speak by her silence. 'There are fewer people about, and since I was coming this way –' of course, he had his dogs to exercise, though, curiously, they didn't seem to be with him on this excursion '– I thought you might like to see the beach. I didn't think you'd have been down there yet. It's really pretty.'

Kara stepped out on to the garden path. Above them, the entirety of the Milky Way was strung across the night sky like a glittering stream. The reflection of all those lights upon the water would make the ocean seem vast and magnificent. Ric's notion remained questionable, though. 'It seems awfully romantic. I didn't have you pinned as that type.' He hadn't done anything up to this point to suggest it, quite the opposite in fact.

'Well, don't come out if you're expecting odes and sonnets. I like the stars, but I'm not much for flowery sentiments.'

'Likewise.' She'd been taken in by a heap of romantic nonsense in the past. Then she'd woken up and realised Gavin's romanticism and coddling were simply designed to keep her in her place. The crunch had come the day she'd lost her job and she'd caught him smiling because she was finally dependent upon him. 'Very well, I'll come. What should I expect?'

Ric's brows briefly furrowed. 'A scramble down the cliff face followed by sand between your toes.'

That's it? He had to have an ulterior motive. 'Did you bring your camera?'

'No.' He quizzically cocked an eyebrow. 'I'm sensing disappointment.'

'Well, after last night, I'm not sure what to expect. I thought perhaps you were going to spring some ancient tithe on me?'

'Oh!' His mouth rounded. 'I wasn't planning to. Besides, none of the ancient documents refer to photography. Maybe I ought to add a codicil.'

God, he both vexed and charmed her. It wasn't as if she wanted lewd photos of herself floating about the place – the locals were gossiping about her enough – although the idea of having a permanent record of some of her experiences did kind of appeal. She had always loved the more visual aspects of sex.

Actually, she'd like to turn a camera on Ric. He'd make for a far more evocative picture than she would, with his silk-like hair and pale hypnotic eyes, not to mention that feral, fox-like smile. Plus, she liked to see muscle and cock, not feminine curves.

'Clothing recommendations?'

'Thigh-high boots and nothing more.'

Kara gently tapped his cheek. 'It's a little nippy for that, don't you think?'

'You asked.' His lips pursed. 'And I'm sure I could dream up ways to keep you warm.'

Blazing, she imagined. Unfortunately, she didn't own such footwear. Maybe Ric did, amongst his studio props. If so, perhaps she could play dress-up next time she dropped by the fort. 'I thought you said we were going on a stroll.'

Maddeningly, he just grinned.

'OK. Look, come on in.' Kara pushed the door wide, making space for him to cross the threshold. With any luck, Zach had already come and gone, and she'd slept through it. She liked Zach, and didn't want him stumbling upon her engaged with Ric. Right now, it seemed sensible to keep her options open.

Ric flicked on a lamp in the lounge, saving Kara the bother of stumbling around trying to locate the overhead light switch. She left him to make himself comfortable and trotted upstairs to pull on some clothes. Five minutes later they were back on the doorstep, her in jogging pants and a zip top worn over a sports bra.

Ric tweaked the sports ensemble with a pout. 'I preferred my suggestion.'

They headed straight across the heath to reach the cove, where the moonlit water lapped quietly at the shore. The crisp, salty smell of seaweed drifted up to them as they scrambled down a narrow gorge that was cut into the rock face and zigzagged its way down to the shingle-covered beach. Only near the water's edge did the pebbles give way to sand. They stood on the wet shore, letting the tide pull the ground away from beneath them.

'Thank you for the scones,' Kara said, as she watched him skim stones across the waves. 'Robin found me and let me know you'd sorted everything.'

'I'm sure she did.'

The sharp edge to his voice made Kara's attention perk. 'Sorry, I thought you'd sent her.'

Ric shook his head. He began to walk again, following the line of the surf. 'I figured you'd go home eventually.' He stuck his hands in his pockets and focused his attention out to sea. 'I sent Zach a text, in case he ran into you again.'

'You didn't send Robin?'

'Didn't I just say that? Why would I? She's nothing to do with me.'

'She's not your PA?' Kara hurried to keep pace with him. That's definitely what Robin had implied.

'She's not my anything.'

Alarm bells started ringing in Kara's brain. She'd allowed Robin to ... well, to masturbate her, having accepted her for whom she claimed to be, when apparently it had all been lies. What, if any of it, had been the truth? 'Then why would she say that?'

She didn't need Ric to answer. Not that he did. Robin's obsession had been apparent from the outset. She'd latched on to Kara deliberately so she could get a vicarious kick out of reliving Kara's night with Ric. She'd probably seen her leave the fort first thing, or, hell, just made an assumption based on her knowledge of Ric and the rights he claimed over those resident on his island.

'You didn't speak to her about us?'

'I haven't spoken to her in years.'

Kara stopped walking and watched the space between her

and Ric grow. 'That's odd,' she called, 'because she seems very fond of you.'

Ric's back immediately stiffened. He stopped and turned, and then swallowed up the space between them in five long strides. 'Fondness isn't really the right term, is it?' He looked her hard in the face, bending to do so. His expression had become brittle and tiny crow's feet creased the corners of his eyes. 'Go on, ask. Most people want to know why I don't oblige her.'

'Why don't you?' Kara murmured.

He shrugged as he straightened back to his full height, allowing the movement to convey his ambivalence. 'I don't fancy her. She doesn't live here.' He raised his hands in a gesture of indifference, before digging them back into his pockets, so that the denim crept down his hips. 'You can couple that with the fact that she's too clingy. I'm not interested in that sort of dependency. I figured you'd have realised that by now.'

Kara folded her arms across her chest. 'It's why you cut things dead last night. You didn't want me thinking that you were somehow available,' she drawled, extending the syllables of the last word.

Ric had the grace to look contrite. He pulled his hands from his pockets and extended them towards her in friendship. 'I'm sorry. I didn't mean to piss you off. I just wanted to –'

'– make it clear that it was sex and nothing more. I got that. I'm fine with it.' She stared at his hands, unwilling to accept the embrace. 'I'm nonplussed over this, though. Walking? You're not interested in dating me so what is it?'

'Does it have to be anything?'

'Yeah,' she said. 'Yeah, it does.'

He dropped his gaze to the sand for a moment. 'OK.' He

looked up, nodding. 'As you want it. I needed to return these.' Ric fished about in his pocket and drew out a scrunched piece of cloth. 'You left your knickers behind.' He twirled the coloured scrap of cotton he'd stripped from her the night before around the end of her finger.

Kara stared at him, but didn't reach out and claim her undies.

'I suppose you know only naughty girls take off their knickers in a stranger's living room,' he crooned, still twirling the cloth about his finger. His grin split his face, and warmed the blue of his eyes. 'And only really naughty girls walk around in short skirts wearing nothing underneath. I dread to think of all the trouble you've stirred up on my island flashing your muff at the tourists.'

The tourists hadn't given her much trouble. It'd been the inhabitants.

Kara made a backhanded swipe at his torso, not caring about the knickers but irritated by his grin. Ric easily dodged. He grabbed her arm and swung her into his embrace, so that she was standing with her back pressed to his front, both of them facing the ocean. 'Get off me.'

'Shan't.'

'What do you want?' His loins pressed tightly against her bottom, so she could feel the shape of him beneath his clothing.

'You know what I want. It's the same thing you want.'

Was it? Could she genuinely do long-term sex with him without becoming even a little emotionally invested, or knowing the first thing about him? Could anyone do that? Ought she to mention Zach, who seemed altogether more emotionally malleable, and whom she could see building an actual friendship with? She probably should, but wasn't that the point Ric was making? That he forfeited all right to any knowledge of her?

Kara buttoned her lips and kept the information locked up inside her, where it fizzed, making her feel somewhat volatile.

'Strangers,' Ric purred into her ear. 'Not fuck buddies or friends. There's nothing familiar about us except our wants and the shape of our bodies.' His lips traced the pulse point in her neck, lightly at first, though his sucking soon became insistent.

Kara tilted her head, allowing him greater access as her breathing began to stutter. A flood of sexual heat liquefied her insides. That point just next to her collarbone was apparently hardwired to her nipples and her clit.

Her sighs became voluble, and devolved into pleasurable groans.

She turned in his arms, and stretched on to her toes to reach his lips. His hand clasped tight over hers where she held it against his chest. His thigh fitted neatly between her legs as she leaned into him. As for the kiss, Ric's lips were softly demanding. He teased, never quite giving her all she wanted, like he was deliberately winding her up and holding her back.

Craving more, not less, Kara clung to him. She pushed her hands inside his jacket and explored the contours of his back. This time sex wasn't all going to be his way. She intended to take a little of what she wanted, not just wait for him to dish it out.

Her tongue tangled with his, spearing into his mouth in an imitation of coitus, while her hands moved to his button-fly and the wedge of his cock lying diagonally beneath.

'Let me go down on you.' He'd shown her what he could do. Now it was her turn. She pulled away from his kiss, though he tried to hold her there by pushing his hands into her hair.

Kara backed him up against a nearby rock. Her hands passed up and down his body, taking in the hollows and planes. He was broadest across the shoulders, thinnest at the waist, every inch pleasingly firm. Within seconds she had him out of his jacket and T-shirt, his clothing making a shadowy pile by their feet. 'You're not cold, I hope,' she said a second before latching on to one of his stiff little nipples.

'If I were, what would you do?'

Kara unbuckled his belt. She didn't bother with the buttons of his fly, choosing instead to simply tug the denim down until it hugged the tops of his thighs. 'I'd tell you to man up and cope.'

He responded with a soft guffaw that morphed into a sigh as she slid her tongue down the tight contours of his abs to where the head of his cock bucked expectantly against his flesh. His cock stood flushed red and eager, his balls drawn tight to his body.

Kara stood back to admire him. Ric Liddell had to be one of the most beautiful men she'd ever met and just because they weren't headed for something deep and meaningful didn't mean she couldn't appreciate that. Lord, even his cock was pretty, ramrod-straight and streaked with pale blue veins like a Ming-dynasty vase. Only at the tip where the skin was taut and smooth did the colour grow fierce; there it darkened to a pinkish-plum.

In fact, he looked so perfect, so lewd and magnificent all at once, that she got out her phone and took a snapshot.

Ric didn't bat an eyelid at her recording his image, not even when she turned the screen towards him so he could see how proud he stood. He sniffed. 'Definitely one for the female gaze, that. Lighting sucks.'

'Aren't you supposed to follow that with "I hope you do

too?"' Kara smiled up at him sweetly. 'You could ask nicely and I might, you know.'

'How about I ask nastily?'

God, that feral grin of his, it damn near turned her inside out. Somehow he managed to make his subsequent growl of 'Suck my cock, Kara' the sexiest sound on the planet.

Ric hooked a hand behind her head and pulled her down towards his erection. She knelt willingly and took him fully into her mouth. The hot, pungent taste of his body, all male, laced with the salty taste of pre-come, hit her tongue and sent a welcome ripple of arousal through her body. This was simple and straightforward. She knew all the rules. Sex could be so uncomplicated. It didn't need prettifying with unnecessary sentiment. All that mattered was that he shagged her senseless and that at the end they were both satisfied.

God, she hoped he was going to shag her senseless, and that he didn't just come in her mouth and then walk her home.

Ric, it turned out, was a little more than she could comfortably swallow. Kara stuck to lavishing attention on the head of his shaft, swirling her tongue against the delicate slitted eye and claiming each precious drop of pre-come that spilled.

Ric's palm rubbed over the back of her head, not so much encouragingly as though he was keeping a tight hold on where she was taking him. It still came as something of a shock when he pushed her away.

Kara fell back on to her haunches. 'What?' She gazed up at him expectantly. 'What?' She wriggled her jogging bottoms down to her calves so he had only to pull aside the scrap of her knickers to get to her.

'All the way,' he insisted. He kicked off the rest of his clothes, while she tugged her trousers over her shoes. He didn't immediately fall on her, though. Instead he ran into the water.

'Wait.' Kara gingerly tiptoed after him. The surf soaked through her deck shoes, chilling her toes and making her screech. She hated the water, had always done so. She could swim, but only just. 'I'm not coming in. It's too cold.'

'Not even if I promise to warm you up?'

He turned his back towards the moonlight so that he stood facing her naked. Salt spray coated his skin and gleamed with the light from the stars, save where the black lines of ink covered his biceps. 'Come and give my cock another kiss, Kara. Let me make love to you in the foam.'

'You don't want to make love. You just want to shag my bottom,' she taunted. She stuck out her tongue and refused to budge. Ric flicked water in her direction, provoking a scream as she tried to dash out of range of the spray.

'Been thinking about that, have you? I haven't forgotten how hot you were back there.'

How could she not? No one had ever treated her quite so brazenly. No other man had offered to fuck her there, or even really explored the nerve-endings in the way he'd done. Not that that meant she was going to roll over and just let him do it. She clucked at him. 'If you think I'm going to consent to that, you're deluded. You'll have to tie me up first.'

'Damn,' he hissed. 'And I seem to have forgotten my rope.' He padded towards her, edging her back on to the beach, his erection still standing proud and filthy glitter in his eyes. 'You know it really is time to get you out of those clothes.'

Kara shook her head. While the evening was balmy, a breeze still blew in off the sea, and she wasn't looking to gain a reputation for streaking. He might be comfortable frolicking on the sand in the altogether, but she'd rather they took this home.

Hence, when he sprang towards her, she ran.

At first she easily outpaced him, only for her gait to become unsteady as she crossed the shingle and headed towards a track leading back up towards the headland. Ric didn't seem to encounter nearly so many problems, for he had a long slender build, backed up by plenty of muscle, so that he seemed to skip over the pebbles, while her feet sank in them.

He grabbed hold of her jacket as they neared the old way marker stone at the top of the cliff.

Kara squirmed in his arms, shrieking and protesting as he wrestled her up against the rock. 'Got you,' he said, laughing as he unzipped her top. 'Now I'm going to eat you.' He gave a snarl and aimed for her throat. He didn't bite; rather he sucked, right over the sweet spot in her neck he'd found before, where his renewed efforts caused her legs to wobble. Kara pressed tight against his naked body, unable to do anything but groan.

Ric might not appreciate her clothing on a visual level, but it had several bonuses on a sensual one. The jersey fabric hugged tight to her form. Thus, when he rubbed up against her, she felt all his raw power, plus the damn heat of his skin. Kara clawed at his shoulders, suddenly desperate for everything he offered. It wasn't enough. She dug her fingertips into the thickly bunched muscles of his arse in order to bring their loins closer. In return Ric shoved up her sports bra, so that her breasts bulged beneath the elastic, squashed into fullness, and he took possession of her nipples.

'Yes,' she crooned. 'Yes. Oh, please.' He effortlessly stripped off her jacket. To Kara's surprise he claimed her phone from her pocket, and used it to snap her picture.

'This is definitely more my thing. You look positively sluttish.'

'I thought you were into creating art?'

Ric glanced at the image on the screen again, then back at her. 'You and me, babe, we're definitely doing that.' He took a few more shots, recording in explicit detail the lush, wet swell of her cunt as he fingered her.

'I hope you're going to let me photograph you properly. I was serious about that offer to set you up.'

Kara pushed a hand up against his chest, trying to slow him down. He knew just how to fire up her senses so that she was on edge and ready to come in hardly any time at all. She didn't want to explode just yet, and she was trying to keep up with what he was saying.

That, and they really ought to move this indoors, just in case Zach came by, or Robin was out with her binoculars.

No amount of tugging or twisting made any impression on him, though.

Ric spun her around. 'It's time,' his breath whispered against her ear.

'For what?'

Realisation struck the moment he fitted his body to the curve of her back and his erection nudged into the channel between her cheeks.

Apprehension coupled with the pressure of the icy rock against her front caused her nipples to further pucker. In contrast, Ric's naked body warmed her back and promised additional heat. He kissed all the way down her spine to her buttocks, where he lavished attention on the curves of her arse. His big hands took possession of her rounded globes, holding them, massaging them. Thence followed some subtler strokes, gentle caresses that raised the hairs and walked the border of sensitivity. She'd never have tolerated them if not for the rougher handling that came first.

'Is this really the place to be doing this?' Kara's words came out in a rush, betraying her nervousness.

'Absolutely, the view is magnificent.'

Whether he meant the view out to sea or the sight of her doing mermaid impersonations against the rock, she wasn't sure.

'Just say if you're not up for it, Kara.' His tongue made a swift foray into the channel between her cheeks, where he gently dabbed at her furled entrance. 'But –' the word came out as a gasp '– I've got to tell you, you've no idea how much I want to fuck your arse.'

The words to deny him clean escaped her, because the connections caused by his delving tongue seemed to short-circuit the reasoning part of her brain. Suddenly, everything was about pushing back against that pressure, and squirming a little left and right in order to maximise how good it felt.

'Do you like my kisses, Kara? Shall I push a finger inside?'

Should he? 'Yes ... oh, God!' This was crazy, she was chilled and exposed, and somewhere in the back of her mind the fear of being seen lingered. But her nipples were so pointed and stiff that they almost hurt, and yet she knew she couldn't move from that boulder until he'd delivered on his promise.

When his heat parted from her body, she glanced back to find him slathering his cock with lube, pulled from the pocket of his jacket, which she didn't recall him even picking up. He came to her all swathed and shiny.

His fingers slid through her juices. The rough handling only made them run more thickly. Ric used her wetness to further lubricate her hole.

'Ready for this?' He sandwiched them close together.

'No ... Yeah.' She was and she wasn't.

The pressure against her backside grew intense. It almost threatened to overwhelm her desire. Just when her nerves had fired up and she was starting to get skittery, Ric cupped her mons with his palm and gently pulled her back on to him.

'Yes. Fuck, yes!' His hissed exclamation scalded the back of her neck.

Ric curled up his fingers so that two of them teased the entrance to her sex, then he used his other hand to hold her hip still as he gave another thrust.

It felt alien and tight as the springy curls of his loins nestled up against the curves of her arse. At the same time, pleasure seemed to flood her sex, so that the slide of his palm against her cunt became ridiculously smooth. Moisture trickled down her inner thigh. Heat followed, as he'd said it would, but not contained purely within her bottom. Rather the flames crackled and spread right across her synapses.

Kara ached, and he filled her. Or at least he filled part of her, for her pussy clenched at the tips of his fingers, trying to hold on to something that wasn't there. Perhaps it was no surprise that she thought of Zach in that moment: Zach joining them, Zach filling up her cunt while Ric pleasured her arse. Ric knew how to make this good. It seemed totally natural to have him filling her in this way, and far, far nicer than she ever thought it would be, but having both men, that'd be like discovering a whole new world.

'Babe, you're heaven,' Ric murmured. 'I need to speed it up, though. You're too tight. It's too good to hold it off for long.' The way his breathing had become laboured and his hips rolled in ever swifter circles seemed to confirm that.

'Is this what you did with Zach?' she blurted, only to clench her muscles tight and clamp a hand across her mouth.

Ric groaned. 'What did you say?'

Shit! She hadn't meant to speak her thoughts aloud. 'I asked if you fucked Zach this way. He kind of hinted that you weren't picky over gender orientation when it came to collecting on your taxes.'

Ric's laughter emerged in punchy little bursts. 'I bet you just love that idea, don't you?' He wrapped his arms around her and pulled her more firmly against him, so that all that lay between their bodies was a trickle of sweat. 'Mmm, yeah, I can tell you do. Your passage is like silk. You're so smooth, but your pussy is just weeping for more, isn't it? Is that why you're thinking of him? Are you getting ideas from those pictures of him?'

'No.' Dear God, had the guy she thought she'd recognised in Ric's photos been Zach?

The denial made him chuckle again.

'Maybe I ought to haul you both in and do a shoot. He has a prehensile tongue, did you know that?

Did such a thing exist? No matter, just hearing Ric say it formed extra lewd pictures in her brain of what the two men had been doing together in order for Ric to discover it.

'Just watch him licking an ice cream if you don't believe me.' Ric shoved her legs wider apart, so that he could push his fingers a fraction deeper. 'Oh, man. That's really got you wet.' Immediately, her sheath clenched around his digits. His loins slapped hard against her bottom, *thump, thump, clash*, like he was playing percussion. With twin penetrations egging her towards climax, it came rushing up in a lava flow.

'Just a little more, Kara. We're almost there.'

Ric gyrated their bodies as one. For three, maybe four seconds everything was sublimely perfect. Then her muscles tightened and began to pulse. Her climax ripped through her as a stream of white hot darts.

'Oh, hellfire. Oh, sh –' He pressed hard upon her clit, and then seemed to soar for ever, his hips still pumping long after she was all wrung out.

Ric held on to her long after his orgasm had petered out, which she took as a sort of apology for the previous time when he'd been so abrupt. She did wonder though if he wasn't simply holding on because his legs were so shaky he feared toppling over. If he felt remotely as she did, then that remained a genuine possibility.

'Mammoth,' he muttered, when they eventually broke apart.

Kara turned around to face him and caught him mopping the sweat off his brow with his T-shirt. 'Is it true, about you and Zach? You never answered.'

Ric offered up the T-shirt for her to use. 'It's true,' he said simply, and left it at that.

CHAPTER EIGHT

Ric wasn't sure what he was doing; instead of parting ways, he'd somehow ended up back at Kara's, drinking tea of all things. It wasn't even as if he liked the stuff, the tannin always coated his teeth, and they were struggling when it came to small talk. It wasn't like him, but he just didn't want to go home.

Kara yawned into her palm, too polite to show him the door. He was confident she wasn't looking for anything deeper from him. Maybe that's why he felt so safe here. She understood. She was happy with this being a casual thing.

'I ought to let you sleep,' he said eventually, and returned his mug to the coffee table. Kara followed him to the door to show him out. But when she reached out to raise the latch, he turned and enfolded her in his arms instead. Then somehow the exaggerated goodbye kiss he'd meant it to be morphed into a hello-there's-no-way-I'm-leaving-yet kiss, as his blood rushed to his loins.

Thinking with his cock took no effort. It never had, and it was preferable to the crap that was going on inside his brain. Ric scooped Kara into his arms and carried her right up the stairs to her bed.

'Ric,' she squealed, when he threw her on to the mattress, though he noted it wasn't a cry of objection. 'What are you –' Her words petered out as he loosened his fly and then dived on to the bed alongside her.

'You're not too tired, are you?' He zipped open her jacket and headed straight for her breasts. Playtime with Zach just didn't involve such bountiful delights. He mouthed her nipples through the bra, smiling when his actions made them steeple. But it wasn't enough just to do that: he needed some proper visuals, and his fingers were soon working to open the catch.

'Mm,' she groaned. 'What are you doing? What's this about? I thought you were going home.'

'Isn't it apparent?' He wrestled off his T-shirt, flung it to some far corner of the room. Kara's clothing followed, right down to the tiny scrap of lace that was masquerading as a pair of panties. He left that on, somehow appreciating its role as an imperfect barrier. 'Just because it's casual doesn't mean it has to be quick.' He raised his eyebrows questioningly.

Her eyes widened in surprise. 'You're staying ... you're staying the night?'

'That's not a problem, is it?' He looked up at her from beneath his eyelashes. 'I promise I don't snore. I'm an ace alarm clock, and I give the best bedtime cuddles this side of ... oooh, Exeter.'

'Yeah?'

He traced his tongue across her middle, stopping briefly to tease the hollow of her navel. 'Yeah.' He shuffled backwards a fraction more, so that his mouth was poised over her sex. 'Want a demonstration?' He ran a finger, and then his tongue, around the edge of the triangle of lace. It tickled him to bits the way her thighs automatically clenched as if to guard her treasure, and that just made the notion of coaxing her all the more appealing.

'I don't want a demo. I want the real thing.' She reached out to him. Touched him on the shoulders, where the black lines of one of his tattoos wound across the flesh. He kissed her briefly before pushing her back down on to her back.

'Real deal coming up.'

He figured she thought he'd remove her panties. Not so. Ric returned to nibbling around the edges of them as though they were some sort of chastity belt he couldn't work out how to breach, which had exactly the effect he was looking for. Within minutes she was lifting her hips off the bed, making a silent plea for him to take them off, which he didn't, because he'd already decided that they were definitely staying on. Life was all about contrasts. Last night in his study he'd had her fully dressed apart from her panties, and now, in her bed, he intended to have her naked apart from her knickers.

What's more, he absolutely knew it was the right choice from the way she squirmed when he dipped his tongue underneath the barrier.

Yeah, she was an absolute pleasure to torture, just like Zach was. Not that he was thinking about him right now. He pushed the image of Zach's wiry body to the back of his mind. Right now his goal was pussy, not cock.

'God, Ric, please.'

Kara did a crunch and sat up. She clutched his head to her crotch as if that was enough to persuade him he had permission to go further. Maybe he was being a bit of a bastard; after all, her clit was already peeping out of its hood. He could see the outline of the little bead through the layer of lace. He petted it with his tongue, provoking delighted

113

groans, only for her voice to momentarily fall silent when he began to gently suck.

Then, 'Oh, oh!' she sang. 'No fair. Let me touch you too.'

Ric looked up along the length of her body, a grin stretching his cheeks. 'OK.' They could make this mutual. He turned around, so that he crouched on all fours above her. Kara at once pulled him down towards her mouth.

Ric hissed. The muscles of his abs pulled tight as she welcomed him into the warm cave of her mouth. He held himself tense, basking in the glory of the moment. His erection swelled, and he rolled his hips in time with her sucks. Kara clamped her hands upon his arse and took control of his rhythm. Not too far, she wasn't quite up to having him slide into her throat. But then not many people mastered that talent.

Ric drew aside her panties and began to fuck her with his tongue. The taste of her filled his mouth, slightly salty in amongst the sweetness, and so different to the taste of a man.

So different to the taste of Zach.

He ought to have been doing this with him tonight. Instead, Zach was determined to put his nose out of joint. Why did he have to sacrifice everything they had for something so pointless? What did words signify anyway? They knew in their hearts what they felt when they were together. There'd never been any question about the attraction between them. Didn't that make it obvious that something else existed too?

Yes, you could have casual, meaningless sex, but what they had had never been casual. After seven years, how could it be? However, that didn't mean they needed to pin a label on it.

Screw him. If he couldn't see the truth, then let him watch it all melt away.

He had Kara.

She understood him.

She got his needs.

Perhaps got them a little too well. Her fingers uncurled from the flesh of his arse and began exploring the puckered ring of muscle between his cheeks. 'Revenge,' he muttered, knowing this was payback for what he'd done to her. It made him want to hug her tight. Yes, she understood him enough to mirror all the stuff he'd loved doing to her.

It got a little hard to concentrate, of course, when her fingers were dabbing inside his arse. All the little nerve-endings there were instantly alight and sending pulses of pleasure to his brain. Things got harder still when she stopped sucking him long enough to wet two fingers. Ric lifted his head. He knew what was coming, before her fingers wormed inside his arsehole. She really did mean to repay every moment of pleasure he'd given her.

Only, men ... *he* ... wasn't wired in quite the same way. Something slipped in more than an inch and angled quite like that was guaranteed to make short work of anything. Ric pulled away fast and rolled over on to his back, panting.

Kara immediately scrambled over him so that she sat astride his waist. Her hair formed a canopy around them as she looked down into his face. 'Keen to dish it out but you can't take it, eh?'

'I can take it,' he gasped.

She laughed as he brushed the line of sweat from above his lip.

'Does Zach fuck you?' she asked.

He didn't want to think about Zach. He tried to distract her with a kiss, but she just lifted up out of his reach and kept her hands on his shoulders so that he couldn't rise.

'No.' Leastways, he didn't very often.

'Why not?'

'I fuck him. He's my tenant, not the other way around.'
She grinned then, as if this proved she'd somehow bested him.

'Often?'

'Why the questions?'

Her smile wrinkled the top of her cheeks and showed off
all her teeth. 'Just curious.' She tilted her head to one side.
'And picturing it is kind of a turn on.'

He couldn't argue with that. Even if he hadn't been his
lover, Zach would still have been his muse. The guy had
bone-structure the camera just loved, and a frame that again
seemed to lend itself to extreme lighting. More importantly,
he could smoulder with the best of them.

'Tell me about him.' Kara shimmied backwards until his
cock bumped against her pussy. A second later, the honeyed
heat of her sex surrounded him.

Ric's eyelids closed. Fucking sweet. Damn, she was hot.
The walls of her sheath rippled around his cock, tugging,
squeezing, as she began to rise and fall. He wouldn't last. He
tried to catch hold of her, but Kara knocked his hands away.

'Tell me about it,' she insisted, pressing down hard on his
chest with the heels of her hands. 'What's it like when he's
on top of you like this? Has he ever held you down so that
he could ride you?'

Like she was doing now? Taking control, even though he
was ostensibly the one doing the penetrating.

'No,' he said, jerking sidewards abruptly, so that they
toppled over. He grabbed both of Kara's wrists and pinned
them either side of her head. 'With Zach, it's more like this.'
He filled her cunt again, pumped his hips hard and fast,
until they were both slick with sweat and panting, and the

headboard was knocking holes in the plaster.

She struggled, but he kept her pinned. He kept the punishing pace up too. Lost himself in the breakneck race towards satisfaction; in a space where nothing else existed and all that mattered was the steadily intensifying heat in his loins.

Even after his orgasm rushed up and shook him, Ric kept on dwelling in that void. He sank into it, let the blackness there overwhelm him for a while. Not too long, though: he wasn't a complete bastard, after all. He stayed hard inside Kara long enough to rub her to a peak with his fingers.

Then in the quiet that followed, when his cock was spent and a near constant yawn stretched her face, he rested his head between her thighs and licked her to another, quieter climax.

* * *

Tuesday Morning
Text message from Zach Blackwater to Ric Liddell:
Wanker.

Text message from Ric Liddell to Zach Blackwater:
What do you expect when you constantly stand me up?

* * *

Fifteen minutes after Ric left without making any arrangements for a repeat meeting, Kara blearily peeped out of the front door to find Robin on her step. She closed the door and rubbed her face before releasing the chain. Why now? Couldn't she at least wake up a little before facing this?

'I brought you breakfast.' Robin beamed, waving a brown paper bag in Kara's direction. She'd obviously come straight from the mainland, and the smell of warm bacon wafted temptingly from the bag. 'I thought you might appreciate not having to cook. I can boil the kettle for the rest.' She made to step into the house, but Kara remained immobile in the doorway.

'No,' she said simply. 'You're not coming in.'

'Wha – wait!' Robin stared at her, her red mouth hanging open in a goldfish expression. It didn't suit her otherwise perfectly styled outfit. 'I thought –'

'You lied to me.' Kara stepped back to close the door, despite the welcoming growl in her stomach at the smell of bacon. Ric had indeed proved to be a magnificent alarm clock, in that it woke gloriously early. Sadly, providing breakfast in bed hadn't been part of his repertoire. Hence she was totally famished.

'Hang on.' Robin slapped her palm against the closing door. 'In what way did I lie?'

'You told me Ric sent you and he didn't. He barely knows you. He doesn't employ you. I don't like being used, Robin. And you used me. You pretended to be something you're not in order to cajole me into sharing details that I would never for a moment have dreamed of sharing with you.'

Kara shut the door and pulled the bolt across too. She stood with her back to the wood.

'Kara. I'm sorry, Kara. I didn't mean to cause any harm.'

Maybe so, but regardless she wasn't putting herself in a position where she could be abused in that way again.

'I just wanted to know about him, that's all. We had fun together, didn't we?'

No, they hadn't. Not really. 'Go away.'

Robin pawed at the wood. The image of her in Kara's head remained pitiful. 'We can still be friends, can't we? Did he stay the night?'

'I said go away.'

A moment's silence followed. 'OK. I'll let you calm down. I'm going. I'll leave your breakfast on the step.'

Kara waited until she could no longer hear the crunch of gravel, then she let out her long-held breath. She didn't open the door to scoop up the sandwich. Robin's motivations in building their friendship were all too apparent. Why else would she have arrived here just after Ric had left? She'd probably watched him go. Hell, for all Kara knew, maybe Robin had watched him arrive too. That thought killed her hunger and replaced it with a slight feeling of nausea. She just didn't want to share her sex life like that. Her thing with Ric might be casual, but it was still private, something between her and Ric, not anyone else. God help her, she wasn't even sure if Robin would keep the information to herself. The fallout could be horrible if she went blabbing things to folks all around the island. She wanted to be the one to tell Zach what was going on, rather than have him hear it through the island grapevine. It wasn't as if they had a special relation-ship. It was just courtesy to let him know where he stood. Plus, she ought to establish why she'd missed him.

On top of that, it also seemed plain wrong to encourage Robin's obsession. God forbid the woman should start genu-inely stalking the guy. At the moment, Kara prayed her notions of Robin parked on the hillside spying on Ric were just fanciful ideas, and not the actual truth.

* * *

'What do you want?' Zach didn't bother to turn his head in order to confirm the identity of the person who'd just entered the Bunker. The waft of expensive aftershave combined with the yammering of two dogs outside made it obvious, which was why he didn't feel the need to be polite. Ric had ruined a perfectly good evening last night by commandeering Kara's attention. Now he was set to ruin a perfectly good morning by crowing about it. He'd rather hoped his text message had got across his feelings on the matter already. Evidently not. He tensed in anticipation of barney number two.

'Well, good morning to you too.' Ric planted his boots right alongside the box of pink greetings cards Zach was halfway through sorting. 'Nice to see you're so cheerful. I thought I'd drop by and let you know how much I've missed your company and what happens? I get snarled at.'

'Piss off. You haven't missed me,' Zach spat. Much as he longed to believe otherwise. 'I saw you mooning your arse at passing ships last night while breaking in Kara. She's obviously keeping you far too busy for you to be thinking about me.'

Ric covered his mouth with his thumb. 'You know I like to keep my taxes up to date and my tenants on their toes, and, as I said earlier, you stood me up.'

'Backs,' Zach corrected. 'You like to keep them on their backs. And if you want me that much, you know what you have to do. It might not even kill you.'

Ric pretended not to hear. 'Even so, I was thinking about you the whole time.'

'Like fuck you were.'

'Wow.' Ric folded his arms across his chest. 'We are in a bad mood. Dare I even ask why you were around to see Kara and me? You weren't, you couldn't have been, looking for me? I hadn't actually changed your goddamn mind?' Ric gave him a slapdash grin, which while annoying also made him look ridiculously sexy. Ric had stylish charmer down to an art. This morning he sported bed hair and his dog-walking clothes: a jeans and jersey combo that made him look like a catalogue model. It was hard to hate him, when looking at him made Zach ache with longing.

'Fuck you,' Zach muttered again. Anything more eloquent seemed to have slipped right out of his head. 'As if. I've told you how it is. I've no reason to come looking for you.' Damn, he didn't even want to have this conversation again. He'd told Ric dozens of times how he felt, and that he wanted more from their relationship than sex. Fucking was all well and good – and boy, was it good – but you could only live so long without emotional sustenance, and he'd wanted something more meaningful for years. He often figured it'd be nice to share more than grunts for a change, maybe enjoy a nice dinner, or take a holiday and soak up some culture.

'So, why were you on the island so late?'

'Actually, I had a date with Kara.'

Fine, so he was a little pissed off at her too. Yes, he'd been running late. He'd had to drive Heather home and then play chicken with the tide to get back across the causeway. All for nothing, because by the time he'd arrived she was already being screwed by Ric.

'Ohh!' Ric sucked a breath between his teeth, and clutched his stomach at the same time, as though he'd been kicked. 'Smarts. So that's why you're in such a bad-ass mood.' Ric bent at the waist so that his long hair fell forward and obscured Zach's view of the cards. 'Did you set up an alternative date that I ruined?'

Zach flicked a card in Ric's direction, aiming for his face. It flew wide of his ear.

'You know you could have joined us.'

'I can't say I much fancied it,' Zach growled. Besides, it would have put Kara on the spot too much if he'd shown up after she'd agreed to go out with Ric. Conflict wasn't what he'd been looking for. He'd envisaged sharing a glass or two of wine with her and chatting. Just because alfresco sex had featured as part of their first two meetings, it didn't have to be a staple of every encounter he had with her. He actually quite fancied getting to know her as a person. Better that than ending up in the situation he was in with Ric, which amounted to a whole lot of fucking nothing.

'You ought to know she's been angling for that very thing.'
'What?'

'Kara. She thinks you have a sexy butt, and she wants to watch me screw it.'

No. No. They weren't going down that path. Getting involved in a threesome would only lead to further heart-ache. He didn't want to share. He struggled enough as it was, and hated it when Ric insisted on him taking part in multi-partner photoshoots. He didn't believe it either. Why would Kara have even mentioned him?

'You know, while I'm really enjoying the visuals of that pout, I'm sensing a breakdown in communications between us.' Ric moved so that he could encircle Zach's chest from behind. Maybe if he hadn't been kneeling on the floor he'd have stood more of a chance of dodging the hold. As it was, one arm locked tight across Zach's chest while the other angled upwards, so that Ric's hand splayed across the front of Zach's throat, fingertips digging into the underside of his chin. He had no choice but to tilt his head back and look up into Ric's face.

'What do you want?'

'I need you to come and pose. You did agree to do it, and my deadline is getting close.'

Despite his anger, Ric's pale eyes never failed to melt Zach's heart. Ric's eyes were a blaze of ice-cold silver, encircled by a darker sapphire ring. Zach could still remember the first time Ric had turned that gaze upon him, and he'd known immediately that what he thought he knew about himself was wrong. Straight, gay, bi: labels didn't matter any more. He just knew he'd fallen hard for Ric. Years later, he still had it equally bad.

Zach carefully wetted his lips. 'I'm busy. I've stock to unpack.'

'No, you're not.' Ric's lips briefly brushed his. Just that one irritating suggestion of affection set a groan rumbling down Zach's throat. One more kiss and his dick would be hard as rock and he'd be as malleable as clay. He craved that second touch even as he despised himself for wanting it.

It didn't help that for the most part he enjoyed posing too. He just suspected Ric had plans for the session that involved more than simple photography. He usually did. God help him if on this occasion it involved Kara.

'Heather can run the van.'

'She's not here today.' His sister only did alternate days except for weekends.

Ric put on a pout, but he didn't withdraw. The arm locked across Zach's chest shifted sideways. Five teasing digits made a drum roll against his chest, and then walked down the centre of his abs to his belt buckle. 'Come on, you know you'll earn twice as much and have six times as much fun posing than you will sitting in that van selling ice cream to runny-nosed brats and balding, overweight men.'

So true, Zach didn't even attempt to deny it.

Ric's fingertips eased beneath the bottom edge of Zach's T-shirt and into the waistband of his jeans. A shiver ran through Zach's already tensed muscles. He didn't want to respond, but he did. Every bloody time, he did. He also knew Ric thought nothing of crossing boundaries. He'd open up the whole of Zach's fly and rub him off right here, right now and not give a damn that anyone could walk into the shop without warning. Typically, Zach preferred to be a little more circumspect. He tried not to thrust his sex life into people's faces. It wasn't good for business.

Zach shrugged, but he failed to dislodge Ric's hold. 'I told you. I don't want it to be like this any more. I'm sick of games. Offer me something serious. Maybe then I'll feel more like obliging you.'

Ric's index finger flicked back and forth across the top of Zach's loins, where it caught the side of his growing erection, *tick, tick, tick*, in the way a normal person might thought-fully tap their lip while considering.

'Seriously, Ric, there's more to life than sex.'

Woe flashed through Ric's eyes, as though the remark had reawakened a distant memory. There had been a time in Ric's past when he'd allowed himself to feel a whole range of emotions and when he'd been intimately involved with another person on an emotional as well as a sexual level. He just seemed determined never to go there again. Why that was, Zach had never figured. He didn't believe for a minute that Ric was still mourning his wife. Mostly, he got the impression that Ric was grateful that period of his life had passed.

'Tell me one thing that's better than sex.'

Zach blinked, and floundered. He hadn't anticipated the

question. 'Well ... um ...' Damn it, his mind was blank.

'You seem to be struggling a bit.'

'Yeah, well, I can't think. Not when you have your hands in my pants.'

'Oh, Zachy, there's no reason to think. Nothing else comes even close.' A look of sly serenity stretched across Ric's face. Bastard wasn't going to budge over the nature of their relationship, and he wouldn't let up over Zach posing either. 'You know, you are pretty hard. A good wank might calm you down and grant you some proper perspective.'

Zach severely doubted it, but Ric's voice continued to purr into his ear. 'Since I already have my hand down here, I could easily oblige. You'd like that now, wouldn't you?' Ric's agile fingers were already releasing Zach's zip. Worse still, knowing that he ought to shove Ric off didn't help one bit, especially not when his nice big hand cradled Zach's erection. Three minutes, five tops, and Ric would have him happily shooting off. Godamnit, he was going to have to come up with another strategy for making Ric open up to them being a bit more than fuck buddies. Ric just saw his attempts at sexual withdrawal as a challenge.

As for him having sought out Kara again, that was more than likely just an attempt to say, 'Fuck you, I've other lovers to please myself with, Zachy. If you don't like it, you know what to do about it.'

As soon as Ric's hand closed tight around Zach's shaft, and began making those ridiculously pleasant pulls, Zach let his head sag back against Ric's shoulder. 'Bastard,' he growled, before sinking his teeth into his bottom lip. His hips began to roll with the motion of Ric's hand.

'Hello, there. Anyone about?' Kara's voice echoed around the display racks and filled Zach's ears and brain. Behind him, Ric briefly stiffened, so that his chest grew tight against Zach's back. His grip froze too, but he didn't withdraw as most would have done; rather, he paused. Listened, presumably to gauge just how close she was to discovering them.

'Don't do this now,' Zach hissed. He fastened a hand over the top of Ric's where the other guy still held his cock.

'Fine,' Ric kissed him. 'But I'll take that as permission to do it later.'

Whether by that he meant he intended to jerk Zach off later, expose their relationship to Kara, something else entirely or all of the above, Zach really couldn't say. He just managed to unravel himself from Ric's hold and redo his fly before he caught a glimpse of strawberry-blonde hair peeking over the top of the card racks. Seconds later, Kara appeared in the aisle between the display shelves.

She'd opted for another outfit that displayed her legs, this one a butterfly-covered sundress that hugged her breasts and waist, then fanned over her hips to gently fall halfway down her thighs. A pair of wedge-heeled sandals that helped emphasise the length of her legs completed the ensemble. She took a hesitant step towards Zach, an apology already halfway to her lips, before her gaze slid sideways to where Ric stood with one elbow propped against the shelf of light-house moneyboxes.

He could almost hear her thoughts; she projected the OMG part so well. It couldn't be easy facing them together, not when you had to apologise to one for standing him up in order to screw the other. She took another hesitant step. Stopped, and then nervously moistened her lips.

Zach was many things, and he liked to include gentleman among them. Admittedly, he'd been mighty pissed off last night, and he was still narked at Ric now, but he wasn't about to take his frustration out on Kara. He knew firsthand exactly how persuasive Ric could be when he put his mind to it. Who could blame her for falling into his trap? He didn't. Not really. Nor did he fancy making a big deal of it now. The fact was that if you were on Liddell Island then you were fair game as far as inclusion in Ric's naughty games went. If you didn't like that, you didn't live here.

'Good morning, again,' Ric remarked ending the awkward silence.

There he was, Mr Smooth, showing off his charms. Sometimes he wondered if they'd work quite so well if Ric had a bust nose, but he didn't really want to hurt him in order to find out. He wasn't even demanding that Ric become monogamous, just that he accepted some form of commitment between them. He didn't want to be grouped up with Ric's meaningless shags any more. After nearly seven years, he deserved more than that.

What did briefly give Zach pause was the 'again' in Ric's sentence. He glanced over his shoulder at him, rage filling him up. The bastard had actually spent the night with her. If that wasn't meant purely to provoke him, he didn't know what was. He was about to let his anger out, when he realised that Kara didn't actually seem all that pleased to find Ric here. A fact she displayed by gawping at him, while she rocked slowly on her wedge heels.

OK, time he worked some Zach magic and put everyone at their ease before any fireworks went off. Namely, his. He crossed to where Kara stood and wrapped her in a hug. Then he smacked a chaste kiss on her cheek and launched into an explanation of why he'd stood her up – not that he had – so that she didn't have to feel so bad about it any longer.

'So, you were stuck on the mainland until this morning?'

Her eyes opened wide with hope.

'That's right,' he agreed. She hadn't been on Liddell Island long enough to work out the cycle of tides and hence recognise his affirmative for the outright lie it was.

Ric gave him an intrigued frown, clearly puzzled by the deception. He'd just have to keep on wondering about it too, because Zach wasn't about to spill the details.

Kara blew out a sigh of relief. She gave him an enormous grin and mussed his hair. 'That's all right, another time.'

'Yeah, absolutely. I hope your evening wasn't too dull.'

'It was ... it was OK.' She wrinkled her forehead as she spoke, and kept her gaze firmly to the right of Ric.

Zach turned to face his lover, pleased to see hard lines etched into his expression. 'OK' was damning praise whichever way you looked at it, and Ric did so like to flaunt his sexual prowess. What Zach wasn't prepared for was the genuine hurt blackening the centre of Ric's eyes.

It wasn't like Ric to care that much. Unless he'd genuinely decided Kara was special.

Zach's heart started beating overtime at the possibility. Could Ric ... could he be falling for someone else?

'Are you free, or what?' Ric snarled. He pushed away from the display case, dislodging a few cuddly starfish in the process. 'The day's wasting, and if you're not I need to find somebody else.' He didn't look at Kara.

'Yes, I guess I am,' Zach replied. 'Let me lock up.'

'Oh, you're going somewhere?' Kara said, clearly intrigued. 'I'd come for some more coffee, but there was no one in the van.'

'Sorry, coffee shop is closed.'

'Where are you going?'

'He's posing for me,' Ric remarked, having somehow

managed to insert himself between Zach and Kara. 'I suppose you'd like to come along.'

'Well, only if it's no trouble.' She smiled up at Ric.

'Whatever,' he drawled. 'But you'll have to make your own coffee. And don't go distracting him.'

CHAPTER NINE

Did it feel awkward strolling up to the fort with the two of them? Maybe a little, but not once did Kara consider changing her mind about tagging along. She still felt bad about not waiting home for Zach and for getting frisky with Ric instead, but not too bad. After all, it turned out she hadn't really done anything wrong, since Zach had stood her up. Plus, it wasn't like she had an agreement with either of them. Moreover, some things simply outweighed embarrassment, this being one of them. Ric and Zach: one holding the camera, the other making love to it, and both of them sexy as hell. She didn't even mind that she ended up making the coffee.

Armed with three pint-sized mugs balanced on a tray, Kara made her way up the winding staircase to Ric's studio. She wasn't really sure what she'd expected, maybe some soft music playing in the background, lots of mood lighting and some kind of rail of clothing. Instead, the large studio had been reduced by lighting to cosy intimacy. Dust motes swirled in the air, visible in the glow thrown by the lamps. However, much of the room lay in shadows. Ric had drawn the blinds across the window, blocking all but a few shafts of sunlight that formed vivid slashes on the black slate floor.

The two men were by the window. Ric held the viewfinder of his weighty camera pressed to his eye. Zach looked no different to how he'd been when they'd arrived. His hair remained tousled by the wind, lending him a dishevelled charm. His clothing still consisted of a shirt and a pair of frayed jeans. Only when Kara examined him more closely did she realise that he'd removed his shoes and socks, so that his bare toes were curled against the floor tiles.

'Put the tray down over there, and stay out of the way.' Ric absently waved her towards a small coffee table and a collection of leather pouffes. Dutifully, Kara deposited the tray as instructed, then added milk and sugar to order while the men got to work. Unfortunately, her position didn't give her much of a view of the action.

'Where do you want this?' she asked, holding Ric's drink towards him.

'Just leave it there.' His camera made a whirr each time he pressed the button, resulting in a near continuous purr, just as Ric maintained near constant motion as he adjusted his angle and position, sometimes moving up close to focus on Zach's face, before panning back out. Half of his pictures would surely come out blurry because of the movement, but he didn't seem at all concerned by that fact. Maybe the vast quantity of clicks allowed for rejects.

Kara had drunk almost half of her coffee before Ric paused long enough to take a single sip. Zach didn't even receive that. He remained dutifully in position as Ric had posed him.

'That's it, now turn towards me slowly.' The light from the window carved Zach's face with shadows. The effect reminded her of how she'd seen him striped with coloured lights on the dance floor of the club where they'd first met. Same beautiful bone structure, only this lighting infused his expression with a kind of melancholy. That sense of nostalgia and longing grew more profound when Ric barked at him to unfasten the shirt.

It hung open revealing a slice of his chest. His stomach was taut, exactly as she remembered it, with that line of golden-brown hair leading down from his navel, and the extended diamond of fur that covered his chest. Zach stuffed his hands into his pockets. It made him look like he'd just spent a night on a sofa. Now thoroughly dishevelled, he was definitely pleased with himself. It may well have only been a sofa, his expression said, but he'd been well fucked there. That's probably what he'd have looked like last night if he'd come to her house and she'd been there to greet him. They'd sort of agreed to stay out of one another's pants in order to get to know one another, but she didn't think she'd have been able to resist undressing him, seeing how he was so fucking pretty.

Yeah, pretty – but not in the way of the man snapping him. Ric had classical bone structure coupled with an elegance of movement that remained obvious even as he darted about lining up camera shots. Zach was all disproportionate and not quite so symmetrical, but he had those dreamy, wide, deep-set eyes that you could melt into.

Damn, she wished she had a camera so she could snap the pair of them. Kara surreptitiously snuck her phone out of her bag, only to think better of the idea and return it. Instead she crept forward to get a better view. As long as she stayed out of shot, then what was the problem?

Only the nearer Kara got, the more aware she became of the heightened tension between the two men. Prickles spread across her skin. She kept holding her breath in anticipation – of what, she wasn't sure. For though Zach smouldered, and

Ric lapped it up, there wasn't any overt flirtation between them. They didn't speak much at all.

'Sit down,' Ric commanded, making her jump. She froze in position, only to realise that the comment was directed not at her but at Zach, when Ric kicked a wooden chair in his direction. More close-ups followed. Zach did exactly as instructed, pliantly straddling the seat, turning first one way and then the other, frowning and smiling on demand.

'Stand up. Turn around. Now slowly lose the shirt.'

Zach concentrated on the task of unfastening his cuffs first. Only once did he cast a sly look up at Ric.

'That's it. Do it again,' Ric encouraged. The angle gave great depth to Zach's expression. It emphasised his wing-like brows and turned his brown eyes into molten chocolate swirls. 'Now bring your thumb to your lips. Got it. Perfect. You were so fucking made for this.'

He was. She'd thought it from the first time they met, when she'd wanted to snap him clutching the iron railings outside the club.

'Yeah, yeah,' Zach drawled in reply, making it difficult to tell whether he believed in the remark. 'Tell you what, let me have my drink and then you can schmooze me into working my butt off some more. What are these ones for, again?'

Ric didn't lower the camera. 'Primarily, my next gallery exhibit. Although I might use some for an aftershave contract I've been offered. How'd you like to be the face of Wastrel by Thierry Tigris?'

Zach gave a small shrug in reply. 'I'd rather be chief flavour tester for Nescafé. I'm parched, Mr Paparazzi Man.'

Finally the digital whir stopped. Ric lowered the camera to reveal an annoyed pout. 'Fine. Go drink. Kara, bring him his coffee.' While she dutifully pattered over and offered up the mug, Ric zoomed through the images he'd already captured.

'Milk and two, just as you asked.'

'Lovely.' Zach curled his fingers around the cup. She watched him sip. He gave a contented gasp and held the rim of the mug pressed against his lips. 'I hope you're not bored.'

'No. Absolutely not.'

He watched her, his lips pursed against the rim of the mug. *Want to meet up again?* his expression said. *Sorry last time didn't work out.*

Yeah, I do.

A smile briefly flashed in his eyes. 'So do I.' This time his words were for real, though very softly spoken.

Kara cast a swift glance in Ric's direction. He'd slipped the SD card from the camera into his laptop to clear the memory. Images were flickering in a continuous stream across the screen, too fast to review the content.

'When did you have in mind?' Kara asked. She was free later, assuming Ric didn't make another impromptu visit.

Something about Zach's responding grin suggested wickedness that had her totally intrigued. 'How about now?'

'Now? You're ...' Realisation sunk in. 'You mean for the camera. In front of him.'

'It's not like he hasn't seen you before.'

Yes, but ... Hell! It wasn't even the fact that he'd be photographing her that made her pause. It was the realisation that Ric would know about them. If he shot them together, it'd be obvious they'd been intimate before.

Zach's lips rested on the lip of his cup. She didn't think anyone had managed to make cradling a mug seem so provocative before. Kara was hard pressed not to reach out to him. What would Ric think if she suddenly intruded on the shots?

If, instead of spectating, she became a player? While he'd clearly stated that he wasn't interested in anything serious developing between them, might he still balk at the idea of snapping her shagging another guy?

Who was she kidding? Ric had already twice suggested the possibility of setting her up with two guys so he could photograph her being had in both holes. He knew she was intrigued by the idea of a threesome, particularly with him and Zach. This could even lead to it.

'Won't he get cross?' She glanced over her shoulder at Ric perched on a swivel stool by the computer.

Zach shrugged in a loose-limbed way that initially seemed to imply he didn't care, but on further thought perhaps screamed malice with intent. 'He won't bat an eyelid.'

'Yes, but he did tell me to stay out of the way.'

'Hmm.' Zach jerked one of his thick eyebrows upwards. 'And do you always do as you're told?'

'No.' No, she did not. Not any more. After the whole Gavin debacle she was absolutely determined to rule her own destiny, not have it dictated by anyone else.

'Didn't think so.'

'Time's up.' Ric bustled up, camera in hand.

Zach remained where he was and hung on to his drink in order to gulp down the whole cupful.

'That's enough.' Ric snatched the mug away, causing a mocha-coloured dribble to run over Zach's chin, which Kara longed to catch with her lips. 'Kara, take the mug. Get out of the way.'

'I think I should stay in the shot,' she huffed, not appreciating his tone.

Zach's eyes lit with glee.

Ric turned to her. His blond hair settled around his face so that several long strands fell across it. His eyes narrowed. 'In order to do what exactly?'

Kara shrugged. She hadn't thought it out that thoroughly. And she wasn't about to blurt, 'So I can shag Zach.' Somehow she knew that wouldn't get a good response. 'Well, you keep promising me naked butts.' She gave Ric one of her best smiles, all sweetness and tease wrapped into one. 'Maybe I could help undress him.'

'Did I promise you that?' Ric dragged his teeth over his lower lip. He looked thoughtfully between the two of them. 'Actually, I think Zach's perfectly able to undress himself.'

'I'm so-o not,' Zach said, earning him a hard glare from Ric, whose blue eyes flashed. 'Come on, Ric. What's the problem, why not let us have some fun?'

Ric snapped the lens cover on to the camera. 'Because this isn't about fun. It's about art and fulfilling a contract.'

'The exhibition shots aren't. You always claim things turn out better when they're not faked. I can promise you this will be genuine.' Zach snatched a look at Kara's chest, and then waggled his wing-like eyebrows at Ric. 'I certainly won't have any problems getting hard, not like with the scrawny models you normally bus in.'

'Not interested,' Ric snapped.

'Oh! And why is that?' Zach rested his chin in a V he made with his forefinger and thumb.

'Because.' Ric turned his back on them and began fussing with papers strewn across the computer desk. 'I don't have to explain my reasons. Now can we get on? Back to where we left off. You were undressing.'

Zach bent to whisper in Ric's ear as he swept past to resume his position. 'Spoilsport. You've had her. What's the problem with me having her too? It's not like you care about either of us.'

'Fine. Whatever,' Ric snarled through gritted teeth. His capitulation took Kara by surprise.

He snatched the lens cap off again and advanced, holding the camera like a lethal weapon. 'We still start from where we were at. Kara, stay the hell out of the way until I tell you.'

They began again, with Zach expertly nibbling the very tip of one index finger, while he coyly hooked one thumb into the waistband of his jeans. 'That's it. Hold it.' Ric began to jig about, filling up the SD card again. For a moment, her promised involvement was forgotten. 'Now move. Come on, move. Give me something else to work with. Didn't I tell you to lose that shirt?'

Zach had only got as far as loosening the cuffs before breaking off for his coffee. Now, he eased the slate-grey shirt off his shoulders, whereupon it slid slowly down his muscular arms until it hung on to only one wrist. Zach held on to the cuff for half a second before letting it fall and form a shadowy puddle at his feet.

Beautiful. Kara had no other word for how he appeared in that moment. The light, the pose, his expression, everything came together perfectly. Maybe it was better if she stayed out of view and they left this as a study of Zachary Blackwater rather than turning it into some x-rated porno.

'Do it,' Ric said. 'Back on the chair.'

Zach's breath caught so that he made a tiny sound. Without waiting for further elaboration, he planted his bottom on the edge of the wooden chair. His back arched so that his shoulders hit the back rest. The pose, while not perhaps the most comfortable one, did thrust his hips forward and allow him to stretch out his long legs. Zach opened the metal fastening at his waist and let the zipper slide.

Oh, my God, was he going to … With one palm tucked inside his fly, what in the world else could Zach be doing, besides stroking himself? Was this where she came in? Kara stared at Ric, but he had his back to her.

She knew the moment Zach's glans poked above the line of his underwear because Ric's spine straightened for a second before he became a dervish-like whirl. Kara began inching forward. It wasn't that she meant to intrude upon the shots; she just needed a better look. She hadn't seen all that many men masturbate, at least not as close up as this, and definitely not while someone voyeuristically photographed them. If only her careers adviser had suggested Ric's line of work. She'd have been good at it, for sure, and job satisfaction would never have been an issue. Sadly, she barely knew one end of a camera from the other. Even her family snapshots inevitably suffered from glaring red-eye and cropped heads. The digital revolution couldn't entirely counter ineptitude.

Kara hadn't realised how close she'd got in her quest for substantiating visuals, until Ric backed into her. He clamped his mouth shut over a bark of irritation, then stood, the camera held at waist level, and gave her an appraising look.

'So this is what you want, is it?'

'I just …'

He snapped an image of her with her mouth hanging open, and then another of her blinking because of the first flash.

'Hey!'

He kept on taking pictures.

'You said we weren't serious.'

'And we're not.'

'You said I should come in some time for you to photograph.'

'That's what I'm doing.'

It was. He was still mad at her, though, even if she didn't really understand why. 'Come on, then. Look at him.' Ric dragged her closer to Zach, until she stood right before him. 'Work with me, Kara, if this is what you want. See him. Drink him down. Be my extension. Rough him up a little.' He paused before adding, 'But no actual bruises.'

There wasn't any way on God's earth she could resist a command like that, not when Zach looked so utterly delectable.

'What will you do with the pictures?'

'That depends how they come out. I don't know how well you photograph yet, and you've yet to prove there's any chemistry between you.'

There was plenty of that. She didn't think convincing him would prove much of an issue.

Zach didn't move at all, unless you counted the muscle in his thigh jumping as she approached. Facing him square on, Kara found her viewing angle much improved. She no longer needed to strain in order to see what he was doing. All the explicit detail she could wish for lay right before her. Zach's broad-tipped fingers were splayed over the long thick shaft, while his thumb curved over the tip, where it drew concentric circles in the shiny film of pre-come leaking from the slit.

'Think about what he's doing, Kara. Why's he doing it? Are you demanding it? Who is in control?' Ric filled her head with questions.

Who was in control? Not her at this moment. Possibly Zach. He was certainly the centre of attention, given the way he was slowly circling his thumb. Yet she was also raring to see him do so much more. Like squeezing tight his erection and working himself into an absolute frenzy as if it were a race he was desperate to win.

For whatever reason, Zach didn't rush, even when she bent over him, getting as close as she could without making contact.

'Don't touch him,' Ric commanded, only to rescind the instruction immediately. 'OK, one finger, and you'd better sign a fucking release form afterwards.'

Uncertain whether Ric would change his mind again, Kara immediately reached out. She placed the tip of her index finger halfway down Zach's shaft in a space between his splayed fingers.

Zach made a soft sound in the back of his throat. This time it was more than a simple catch in his breath. It constituted a full-on moan. He looked up at her immediately, his brown eyes wide, his mouth too. There was such need, such desperate urgency in his expression. His hand wrapped around her. He carefully brought her whole hand in contact with his shaft.

She'd done daring things and stupid things, but she'd never before been watched like this. Kara's cheeks burned. She snapped at Ric to keep the camera pointed downwards and not at her face. He took no notice.

'You're the model, I'm directing. I'll snap whatever I see fit.'

The heat of Zach's cock filled her hand, causing a corresponding fire to awaken in her cunt. Mingled with that first flush of arousal was an intense buzz of nerves. She wasn't camera-shy, but this was still a first, and lord knows where it would lead.

Zach guided her, his large hand clamped tight over her smaller one. Up slid her grip until his glans brushed the centre of her palm, then down, right to the base, so that his pubic hair tickled her fingers. Around them Ric buzzed like an irate bee. Only the sharp sound of their breathing competed on a noise level. She stared at Zach, knowing without explicitly being told that this is what he'd hoped to provoke, this weird situation where they were all linked and tension flirted close to breaking point ... but they weren't quite in it together. They weren't yet a threesome.

Ric had taunted her with that possibility. He knew what she wanted, what she liked. How far would he let this go? Had he realised yet? Did he know that she and Zach had prior knowledge of one another? It was possible the men had talked. Well, if they had, they were obviously cool with it, because otherwise this just wouldn't be happening.

Zach wouldn't let go of her hand. That was probably a good thing, because if she was free to move, she'd probably end up astride him, or sucking him. If only Ric would give her an instruction.

'Kara.' She continued to work Zach's shaft with firm sure strokes, while looking him in the eye. He only blushed when he started to glow. Then as his breathing slowed to a tremulous pant, he also dug his teeth deep into his lower lip. Too slow – she was reining him in, drawing things out when he wanted to race. Ric couldn't help lapping up the struggle, even though his shoulders were lifted up around his ears and his face had become narrowed and serious.

'Kara.' Zach's plea tore up his throat, sounding so husky that it must have come from somewhere down near his belly. 'I need ... Will you let me?'

She didn't really want to let him come. In her thoughts, she straddled his lap and sank down on to his cock. Ric didn't have a camera either. Instead he was even more naked than Zach and nuzzled up against her back as she bounced astride

Zach's cock. He took possession of her breasts, rolling them in his palms as he kissed the side of her neck, and when Zach came Ric claimed her for himself. Entering her when she was slippery and wet, yet still making her groan.

'God! Kara, please.'

Ric captured Zach's plea in close up. Its weakness was pitiful, yet it still had enough power to tie Kara's stomach up in knots. Everything came down to her actions. If she let go and backed away, would Zach finish things off himself or beg Ric for a helping hand? Should she kneel down and suck him? What?'

'What should I do?'

Zach groaned. His eyelids fluttered closed only to open again at once.

Kara sank into those two molten chocolate pools as she pumped her fist. There was little grace in the motion. She sensed what he wanted, could feel the strain in his muscles, in both his thighs and his stomach. The fact that she knew he was straining towards that goal increased the feeling of slickness between her own thighs, so that she jigged her hips as she stroked him, bringing her pussy lips together and giving her clit some welcome relief.

Oh, God! She needed him so badly.

Kara lifted the skirt of her sundress so that Zach could see what lay beneath. She had on the prettiest pair of panties in her possession. Just a tiny triangle of silk held on with ribbons that he took no time at all to undo. Kara shimmied forward. Their mouths met as she straddled his lap. Zach's cock felt so smooth against the silk of her pussy. Her clit damn near burned with eagerness. Ric was in the way, though. He was damn well in her face and between her thighs with that camera. His instructions having completely dried up, he was sucking down sharp anxious breaths.

Any moment ... any moment, she swore, he was going to join them. Then when Ric's fist did wrap around Zach's cock, effectively stopping her from sliding down on to him, she damn well nearly screamed with rage.

Stuck between them, unable to see what Ric was doing yet perfectly able to feel it, Kara ground her teeth in frustration. To the side of her she could just make out their reflection in the glass-covered line of mounted prints. Ric was jerking Zach's cock. No. Hellfire! He was on his knees sucking Zach, and still taking pictures.

That was so unfair. She strained her neck, trying to look over her shoulder at him. No use, she could just see the back of his blond head.

Zach broke eye-contact with her as he came. His chin tilted up, his head rested on the back of the chair so that he gazed up at the whitewashed ceiling, ecstasy stretching the tendons in his neck and adding a layer of savageness to his face. His body spasmed a millisecond after each jerk of his cock.

'Fuck!'

As for his cry, it seemed that each note was torn from the bottom of his soul, as if he were a wounded animal and not a man at all. Either way, he was undone, and Ric, not she, had got him there.

CHAPTER TEN

Ric's camera had finally fallen silent. He placed it on the stand beside his open laptop.

'Why? What the hell did you do that for?' she asked as she removed herself from Zach's lap. There had to be a reason beyond the fact that he could.

'Why is it a problem?' he shot back at her. 'It's meaningless after all.'

To Ric, maybe. But not to her. Sex had never been meaningless. It had always had a purpose, even if it was as simple as finding a release.

Beside her, Zach remained silent. He slithered from the chair, and sprawled with his head resting against a chair leg. He touched her ankle, but she didn't look at him. Her gaze remained fastened upon Ric's back.

'There are some forms I need you to sign.'

'Are there?' He could stuff his consent forms where the sun didn't shine. How dare he derail things like that, just because he hadn't wanted it to happen? He hadn't capitulated at all. He'd fooled them. And now he dared to talk business with her as if nothing had happened.

'I'll arrange payment for the modelling work the same as

I do for Zach, but you forfeit all rights to the pictures, OK?'

No. It fucking wasn't OK.

Despite her anger, desire still ran through her body in hot streams, but Zach lay spent and all the hints of a threesome happening had evaporated – assuming there'd been any chance of that in the first place.

Ric placed the contract on the edge of the computer desk along with a ballpoint pen. Something told her he wasn't going to let her out of the building without signing. Kara gritted her teeth and scrawled her signature. 'Tosser,' she hissed under her breath as she made the final flourish.

'What did you say?'

'You heard me.'

'My studio, my rules.'

Kara raised her hand to strike him, only for him to catch her wrist before she'd properly made a move. He backed her up against the wall.

'Bastard,' she cursed.

'Rules, Kara. I make them for a reason. While you're in here what I say goes, and you accept that or you don't get invited back. Now, maybe you'd like to explain what's got your knickers in such a twist?'

As if he couldn't guess. They'd been just shy of penetration when he'd taken it upon himself to get Zach off; now her nerves were in shreds, her temperature was running hot and cold and there was no sign of satisfaction in sight, and that was before she got on to the derailing of her major fantasy.

Suddenly, Ric's expression softened. His grip slackened a fraction too, although he still held her so close that his mouth lay just shy of her lips as he spoke. 'The shots I have of you are good. This was always about work, Kara, nothing else. I'm sorry if you feel I've been cruel.'

'You didn't have to do that.'

'No.' He kissed her softly, thus transferring the taste of Zach's seed on to her tongue. 'Perhaps not, but I always like to incorporate a little of the unexpected.'

'You weren't trying to stop us?'

'Of course not.' The taste of Zach made her groan. 'Why would I?' His hand cradled the swell of her breast. He caught her nipple between the sides of his fingers and gave it a welcome squeeze. 'You need to come. I understand that. There was never any question of leaving you wanting.'

Wasn't there? She blinked at him, bewildered by the way he made her emotions ebb and flow. Ric turned her hand so that the swell of his erection pushed up against her palm. He was hot and needy too. Of course, he hadn't come either.

Damn him! For someone so pretty, he was a proper devil, but she couldn't … didn't want to resist.

Arousal thickened once again between her thighs. The blunt tips of Ric's digits speared between her curls, heading right to the source of her pleasure. He rubbed, focusing solely on her clit, until she was stretched up on tiptoe, one hand splayed against his chest as if to hold him back.

Kara released his fly. When he lifted her, she wrapped her legs around his waist, so that he could thrust right up into her, filling her in a way that caused a delicious rush.

'Yes!' This was what she needed, what she'd desired all along. Her heart flapped wildly. The pulse between her thighs grew ever stronger.

Ric moved a step further away from the wall, so that she was leaning away from him, her back supported by the brickwork. It was a position worthy of a circus performer. More acrobatic than she'd ever attempted before, and definitely somewhat precarious, but boy, did it feel good, especially when the head of his cock tap-tap-tapped against the front wall of her pussy.

His hands kept her steady. Kara's muscles strained as her breathing transformed into a pant. She kept her eyes open, looking at him, loving the fact that he maintained her gaze, and that he was feeling the same build-up that she was.

'That's right, baby. Give it up.'

Her hand clasped and opened. Her fingernails tore against the wall.

'Let go.'

Her head jerked back. She came hard, inner muscles squeezing tight his cock until she felt him peak too.

His mouth opened, gasping her name. He panted throughout the whole ejaculation. Then, all done, he closed up the gap between her upper bodies and gave her a long deep kiss.

It was only when Ric lowered her back to the floor that Kara realised Zach had watched the whole performance. His dark eyes were two shiny black pools that writhed with shadows. It didn't take a genius to work out that this hadn't been the outcome he'd been looking for when he'd suggested they got it on.

'I'd better go,' Kara said, not sure what else to do. Tension saturated the air, producing a static-like charge that caused prickles right along her spine. She didn't want to be here for whatever row was about to break out. 'I'll see you both soon.'

'Count on it.' Ric guided her towards the stairwell.

'Zach?'

He nodded, and managed to form a tight grin.

Kara shakily trotted down the steps. 'Are you two going to be all right?' she asked Ric as he showed her out of the front door.

'Of course.' He kissed her. 'Goodbye, Kara. I'll bring some of the photos over to show you.'

'Thanks. See you soon.'

Ric closed the door behind her.

Zach went up to the battlements when Ric and Kara left the studio. He needed air. It didn't matter how hard he rubbed, he couldn't work all the cricks out of his face. Hunched into a wind-resistant ball perched beside the canon emplacement, he watched Kara worm her way down into the valley.

It was his own fault, what had happened. What the hell had he expected? He'd foolishly thought he could provoke a reaction out of Ric. Well, he had. Just not the one he'd wanted.

The idea was to incite jealousy, not to have Ric turn the tables on him.

He'd always hoped that Ric felt more for him than he let on. Now he was no longer sure. Things had gone to plan to begin with. Ric had seen how much fun they were having, and had probably realised that they were both into the idea of having one another. That's why he'd got down on his knees and given Zach head. He'd come – man, had he come – and Ric had supped him right down. That should have been the end of it. Point proved. Ric cared enough to act. They could squabble over the details later. Only Zach hadn't properly factored Kara into the plan.

Ric had soothed her.

Ric had fucked her in front of him. Something he never ever did. Ric had never hidden the fact that he had other women, even sometimes other men, but he'd never flaunted that fact quite so brazenly in front of Zach.

It cut. It hurt like he was being stabbed repeatedly in the guts. He'd watched them both come and then share a post-orgasmic kiss. He'd realised as their tongues tangled and they clung to one another that Ric really didn't care. No, worse than that. He didn't care for Zach, but he did care about Kara.

Ric had spent the night with her. Something he never did with any lover. Zach could count on his fingers the number of nights he'd spent in Ric's arms. All of them had happened by accident because they were too exhausted to move. Maybe that had been the case with Kara last night and maybe not. Not being sure was eating him up.

Reviewing things again in the light of the fact that Ric seemed to prefer Kara, well, the whole scenario took on a different aspect. Suddenly it wasn't a case of Ric blowing him in order to stop Kara having him. Rather, Ric had done it to stop Zach having Kara. The difference might seem small, but it was significant.

The stairwell door creaked as it swung open to let Ric on to the battlements, carrying two bottles of beer. 'What have you come up here for?' he asked, as he passed one of the drinks to Zach.

Zach tactfully kept his silence. He took a sip of beer and watched Ric rest his bottom against one of the crenellations. His lover tucked his legs up against the side of the cannon so that he hung in mid-air with minimal support.

'I could still use a few more shots of you.'

'Tough.' Zach rubbed his nose. 'I'm going back to work.' He stood, only for Ric to stand too.

'Are you going to tell me what the problem is?'

'Why did you interrupt, Ric? It's not your usual way.' Normally Ric let things develop naturally when he had a camera in his hand. He believed in fluidity and rarely got involved once the action was underway. Today, his direction had crossed that boundary and they both knew it.

'Isn't that what you wanted – me to show you some love?'

'It wasn't me you were loving.'

Ric flicked his hair away from his face. He lifted his beer and took a quick swig while watching Zach closely. 'I must have imagined swallowing your come,' he remarked.

'You only did it in order to stop me having Kara, not because you wanted me. Couldn't have me actually fucking her, could you? Not when she's your precious new playmate.'

'Zach. Hello.' Ric snapped his fingers under Zach's nose. 'Are you suggesting what I think you are? That I acted out of jealousy? When have you ever known me to be jealous? It's no skin off my nose if you want to fuck her.'

Just as well, since he already had, and he was going to make a point of doing so again at the first opportunity, like right after he left here.

'I figured it wasn't such a problem since you were quite happy to have her in front of me. That's a bit of a turnaround from your position of yesterday, when you were demanding exclusivity. Would you prefer I'd left her wanting? You weren't really in a position to satisfy her any more.'

'Because of you,' Zach growled. Prior to Ric stepping in, he'd been perfectly positioned to give Kara exactly what she'd been looking for. 'You didn't need to step in. You could have stayed back and kept taking pictures.'

Ric shook his head. 'You're talking such shit. I already told you that she's angling for the three of us getting it on. I was just testing the waters, to see how you both reacted. I didn't see any objections arising from either of you.'

'I don't want a threesome,' Zach said. 'I want you.'

'And we've already had this discussion. I'm going back

151

in.' Ric turned around. He pushed open the stairwell door. 'Follow when you're finished being dumb.'

* * *

In the silence that followed Ric's departure, Zach remained cocooned in his coat. Doubts still riddled his mind and brought a hint of bile to his tongue. What if Ric really was more interested in Kara than he was in him? What did he do then? Could he use that desire somehow, transform it into something else, so that he didn't get left out? Maybe if he wasn't asking Ric to come out as gay then he'd relax more of his guard. Then again maybe Ric was just fucking him about and he was allowing himself to be walked all over. Maybe what he ought to be doing was issuing ultimatums or proving to Ric that he really didn't need to fuck anyone else.

The rage Zach had felt when he'd realised that Ric had sucked him purely to stop Kara having her way with him flared white-hot again. Agitated, he jumped up and began to pace. They needed to have this out properly. The problem was that Ric knew Zach's threats were idle. He wouldn't walk away. He couldn't. He just didn't want to.

There had to be some other way around the situation, but he was damned if he knew what it was.

Right now, he was going back to his van, where maybe, just maybe he'd find some clarity.

Zach got as far as the first turn in the stairs before he ran straight into Ric on his way back up. They glared hostilely at one another. 'Why did you do it?' Zach demanded. 'Why did you need to rub it in my face that you fancy someone else?'

Ric mounted the next few steps so that they stood more on a level. 'Why did you need to fuck her? That was never part of that shoot. What am I supposed to think, Zach? One minute your giving me the whole "let's commit" spiel and then you're all up for shagging Kara. Seems to me you're not entirely sold on the notion of commitment yourself. It wasn't the first time with her either, was it? When were you going to mention that? Fast work on your part, don't you think, considering you only met a few hours after you told me we were done.'

Zach didn't correct Ric's assumption. Pinpointing the exact start of his relationship with Kara wasn't relevant to the issues of the moment. He ran his tongue over his teeth instead. 'Kara and I just happened to cross paths and hit it off.'

Ric's blue-grey eyes narrowed, while his lips formed a thin line. 'Doesn't explain why you needed to make a repeat performance in front of me.'

'Well, maybe I was trying to fucking provoke you.' An irritating tingle filled Zach's sinuses. He pinched the bridge of his nose hard. 'Hell, it'd be nice to think you cared. It wasn't why you stopped us, though. You proved that fast enough when you stuck your dick in her.'

'She needed the release. It'd have been cruel not to oblige,' Ric said.

'Bullshit!'

'Well, maybe if you hadn't looked so irate, she might have stuck around and we all could have had some fun.'

That was it. He'd had enough. Ric just refused to see his point of view. It was like talking to one of the dopey Dalmatians that lay all day before the study hearth. Zach took a step forward, meaning to push past Ric and leave the building. Only Ric grabbed hold of him instead and shoved him up against the curved wall.

'Do you want to know why I like Kara?' he growled into

Zach's face. 'It's because she gets it, that's why. She's not constantly mithering me over whether I want to hold hands in public –'

'I never –'

'I don't, OK. I don't want to be your fucking boyfriend. I'm done with the whole partners routine. I've been there and still have the ring to prove it. I don't see why we can't be happy with things how they've been. What exactly is wrong with screwing each other senseless whenever we fancy, but not living in one another's pockets?'

'It's not enough,' Zach mumbled.

'What?'

'I said it's not enough. I want more of a relationship than that. I want someone to be there for me.'

Ric's eyes blazed with nervous intensity. His grip around Zach's biceps relaxed a fraction. The smell and taste of wintergreen caught on Zach's tongue, sharp and slightly minty, as if Ric had been gargling mouthwash. 'In what way am I not there for you?' Ric asked. 'You know I'll give you whatever you need.' His lips closed on Zach's mouth. 'Whenever you need it.'

Damn, they were back on sex again. It was the bedrock of their relationship and, much as Zach cursed himself for it, he couldn't resist. He really, really couldn't resist. The tension in his muscles melted away as Ric's soft lips moved against his. Slowly, steadily, the kiss became wetter. It incorporated a hint of tongue, grew deep and savage. All the while, Ric held Zach tight against the wall, their bodies pressed together from chest to thighs. He strained a little against the hold, but didn't break it. In terms of pure brawn, he was more heavily built than Ric, though Ric was taller. The scrape of stubble caressed his chin.

Ric carefully released his grip on one arm. His hand moved down to Zach's fly, though he hesitated before releasing the zip. 'You really don't need to be jealous.'

Maybe he did. Maybe he didn't. The fact remained that he was. Even as Ric's hand curled around Zach's shaft, images of Ric and Kara fucking bled across his field of vision. It hurt. More than it ever had before.

Ric worked his cock with practised precision. He encompassed them both with one palm, so that their pricks were pressed together. It implied intimacy, but it was just an act. Zach couldn't believe there was any heart behind it.

'Turn around,' Ric coaxed.

Zach did so. He fell on to his knees so that he was facing up the stairs and let Ric wrench his trousers down around his thighs. Within seconds Ric's head lay on a level with Zach's arse. His tongue nuzzled between Zach's cheeks and performed a merry dance against his anus. Sweet! Such stimulation was always sweet and yet this time sour too. He groaned when Ric's tongue delved inside a little way. There were too many nerve-endings in that region for him not to find pleasure in such exploration. Ric didn't bother to prolong the warm-up by using his fingers first. They'd done this often enough that, in fairness, it probably wasn't necessary. A little spit, a little lube and the promise of some fun were generally enough to relax him. Indeed, Ric slid inside him with minimal effort, right up to the hilt.

Zach pushed back, enjoying the sensation of having Ric's balls pressed up tight to his perineum. This was the closest they ever got, both physically and emotionally. For several minutes, Ric held still and let Zach use him like he might a toy to work himself into a lather.

Nothing really felt the same as this, thought Zach. Fucking

a woman was akin to being squeezed inside a hungry glove. It was fantastic but the focus of pleasure was all upon his cock. Being penetrated involved whole different sets of nerves. The apex wasn't as acutely centred. His entire body seemed more involved in the act. Leastways it did until the pace built, and consequently so did the angle of assault. The shift was subtle but explosive. Red heat swam on the inside of his eyelids as the tip of Ric's cock nudged up against Zach's prostate. Sweat broke out across his body, and a keening wail rose from his throat.

'Easy there.' Ric shoved Zach's jacket and shirt up towards his shoulders so that he could press his body tight to Zach's bare skin. 'Tell me when you're almost there.'

Tell him because they were doing this bareback and Zach's muscles would squeeze tight around Ric's cock, milking him for all he was worth. Zach bit his lower lip, determined not to speak. Hell, yes! He wanted Ric to come inside him. He wanted Ric to lose control like that.

'Zach,' Ric purred. 'Zach. Oh, God! You fucking stu— amazing fool.' His words lapsed into a croon that Zach felt the vibrations of through his back. Just … another … thrust … or two and that was going to be it.

Hot streamers of joy flowed along the length of his cock. Zach jerked over and over as his seed shot from his body, while at the same time Ric came inside his arse. His orgasm lasted a good long while. When he was finally spent he rubbed his brow against his arm to dry the sweat. Ric continued to breathe sharply against his back for several seconds longer.

'Don't ever think that I want to give this up. Know that it isn't true. Don't let's make Kara a wedge between us.'

Zach wondered how literally he meant it.

'Come back to the studio. Let me take some more

photographs. I love how you look just after sex.'

'I don't think that's a good idea,' Zach croaked with a parched voice. 'It's probably better if I leave.'

'No. It's not better if you leave. It's better if you stay. Stay and we'll do stuff together.'

Zach blinked back tears, afraid of what was being offered. He wasn't going to be fooled into thinking Ric had somehow had a change of heart. He was just protecting his interests with a calculated show of compassion. Zach turned around, pulling his trousers up as he moved so that there was a layer of material between him and the stone steps. 'I'm going to leave. I know when I'm being buttered up. Maybe we should spend some time apart and you can see if you really miss me.'

'I miss you already.'

'Prove that, by not shagging Kara.'

'Zach, you know I'll go stir crazy without sex.'

He gave Ric a cold, hard stare.

'I promised I'd take some pictures round.'

Zach gave a sigh. 'I'm gone. See you later.'

* * *

'Shit!' Ric knocked his head against the wall the moment he heard the front door slam. He didn't want things to change. He liked the status quo, the freedom he had to do as he pleased without having to constantly attend to someone else's feelings. He refused to be beholden to anybody. He'd been in that position before and didn't want to go back. His life back then had been a mirage fuelled by alcohol and excess. He didn't like to dwell on the type of excess. Suffice to say, if you named it he'd probably indulged in it.

Ric liked to believe he'd become a good deal smarter since

Scarlett's death. His old friends believed him grief-stricken, and humoured him as a recluse. They still bought his work, but, thank God, no longer considered him part of their set. For a while, he had wallowed in his loss; now it was altogether too easy to let people believe that's what kept him on Liddell Island. It meant there was no pressure to return to the old ways.

Zach wasn't exactly asking for that, but he was asking for more commitment than Ric cared to give. If he was as emotionally detached as Zach seemed to think, that wouldn't have been a problem. He'd have simply cut Zach loose and found a new playmate. The truth was that he cared more than he liked to admit. Zach had been there for him since the dark days following the coroner's report, when uncertainty had plagued him and caused his every act to be scrutinised. Death by misadventure might have been the final verdict, but folks had still questioned his involvement in his wife's demise. Everyone except Zach, who never harangued him over his past.

Damn it, but he didn't want to be shackled to someone in the way he'd been back then. Staying friends with benefits meant they skirted that pitfall.

There were other factors too. He didn't want to be labelled as yet another gay photographer. His sexual preferences were irrelevant to his art. Besides, he wasn't gay. He liked fucking both men and women.

Ric lifted his forehead out of the dint he felt he'd made in the stone wall. Visually, there was no appreciable difference in the stone. He guessed his head hurt more than the wall. So maybe he didn't want them to officially hook up, but he didn't want to completely piss Zach off either. He'd just have to consider it a challenge – the Stay Out Of Kara's Pants

Award. A week would involve a Herculean effort, but if it calmed things down ... well, he could hope that it would stop Zach being so antsy. In the meantime, he'd stay home and work, so that he didn't happen upon Kara by chance.

The dogs followed him as he padded into the kitchen. They wolfed down scraps of pork he threw to them as he made a sandwich. After he'd finished and wiped up all the crumbs, Ric made a fresh flask of coffee to take up to the studio. Loading the rest of the photographs on to his laptop took a matter of minutes; weeding them down to the usable images would take a whole lot longer.

He paused only a few shots into the task. So much for Zach swearing undying love, and all his damn accusations. The camera didn't lie. Zach only had eyes for Kara, which meant his snit was definitely over the fact that he'd only gotten a hand job when he'd really wanted the full works.

Damn bastard had accused him of his own crime.

Ric clicked his way through more of the images as he mulled over that point. Had he been as possessive about Kara as Zach accused? No, of course not. He liked her; appreciated that she understood him. No strings, and fluid boundaries. He rarely encountered a woman like that. But that didn't mean there had to be any depth to their relationship.

Ric stared at one particular shot of Zach and Kara. Zach's head lay tilted back, his mouth partially open, though his expression was slightly out of focus. Kara leaned over him, lips plumped and equally hungry for a kiss. What she was doing with her hands wasn't immediately apparent. Then again, it didn't need to be. The chemistry leapt right off the screen. Any moment, Zach would reach up and slide his fingers into her blonde hair, then drag her on to his lap and envelop her in his embrace. For all its intensity, he might

159

have captured that first moment of penetration, the one that always came as a shock no matter how many times you did it. The one that set the precedent for everything that came next. Damn, he needed them both back here so that he could try to capture that for real. Except they'd both left and he wasn't about to see either of them again in a hurry.

CHAPTER ELEVEN

The wind whipped Kara's hair around her face as she scrambled over the seaweed-strewn rocks west of the Bunker. She'd come this way in order to avoid the main coastal path, where she'd recognised Robin from a distance by her flame-red hair.

Ever since she'd turned Robin away from her door, she'd sought to avoid another meeting. Robin had caught her off-guard that first day. Now, if there was one thing she wished to undo since landing on Liddell Island, it was encouraging that intimacy. Though she did wish she had someone to confide in who didn't have quite such a salacious interest in the subject. Robin's obsession with Ric crossed a whole lot of lines. The more she thought about it, the creepier it seemed.

Zach was avoiding her too. Although she'd trekked down to the Bunker daily to see him, Zach always contrived to be busy when she arrived. Three grunts she'd had out of him since Tuesday and that was it.

She had left Ric's studio because she suspected the two men were going to row. Now she wished she'd stuck it out. At least then she'd have known the outcome, and what exactly the issue was.

She stopped to fish her phone out of the bottom of her

bag. Maybe this wouldn't be the wisest of moves, but she needed some answers. Within seconds she'd sent text messages to both Ric and Zach.

Do we need to talk? Drop round when you get a chance. Kxx

Much to her surprise, when she arrived home Ric's two Dalmatians were tearing around her property and knocking over pots. Ric stood slouched under her porch, dressed in his ubiquitous black jeans and leather jacket combo. He'd pulled his long flaxen hair back into a ponytail today, which drew attention to the narrowness of his face.

'That was quick,' she said, walking up the path to greet him. The two dogs immediately bounded towards her.

Ric squinted uncertainly at her, using his expression to convey his unspoken 'Huh?'

'You got my text, I take it?'

He shook his head slowly only for his phone to beep inside his pocket. He pulled it out and hit ignore. 'Horace, Toby, heel.' The dogs changed direction mid-bounce and danced between Ric's legs, almost knocking him over. 'I was walking this way, so I brought you those pictures.' He dug into the pocket of his tight jeans and pulled out a thumb drive. 'Here … I picked out the best ones.'

'Aren't you coming in?' Kara asked. He'd passed over the little stick and turned away, rather implying that he was leaving immediately.

Ric cast a brief glance at her door. His shoulders lifted slightly. 'I have the dogs.'

'But they'll be fine out here for a bit, won't they? I can get them some water.' Something clean, rather than the brackish slime one of them was lapping out of an old birdbath.

'I don't know. I can't stay long.' He wriggled his hands into his front pockets, which made the jeans even tighter across his hips. 'I suppose a few minutes. What did you want to say?'

'What happened between you and Zach? Why isn't he talking to me? Why have you been so scarce?'

Ric shrugged. 'I've been busy. Can't speak for Zach.'

One of the dogs pushed its nose inside the door as Kara opened it.

'Horace, no.' Ric tugged him back by his collar. 'Sorry.'

'I don't know how you tell them apart.'

'Easy. Toby has a heart on his butt.'

Sure enough, the other dog had a heart-shaped ring of dots on his rear.

'Stay. Wait.'

'Will they actually do that?' Kara asked, giving the two tongue-wagging fiends a last glance before she closed the door.

'Sure.' Ric gave the hall a once-over, presumably in order to digest the changes a week's habitation had made in his former property.

'My laptop is in the lounge.' Kara led the way through to where she'd set up a workstation in one of the alcoves. 'Go ahead and boot her up. I'll make us some tea.'

Hm, Ric seemed a little twitchy, but maybe he was apprehensive over what she was about to say. Casual partners, Kara reminded herself as she stuffed teabags into the pot. We're not dating, so he doesn't have to call or spill the beans on his life. She'd spent too long with Gavin, who checked up on her all the time.

Leaving the kettle to boil, she returned to the room with a plate of biscuits. Ric had taken off his jacket and hung it over the chair, and sat hunched over the screen with his back to her. A list of gig dates written in white stretched across his shoulder blades. Kara smiled, remembering the elaborate inked design that lay beneath the layer of cotton, and how she'd traced each sable swirl with her tongue the night he'd slept over.

The ponytail she couldn't decide upon. It meant she could see the back of his neck, one part of a man that she'd always found fascinating, but on the other hand it took some effort of will not to tweak the cord so that the knot would unravel and set free the silky strands.

She pressed two fingers to his skin just above his collar line and Ric turned around.

'Biscuit?' She thrust the plate under his nose.

'No, thanks. Is there another chair?'

Kara shook her head. There were stools in the kitchen, but she couldn't be bothered to fetch one. 'Shuffle along. We can cosy up.' By the time the imaging software had opened, they had one bum cheek each perched on the seat.

'Did you get anything you can use?' Kara asked. She blinked in astonishment at the impossibly crisp images loading on to the screen. That Ric possessed talent had never been under dispute, but she hadn't expected him to have made *her* look so gorgeous. Somehow, he'd transformed her from an ordinary woman into a wildly erotic creature.

She and Zach looked fucking amazing together.

'One or two things,' Ric remarked. A slight smile tugged at the edges of his lips. 'Would you like me to blow a couple of them up for you?'

'Yeah,' Kara gasped, though lord only knows where she'd hang such an image. She hardly thought Christopher would appreciate having a picture of his sister's naked butt in his lounge. 'I mean, if that's not a problem. It's not going to cost me, is it?' She had no money to speak of.

Ric shook his head. 'No, providing you agree to coming

back to the studio. Any thoughts on which one you'd like?'

'You choose.'

'You,' Ric insisted.

The more Kara looked, the more difficult it became to pick between them and to remain unmoved. Kara surreptitiously squirmed on her part of the chair, trying to negate the flare of arousal that was gathering like dew between her thighs. Ric remained still, she guessed, inured to the effect of the images by years in this line of work. Then again, he'd not been quite so untouched by the eroticism in his studio. Not that the photos showed the whole story. They stopped short of the grand finale.

'Do you ever photograph yourself?' she asked.

Ric shook his head. 'Narcissism isn't an endearing trait. If I want to look at myself, I can look in the mirror. Besides, photography is about catching a moment. Any pictures I took of myself would only reflect what I was thinking about, namely angles and lenses. They wouldn't be very erotic. Why do you ask? What's up? Is Zach not doing it for you?'

'It's not that.' She settled on an erotic but non-explicit picture of her and Zach on the verge of kissing, even though she secretly wanted the one of her masturbating Zach where his hand was folded over the top of hers. 'It's just that these are much nicer than the snapshots I have of you on my phone.'

'I bloody well hope so. What's the lens on your phone, about five megapixels?' Kara took out her mobile to have a look, but there were no markings to verify Ric's assertion. He began to laugh.

'I ought to get you both together so that I can snap you side by side,' she said.

'Are we back on that again? Honestly, I've never known anyone quite so obsessed with the idea of being spit-roast.'

'Ewww!' Kara slapped him across the arm, and then stood up. 'There's no need to be gross. Anyway, you're just as fixated as I am. You're the one who keeps bringing it up. And you're the one that made such a point of having both of us the last time we were all together. It wasn't Zach or I who turned it into a threesome.'

'That wasn't a threesome.' Ric ejected the memory stick and slipped it back into his pocket. 'Nothing like.'

Presumably he was talking from experience. She couldn't make eye-contact with him, so instead focused on the neck-line of his T-shirt where the ridge of his collarbone peeped out. 'Did you two have an argument afterwards?' she asked. It was bugging her. She had to know. 'Is that why Zach's being weird with me? He already knew about us. I didn't anticipate a drama.'

Ric spun the swivel chair to face her. 'That's not what he's pissed off about. At least he claims it's not.' He folded his arms across his chest.

Kara raised her hands in surrender. 'What then?'

Ric got up. He walked around the sofa until they stood face to face, nothing between them. 'What's he told you about us?'

'Only that you had him when he first came to Liddell Island too.'

A small hmm echoed in Ric's throat. 'That was six-seven years ago. I've been shagging him ever since.'

Kara's eyes widened. She reached out to the sofa back for support. 'So you're a proper item?'

'No.' He shook his head. 'No, we're not. That's the issue. Zach wants us to be.'

'But you don't?' She couldn't for the life of her see why. Zach was a complete hottie and even thinking about it at this tense moment was making arousal bloom between her thighs. It still irked her that she hadn't been able to see Ric sucking Zach off. 'Why not?'

'Because.'

She cocked her head to one side, hoping for a more expansive explanation. 'Don't you love him?'

From the way Ric sucked in a gasp and held on to it, she surmised otherwise. Ric cared all right. There was something else holding him back from making a commitment. 'Please tell me this is nothing to do with me.'

'It's not.' That was both a relief and a slap in the face.

'Good. Then what is it?'

'I just don't want any strings.' Ric bowed his head, making the lie obvious.

Kara gently touched his shoulder. 'I understand that. It's why I held off contacting you, even though I wanted to see you, and I had your number.' She didn't really understand it. It made no sense at all. Surely Ric wasn't so foolish as to cast aside love in favour of pointless, faceless sex with whatever strangers happened by his door. 'Listen, I know it's none of my business, but is this something to do with your former wife?'

Ric's head snapped upright so quickly she feared for his neck. 'Don't ever mention her again.' Blind fury transformed his handsome face into a web of lines and darkened the blue of his irises to near black. He sucked down an even deeper breath. 'I see you did your homework on me.'

Did he honestly believe she'd Googled him? Admittedly, she had checked out his web presence, but she hadn't delved into his private life. 'Robin mentioned her.'

Ric pressed two fingers to her mouth to silence her before she said any more.

'I know what it's like,' Kara continued, despite his fingers. 'I just split with my boyfriend. He was a controlling jerk. I've no idea why I stayed with him.'

'Kara.' He cupped her face in his hands. 'I loved her. Quite desperately at one stage. But we were bad for one another. Getting messed up like that is not something I'm about to repeat.'

Flabbergasted, she simply stared at him for a minute. 'But would being with Zach even be like that?'

'It's not worth the risk.'

Kara wasn't so sure, but was it her place to say otherwise? Fuck buddies, she reminded herself for the second time that day. Not that they were really even that. 'I'll go and make that tea.' She needed a minute to compose herself. What was she doing getting involved with them both? She didn't want to screw things up for them, and it was obvious that they were meant to be together.

Ric followed her through to the kitchen. 'Don't bother. I don't like tea.'

'A stiff drink, then?' The demijohn of cider he'd sent over still sat on the countertop. Kara poured out two glasses, but left hers untouched. Ric downed his in one. When she offered him hers, he accepted the glass but put it aside at once.

'Come here, I've a better idea.' He pulled her into his arms. 'I don't really do the whole getting drunk thing any more, but I do know how to raise my spirits.'

Kara splayed her hand over his breastbone to hold him back a minute. The dark sheen of his pupils betrayed his intent. 'Won't this make things worse?' It wasn't that she didn't want him, but she probably ought to leave him to his happy-ever-after with Zach.

'Worse in what way, exactly? I'm not going to change my

mind, and Zach is going to have to accept that. Plus, you're right –' he traced the shell of her ear with his tongue '– I am just as obsessed with the idea of a threesome.'

His lips tasted of overripe apples. She caught the scent of his aftershave as his hand crept up her thigh.

'Tell me, Kara, are you wearing any knickers today? Do you realise you left another pair at my place?'

A silken thread of his hair had escaped its fastening. Kara twirled it around her thumb. Sod it; maybe they could work together on persuading Zach into accepting things. 'Why don't you find out for yourself?'

Ric chuckled, which caused a low rumble deep in his chest. 'What a splendid idea.' His grin turned feral, showed just a hint of teeth. Apparently, that was all the permission he considered necessary. A second later he had her sprawled over the table-top, with her bottom in the air. Ric flipped back her skirt.

'Ah-h, a thong, is it?' He hooked a finger under the narrow ribbon of fabric that ran between the cheeks of her bottom and tugged until the fabric slithered downward and hung around her calves. 'A little damp and eager for it, aren't you?' The blunt tip of his finger briefly swept along the seam of her pussy lips, making her blood run like hot sauce through her veins.

Ric smacked his lips and she knew he'd tasted her. That alone caused another gush of arousal. She glanced back at him. His tongue briefly swept over his lips, moistening their surface. He fitted his palm to the curve of her right buttock as though testing the fit. 'Do you know what I'm going to do?'

She glanced at his palm again. 'Oh, God!'

'It's what I do to all the naughty girls.'

Kara gripped the table edge tight.

'You know that this is going to hurt, right?'

She tensed the muscles in her legs, but even that didn't brace her enough for the tremendous crack his palm made as it connected with her flesh. She jolted forward, gasping with shock. Damn, it hurt! Fucking ow! Yet the fire that streaked across her skin also flowed inwards towards her belly. Ric slicked another finger over the lips of her sex, which made her cunt ripple and throb.

'Ten, shall we say?'

'Five,' she whimpered. No way on God's earth would she ever tolerate another nine. Frankly, even five seemed optimistic.

'Eight,' Ric decided. 'You should be glowing nicely at both ends by then.'

She was doing that after another two. Both sets of cheeks were berry bright and her breathing had become a series of jittery gasps that failed to provide the required oxygen levels. The worst part was not the blow. It was the after-math, when Ric gently caressed the tender spots he'd created, rubbing life back into her injured flesh. That shot tremors right through her body and made her clit nag so much she couldn't help chafing her legs together to cause a little friction. Of course, that only provoked him into punishing her some more.

He reached six before she begged him to stop. Her limbs ached, and the skin of her bottom felt so tender and tight she could almost believe it blistered.

'Are you nicely warmed up, Kara?' He didn't allow her a moment to recover. 'Shall we see how eager you are for me?' His thumb immediately rode the split between her labia. Two fingers pushed straight into her eager cunt, causing her to release a desperate groan. Kara gripped him tight with

170

her internal muscles. She had to concentrate, and blow out each breath.

Ric's hands left her. Momentarily bereft, Kara glanced back at him in time to see him tug off his T-shirt and then unbuckle his belt. Ric shoved his tight denim jeans down his thighs along with his underwear. His cock reared proud, pink-flushed along its entire length – beautiful. It seemed a shame he had to hide it with wet-weather gear.

He bent and kissed her cheek before his cock finally slid into place between her thighs. He filled her up as he had the first time, stealing her breath as he thrust and going deep from the outset. The slap of their flesh made the sting in her rear burn with renewed intensity. White heat fanned out from her bottom and into the rest of her body. Her breasts ached so much she found a way to support her body without her hands in order to squeeze her own nipples. The throbbing in her clitoris wasn't so easily quelled.

'Harder. Harder,' she begged.

'Like this?' Ric curved a hand over her shoulder so that he could tug her backwards on to his shaft as he thrust forward.

Holy-damn-hell-yes! Even though the increased vibrancy of the way their bodies met made her reddened bottom sting. Kara released one nipple in order to wedge a hand between her legs. Heaven swelled within her cunt as she rubbed her clit. Ric continued to drive her up against the table-top. She was going to come hard; already her muscles were tightening with expectation.

When the chime of the doorbell cut through the sexual haze she was drowning in, Kara jumped half out of her skin.

'Easy.' Ric held her firmly, his demanding pace not easing in the slightest despite the racket his two dogs were making outside. 'Were you expecting somebody?'

'Nnnnr.' She shook her head. When a moment later her phone began to beep, she realised she *was* expecting someone. She'd sent Zach that text. 'Zach. Oh, fuck. It's Zach.' They hadn't time to disengage and straighten things out before Zach was peering through the old distorted glass of the uncovered window, straight at them. His thick eyebrows hitched immediately. Then, slowly, terribly, he backed away.

'Fucking shit!' Ric leapt away from her like a scalded cat. 'Shit, shit, shit.' He hoisted up his jeans, his erection apparently gone. 'Oh, bollocks,' he added somewhat more calmly.

Kara twisted round so that she faced him. 'What just happened?'

'He asked me not to fuck you.' Ric wagged his finger at her. 'I'd been doing well. I'd made it to day four. I knew coming here was asking for trouble.'

'I hope you're not waggling that finger at me in order to point blame.'

Ric lowered his hand and shook his head. 'No.' He came and rested his bum against the table beside her. Kara slid her arm around his shoulder. She didn't really understand the relationship between the two men, or the way she'd become embroiled in it, and she didn't wish to see either of them hurting, but nor did she really want to back away. 'Should we go after him?' Maybe if they all sat down and talked like adults they could straighten things out in a way that was acceptable to all three of them.

Ric produced his mobile from his jacket pocket and put it to his ear. After a moment he put it down again. 'He's not answering. I better go after him on foot and talk to him.'

'We'll both go,' Kara insisted. She ran upstairs to find some sensible clothing. It was already heading towards evening and twilight seemed to vanish in the blink of an eye. Ric had pulled on his T-shirt and jacket by the time she came back down. He stood on the doorstep with his dogs.

'We don't know which way he's gone. I'm going to head over to the cove and then across to the fort and the eastern tip of the island. Are you OK taking the other route and heading down to the Bunker in case he's gone there?'

'Yeah, sure. We'll keep in touch by phone.' Kara pushed hers into the pocket of the cargo pants she'd pulled on along with clean underwear. 'Let me know as soon as you find him.'

She set off, fully expecting Ric to find Zach first. They'd known each other for years, and presumably knew all the hiding places and contemplation spots each of them favoured. Plus, presumably the dogs could follow Zach's scent.

CHAPTER TWELVE

The sky had greyed over and spots of rain were already falling by the time Kara reached the bay. She'd exchanged a couple of text messages with Ric. Neither of them had seen so much as a glimpse of Zach. Kara wondered if they would. She'd tried calling and sending him messages too but his number came up as unavailable. Perhaps that was for the best, for she wasn't quite sure what to say to him. She didn't really owe him an apology. She hadn't even known about the request he'd made of Ric, nor did she understand his motives. If Zach was so set upon him and Ric pairing up then why had he been so interested in fooling about with her?

Heavier raindrops began to splash into the rock pools as she descended the cliff path. The typical gaggle of tourists was absent from the shingle, presumably chased away by the incoming weather front. On the mainland, the sea-front lights were just bursting into colour, the reds, greens and blues blurring in the coastal water. Below her, a set of yellow headlights blinked into life, revealing the pebble-strewn bank of the causeway. An engine growled, then Zach's ice-cream van began to slowly trundle forward.

'No. Oh, no. Zach, wait up.' Kara broke into an

unsteady run, wary of her footing on the loose shingle. Her hair lay plastered against her cheeks by the time she reached the shore. Zach was already halfway across the causeway, and the sea was looking choppy, stirred up by the thickening downpour. 'Oh, shit!' Now there'd be no chance to talk to him until tomorrow. But a moment later he stopped. Perhaps he'd seen her waving. Kara trekked a few paces along the causeway, only for a wave to wash over her feet, leaving her deck shoes completely soaked and her feet cold.

The lights on the van went out. Zach got out of the driver's side door and walked round to the front of the van. He lifted the bonnet. What the heck? That was one crap place to break down. Kara splashed forward another few paces through the icy water. The wind was steadily rising and pushing the waves up against the sides of the ramp so that they lapped over the top with increasing vigour.

Kara still hadn't mastered the rhythm of the tides. She wasn't sure when high tide was, or how deeply the path to the mainland was submerged. Was this tide coming in or out? She did know that unless Zach got the engine started again soon, he was going to get swept away. She watched him hit something – the starter motor? – under the bonnet. The van made a very brief choking sound, then nothing.

'Fuck!' Zach's exclamation carried to her on the wind.

Damn. What could she do? Who could she contact? There weren't any useful local numbers in her phone besides Ric's. He was apparently out of range. Reception had always been crap on this craggy lump of rock. Kara's mouth went dry as Zach continued to tinker under the bonnet. She could tow him, except she hadn't brought her car keys. 'Leave it,' she yelled. 'The tide's coming in.'

It was definitely coming in. Each successive wave pushed further up the beach.

Either Zach didn't hear or else he plain ignored her. If there'd been a boat she'd have rowed out, but the only thing of any use was the life ring on a board by the water's edge. Kara grabbed it. She pushed her head and one arm through the centre, and then began to wade. The sea had reached knee level by the time she reached Zach. It stood halfway up the wheel arches of the van.

He finally saw her when he poked his head up from the inner workings of the vehicle. He frowned in a most unwelcoming way that drew his eyebrows down low over his puppy-dog eyes. 'What do you want?'

'You need to get out of here.'

'Yeah, think I figured that one out for myself.'

'No, I mean leave it. You're going to drown.'

'You leave. I just need to ...' He lifted his hand as if to strike another blow with the hammer, but Kara grasped his arm.

'You're not getting it,' she said. 'We need to run. It's just a van. It's insured, right?'

Zach nodded, though he still tried to dodge around her to get back to the engine.

'Seriously, Zach. Don't make me hurt you.'

'More than you already have?'

Kara sucked in gasp. 'Look, I'm sorry you got such an eyeful. It's not what I invited you over for. Ric was waiting when I got home, and things happened. I didn't realise you had a problem with that. You hadn't had a problem with it in the past.'

Zach grunted at her in response.

'Damn it, you idiot man, another few minutes and it's

going to be up to my thighs.' She slammed down the bonnet lid, nearly trapping his fingers. He seemed to see her properly then, wet hair, sodden clothes, life ring and all. Maybe it was because the water level rose higher up her legs than it did on him that the peril became real. 'I'm sorry. I don't really understand, but I never intended to hurt you. If you'd explained how it was between you and Ric ...' Her words petered out. 'Let's get back to the shore and discuss this. Leave the van. Even if you get it started, how far are you going to get before the engine floods?' And then a wave crashed over them, filling her ears with the roar of the ocean.

She surfaced screaming. Icy wet clothing clung tight to her skin from her toes to the band of her bra. Her sputtering seemed to galvanise Zach into action. He grabbed hold of her hand and took the lead in wading back to shore. It wasn't far. They'd easily make it. Only the weight of her clothing dragged upon Kara's shoulders, as though she were carrying an army-sized backpack instead of nothing at all. The life ring got in the way of swinging her arms. Each wave seemed to come in a little stronger too and find a new way to seep inside her clothes. Still, panic never entered the equation until one big wave knocked her sideways so that she lost her footing and got pushed off the causeway into deeper water.

The life ring lifted clean over her head. Thank God, Zach held her arm tight. He pulled her close to his body when she surfaced, spluttering seawater into his face.

'Kick your shoes off and swim,' he insisted. He'd followed her off the ramp and was also out of his depth and treading water.

Kara toed off her deck shoes. They were sodden enough that gravity helped tug them away, but the rest of her clothing clung to her. There was no way she could take it off. Each minute in the water made doing anything beyond shivering a supreme effort.

'Swim.' Zach released his hold to free her arms. 'Keep at it. It's not far.' He kept behind her, so that he could propel her forwards and use his mass to stop the waves from pushing her further off course. 'Come on, kick.'

No matter how hard she strove to propel herself forward, the shore seemed to grow farther away. She'd never been a strong swimmer. She wasn't even a great lover of sitting on the beach. Wave after wave crashed over her head, making her blind to the direction she should be following. Zach remained with her, tugging at her, encouraging her. If they lived long enough she'd owe him for ever.

If they lived long enough ...

Something sharp grazed her knees. Kara winced, brought her arm down and her hand hit the wall of pebbles that lined the shore. They slipped and slid beneath her fingers and toes, but they were out of the depths and into the shallows. Zach dragged her the last few metres up on to the beach.

For several moments, Kara lay face down, panting. Her lungs refused to expand properly. Seaweed clung to her ankles as though the ocean meant to drag her back into its embrace, and her muscles burned from the cold.

Zach knelt beside her, his bare knees level with her ear. Somehow he'd managed to strip off his trousers while they were in the water. He tugged his shirt over his head as she watched and cast it on to the stones. Out to sea, the ice-cream van bobbed just above the water like a giant pink and cream hippopotamus. It was hard to imagine it would ever go again.

'Come on, up.' Zach disentangled her from the seaweed clinging to her legs, and then supported her attempt to stand.

The sharp wind clawed at her waterlogged clothing. The steady rain added to the weight. 'Let's get inside and get dry.'

'Your van,' she managed to mumble.

Zach hugged her tight to his body. He cast one last forlorn look out to sea. 'There's nothing I can do about it now. If she's still there at low tide, I'll call out a tow truck, but she could be half a mile down the coast stuck in a mudflat by then.'

'I'm sorry.'

'Not your fault. At least I have stock still at the Bunker. I'll just have to serve from out of there.' Being dowsed with icy water seemed to have knocked some of the wind out of him, but perhaps his anger would spark again later. She cast a shivery glance back at the choppy sea, and then followed Zach towards his shop.

Zach retrieved the keys from the breast pocket of his discarded shirt. Hell knows what sort of craziness was going through his head about her, Ric and the situation with the van, but somehow he'd managed to maintain enough of a level head to hang on to his keys and not leave them in the van or let them go along with his trousers.

'There's not much in the way of light in here.' He pushed her inside the Bunker as two spotlights flickered into life. They lit up the rack of postcards, while the rest of the gifts remained bathed in shadows. 'Get your clothes off.' He scooped up a heap of beach towels out of a basket marked *£8 for 2* and then busied himself with getting the gas heater lit. 'Everything. We don't want you catching your death because of sitting around in wet knickers.'

Kara managed a feeble snicker through her chattering teeth. Apparently determined to lead by example, Zach rolled off his underwear, which did elevate her mood a little, even if all she got was a two-second glimpse of shiny wet skin, before he wrapped a towel decorated with an angel fish around his waist.

'I'll make us a drink.' He disappeared into a room out back.

Still trembling, Kara managed to peel off her clothes. She threw them as far away as she could, before wrapping herself in the pile of towels and hunching right before the heater. Zach stooped down beside her a moment later. He offered her a huge mug to wrap her palms around. 'Coffee. I hope you like it strong.'

As of now, she liked it any way it came.

Zach rubbed a towel over his hair, leaving it standing on end. 'What were you doing on the beach? Were you looking for me?'

Kara gave him a nod. 'I wanted to talk. Ric's out looking for you too.' Her teeth chattered when she spoke. She ought to phone Ric and let him know.

'Oh?' Zach discarded the towel. He looked at her with his brows furrowed.

'I should let him know that I found you.' She shuffled over to where she'd thrown her clothes and fished her phone out of her trouser pocket. The screen had turned a dirty grey, and nothing happened when she pressed the buttons.

'Good,' said Zach. 'I'm not sure I want him here.' He cast her dead phone away from her. Maybe it would dry out.

'Zach, I've heard Ric's side, so let's hear yours. One minute you're fine with the fact I'm fucking him, even encouraging it, and then –' she spread her fingers wide '– what? And if you're so in love with him, why were you coming on to me? Were you using me?'

Zach's expression froze into dour lines. His beautiful lips pursed so tightly that they'd lost some of their colour.

'I – I was looking for a way out. I didn't mean to use you.

181

I genuinely like you. I just had some mad idea the night we met that I could find someone else to love. Only then you turned up here and Ric had you, and that wasn't fair, because you were supposed to be nothing to do with him.' He covered his face with his hands, and then peeped at her through the gaps between his fingers. 'I was wrong to use you the other day. I wanted to make a point. I thought I could make him jealous. All I succeeded in doing was highlighting the fact that he cares more about you than he does about me.'

Kara gave an almighty splutter, causing coffee droplets to fly. They hissed as they hit the heater. 'Zach, that's so not true.' She wrapped her arms around him and pulled him against her body. Somehow, she ended up kneeling between his legs. 'Ric loves you –'

'Is that what he said?' Zach asked, looking her straight in the eyes.

'It's true.' She wasn't sure if he'd said it specifically or not. 'He's just afraid that if you're together like that it's going to mess things up.'

'He said that?'

Kara turned so that she sat side on to Zach, her legs curled over the top of one of his hairy ones. 'I'm not interested in creating a rift between you. I'm just out for some fun. If my actions are going to cause heartbreak then we can stop doing this right now.'

Zach's gaze strayed down to her ankle, where he placed a hand over the ridge of bone. Kara looked down at her legs, and for the first time noticed a graze on her knee. One long scratch traversed her patella. Around it, the skin looked raw but clean. The wound reminded her of the close call they'd had in the water, which immediately tightened all her muscles.

'That won't change anything. It doesn't matter what I

182

want, he won't compromise. It just means I'll lose any chance I have of being with either of you.'

'Either?' she quietly echoed. She pulled the towel more tightly around herself, covering her injured knee with the bright-blue cloth. 'Are you saying you're still interested in me?'

Heat rolled off his body, warming her, and the stubble around his jaw grazed the skin of her shoulder as he snuggled closer. 'I don't know what to wish for any more. If you've any brilliant ideas … I just know that it's not going to work out how I want it for Ric and me.' His chest hair tickled as he moved. His lips gently nuzzled her shoulder. 'I know you prefer him to me.'

'That's not …' she gulped. It wasn't true. She had no preference for either man; they were different and she'd been enjoying living in the moment. Zach was earthy and genuine. If they'd been neighbours while growing up, they'd have been best friends and she'd have crushed massively on him, whereas Ric almost felt like an alien being, his interest in her kind of amazing and otherworldly. The other thing was: she liked the fact that Ric wasn't looking for commitment, as she didn't want to fall into another claustrophobic relationship, after spending so long marooned on Planet Gavin. Matter of fact, she rather liked being a butterfly, having both Ric and Zach to fly between. 'It's not fair or true. I'm not looking for anything more than fun from either of you. Zach, I only just escaped getting hitched. I'm not interested in making any sort of commitment yet.'

Zach scraped a hand through his wet hair so that it lay slicked back against his skull. 'OK. But you can't deny that there's real chemistry between you and Ric. I should know. I've seen you fuck often enough.'

'I beg your pardon?'

Zach held her gaze, almost daring her to argue the point, but failing to discern the cause of her outburst.

'You've seen us once … twice,' she corrected, recalling what had prompted this meeting.

'Three times,' Zach countered. 'I lied about being stuck on the mainland that night I was supposed to call.'

Christ! He'd seen her. What had she and Ric been doing at the time? She didn't even bother wasting thoughts on hoping that he'd just seen them fooling about on the beach. The glitter in Zach's dark eyes said he'd watched the lot, and that he'd seen her bent over that rock having her bottom thoroughly warmed. 'Fuck!' The exclamation escaped her lips as a string of colourful expletives echoed inside her head. It was her turn to hide her face in her palms.

'Kara.' Zach's fingers gently curled around her shoulder. 'I know you didn't plan it, and I know how persuasive he can be. I know it, because I love him. I don't blame you. We barely knew one another, and I was late.'

'And I knew I was doing something wrong.'

He continued to shake his head. 'No, you weren't. It wasn't a date. It was just coffee.'

'Yeah?' She wrinkled her nose into a grimace, and then buried her face in her coffee cup. The hit of caffeine made her heart thump. 'Just like this is coffee, I suppose.'

Zach gently batted her arm. He glanced away and then back at her.

'There is one way.' Kara brushed away Zach's continued caress, which knocked the towel from around her shoulder. 'But I'm not sure you'll like it. I don't know that it'll even work.'

'Go on.'

This was madness; it wasn't so much a plan as stating her desire, but the possibility of actually having a threesome with him and Ric was too delicious to be ignored. The mere prospect of it set her heart pumping nineteen to the dozen. All those fantasies she'd entertained since meeting the two men were suddenly at the forefront of her thoughts. In some ways it made sense. Why not, as they were all already intimate. Even if it was just the once, so they could see what it was like and if it would work.

Kara opened her mouth and closed it a few times. 'We could all be together,' she muttered. 'He might be more prepared to commit if there were three of us involved. It wouldn't be so claustrophobic.' She didn't know Ric very well, but the few glimpses she'd had into his heart suggested that he did actually care for Zach. He was likely still out looking for him. God only knows what he'd think if he saw the van out to sea.

Zach gave a sharp cough, and then back-pedalled on to his knees. His brown hair whipped back and forth spraying droplets of seawater as he shook his head. 'One of us would get burned.' From his look she knew he thought it would be him.

Kara reached out and placed her palm against the diamond of hair upon his chest. His heart pounded beneath her fingertips.

'Is that what you want?' he asked warily.

'Maybe.' She felt her cheeks burn and turned away. 'Look, forget it. It was a silly suggestion.'

Zach took her coffee cup off her and then tugged her down on top of him, so that she lay pressed against his torso, her hips straddling his loins, with nothing but a few bits of towelling between them. It was far too intimate a position for serious conversation.

'It's not something I've done before.' She couldn't entirely shake the idea. Something about the prospect of having the two men and seeing them together fired up her senses.

Zach rolled them over, so that he was on top and she lay beneath him on the mound of towels.

'If we did it, we could gang up on him,' she said.

'Explain.' Zach's brows furrowed. 'Are you suggesting we both pin him down and roger him until he's too tired to resist and makes a confession?'

'I'm suggesting we don't force the issue. We just let things play out. Think about it. Individually, he won't commit to either one of us – not that I'm looking for that – but if we're both involved with him, he won't even realise what he's buying into until it's too late. Then if he has any qualms, he'll have to decide if he really wants to walk away from us both, leaving us to content one another.'

Zach nodded, implying he understood and agreed, which probably meant they were about to put their truly terrible plan into action. He shifted on to all fours over her.

'Zach.' She held out a hand to ward him off. His dark eyes screamed his intent, even before the knot in his towel unravelled so that she had a clear view of his loins. He wasn't erect, but the sight of him brought back memories of previous times together and how at the photo shoot she'd so desperately wanted to straddle his lap and feel him inside her. 'Why are you doing this now? What do you mean to prove?'

He peeled away her fingers from his chest one at a time. 'I'm curious. I think you have some demented notion of controlling Ric and I'm wondering how you think that will work when he can't even handle me.'

'I can handle you.'

'Yeah? Prove it. Stop me doing exactly as I please.'

He splayed his fingers wide across her hip. Kara's breath caught in her throat. With a series of little jerks, he tugged the edges of her towel apart so that her breasts and the flat of her stomach were exposed. Zach dipped his head and pressed a kiss to her skin close to her navel.

Stop him! She didn't need to stop him. Kara's lips curved into a grin. Zach was a giver, not a taker. If she said no to him, even once, that would be it. He'd stop, take himself off somewhere to sulk and possibly never speak to her again, but he wouldn't force her into anything. Zach wasn't the type to blur the boundaries of consent. She reached down, curled her fingers around his chin in order to coax him into raising his head. His lips broke contact with her skin and he looked at her along the length of her body. 'Come here.'

He wormed over her, snake-like, until their hips lay stacked and his mouth was millimetres from hers. The sheen of tears clung to the corners of his eyes. They'd both been tossed about in the water, and he'd lost everything, including the clothes upon his back. Hers at least lay drying. This was all about comfort, not Ric. She was offering him what Ric ought to be giving.

On which subject, she really ought to find a way of letting Ric know that Zach was safe. Presumably, the Bunker had a phone.

Her lips stung as Zach tickled their surface with his tongue. Kara hooked one leg up around his thighs, though she remained convinced that they were doing this for all the wrong reasons. At least Zach was. She wasn't sure it was about mutual attraction any more. He just needed to prove that he could give her exactly what Ric gave, without realising they were like chalk and cheese. She wanted them because they were different, and because she knew there was a bond between them. Two Rics together wouldn't be half as much fun.

Zach raised his hips and then slid his hand between them. Agile fingers guided his cock into place. He nudged against her labia, but didn't immediately push inside. Instead he turned his attention to her neck, and then to her breasts. Her dark areolas crinkled into hard points. He suckled them until she ached, and her hips began to lift in order to seek out deeper satisfaction.

'Tell me you want me.'

A long acquaintance with Ric apparently hadn't done Zach's self-esteem much good, if he needed to hear her say what was surely apparent from her body language.

'I want you.'

'I'll have to pull out before I come.'

Ric would have just rolled with it and bypassed an explanation. Still, she loved the way Zach slid effortlessly into her. He filled her so perfectly that for the first few strokes she hardly dared to breathe. Kara clung to him as they moved, digging her nails into his buttocks and the muscles of his back. So gentle, and so smooth, yet the pace still turned her breathing into a pant. Zach licked a line up her throat that ended at her chin. Braced upon his hands, arms locked at the elbows, he lifted himself in and out of her in a steadily increasing rhythm.

This was the first time sex had been anything other than frantic since she'd said goodbye to Gavin. One-night stands and fucking on street corners didn't exactly lend themselves to a slow build. Though Gavin would never have done this, any more than he'd ever have suggested they fuck by moonlight braced against a rock overlooking the sea. He never scrambled around on the floor. The closest he got to adventure was spreading her over a dining table dressed with overpriced china and crystal. Maybe that's why this felt so much warmer and far more real. It wasn't about their surroundings – an old military bunker. This was about what comfort they could give to each other.

'Oh, boy!' Zach's previously smooth movements took an arrhythmic turn. 'I'm not sure I want to share you, even with the man I love. I think I'd like to keep you all to myself. Will you give up fucking him, Kara? Give me sole use of your cunt?'

'What about my arse?'

She felt rather than saw his grin.

'Are you splitting hairs?' He puffed the hair out of his eyes with a quick breath. 'You know he likes to fuck me there too.'

'Here?' she asked, stretching out her fingers so that they dipped into the crevice between his buttocks. Her middle finger brushed against the whorl of muscle there, which made his cock flex with increased vigour inside her. Kara squeezed him tight with her internal muscles. 'Do you like being touched here, Zach?'

'What do you think?'

She wriggled her finger a millimetre or so into his arse, which made him crow in a high-pitched falsetto.

'If you do that, I'm going to have to pull out.'

'Soon,' she murmured into his ear. She held him closer, dipped her shoulder so that she could stretch her arm out further. His body ate up her finger to the second knuckle. 'Wow, you're really smooth and tight back here.'

'Kara!' he warned.

'Come on, you want me to push another finger in there, don't you?'

'Don't you dare. Don't you fucking dare.' Unlike him, she was prepared to push boundaries. She wriggled her index finger in alongside her other digit.

The heat of Zach's breath hit her face. He reared up quite suddenly and pulled out. Sitting on his haunches, he embraced his shaft with his fist. Kara curled her hand over the top of his. 'Let me.' She dipped her head and took him in her mouth. Within seconds his seed spilled on to her tongue. She held him until he was completely spent. The moment her lips parted contact with his cock, Zach grabbed hold of her and claimed her mouth for a deep, ferocious kiss.

'Lady,' he said, 'wrap yourself up. We're going back to yours, and I'm going to make love to you all night.'

Kara shook her head. 'Not before I've told Ric that you're safe.'

'If you do that, he'll come straight over.'

'Then we'd best make sure we're ready for him.'

CHAPTER THIRTEEN

Kara emerged from the shower at Beachcomber Barn to find Zach on the bed, drying his hair, his nakedness covered by a towel fastened around his waist and a second draped around his shoulders. 'I thought you'd be over that look now,' she said. He'd hiked all the way from the Bunker to her cottage wearing two towels and a pair of flip-flops, not an ideal or the most elegant get-up for a long walk over rough terrain. Even now, the rain still lashed at the windowpanes. Hardly surprising that Zach was now contemplating stocking a line of T-shirts in his shop. Not that her outfit for the trek had been much better. She shivered, recalling how her sea-sodden clothes had clung to her skin as she'd wriggled back into them. Despite having washed the cold and grime away in a hot shower, she still felt chilled, although hopefully an evening of sport with Zach and Ric would change that.

'No sign of Ric yet?' she asked. She'd phoned from the Bunker and told him she'd found Zach and that his van had broken down, but had omitted the details about the brush with death. No sense in being alarmist, or getting the evening off to the wrong start.

Zach shook his head.

Kara trekked over to the landing window and glanced out regardless. She didn't put it past Zach to leave Ric standing on the doorstep. He might profess to love Ric, but that didn't change the fact that he was pissed off at him, and presumably considered him at least partially responsible for the tragedy of the ice-cream van. She could hardly blame him. The fact was if Ric hadn't come over and fucked her, then Zach wouldn't have gone off in a huff, and he wouldn't have ended up stuck in the middle of the causeway while the tide rolled in.

'I unfastened the latch,' Zach said, coming up behind her. His arms encircled her waist. 'I might not have opened the door for him, but I do want him to come in. Though I've still reservations about whether this will work.'

'It will,' Kara reassured him. 'Give it a chance.' She looked at his reflection in the rain-streaked glass. Worry-lines creased his brow. 'I could just leave you to talk if you prefer.'

'Talking won't work. It never has. No, you're right. We need to come at this from a different direction.'

Perhaps her biggest reservation was the fact that Zach had been so easily persuaded to give this a try. His desperation made her uncomfortable, but she was also confused by his continued shows of affection for her. Zach, she decided, simply craved affection of any sort. Ric, it seemed, had a lot to answer for.

'I don't want this to start with a row,' Zach said. 'If we're just standing around waiting for him when he arrives it's going to be awkward.'

'What then?'

He forced a smile out of nowhere, before turning her around. 'You're joking, right? We have a whole world of entertainment available at our fingertips.'

'Don't tell me you've found that mouldering set of Scrabble, and you're just desperate for a game.'

He wagged his finger at her and then pushed his nose in the air. 'I could be quite hurt. I flaunt my nakedness at you, and you suggest I'm only interested in playing word games. How many other men of your acquaintance dress exclusively in bath towels for your entertainment?'

'It is a good look,' she admitted. 'Although it's not really the towel that does it for me. It's more what I can find hiding beneath.'

This was more like it. They were headed in a fun direction, rather than wallowing in seriousness or dredging over the issue of what would happen to his van.

Kara rested her hand upon his thigh, and then stroked upwards under the terry until her hand rested near the top of his leg, where the hair grew more thinly. Silky smooth skin surrounded the area just shy of his groin. Kara gently explored the area while holding Zach's gaze. Anticipation danced in the heart of his pupils, until at last her fingers teased the curve of his balls. Immediately he stood a little straighter, bringing his shoulders up and back. He inched his thighs a fraction further apart, giving her space to more thoroughly explore him. 'Do word games not do it for you, Zach?' she asked, returning to the idea of them both hunched over Scrabble. 'Shall I try a few and see how you react?'

He merely flicked his eyebrows up towards his hairline.

'Cock,' she said giving the syllable particular emphasis. 'Shaft.' Her hand swept upward to where his cock was beginning to swell. 'Pussy. How would you like to put your cock in my pussy? How would you like me to suck your nice big cock?'

That one prompted a faint but discernible mewl in the

193

back of his throat. 'Is that right, Zach, do you want me to get down on my knees and suck your cock?' That would certainly make things interesting when Ric arrived.

She tugged on the towel, causing the knot at Zach's waist to unravel. The edges fell apart revealing the glory of his swelling erection. Kara gave him a playful squeeze. The towel landed on the carpet behind him.

'You know I mean to have my wicked way with you now. If you'd just back up a way, I'll give you something nice to hold on to.' She backed him into the master bedroom and up against the footboard of the bed, which she ordered him to grasp hold of. The iron frame meant he could lace his fingers around the bars.

Kara bent her head. 'I'm going to kiss your cock first, and tease my tongue over that pleading little slit.' She dabbed her tongue against him as though she was tasting ice cream. 'Are you weeping a little for me already? Gosh, yes, you are.' Zach immediately groaned, and a drop of pre-come seeped from the little hole. Kara collected it with her tongue. She liked the taste of him, always had. Slowly, she opened her mouth and allowed him to fill her. She encompassed the lower half of his shaft with her hand and worked with the roll of his hips, allowing him to fuck her mouth for several strokes before she pressed a hand against his stomach to still his motion.

'Not so hasty. I think I ought to make this a thorough exploration.' Her attention turned to his balls. She cradled them, and ran her tongue along the split between the two sacks. 'Open your legs wider.' He did so, and Kara shimmied between them, so that she came up behind him, sandwiched between the footboard and his deliciously muscular arse. Her tongue explored the underside of his balls, then the smooth piece of skin behind them that led towards his anus. Zach danced on his toes as her tongue explored the knotted whorl of muscle. He really was sensitive there, although he didn't start cursing her this time. Instead, he groaned long and piteously when her tongue-tip teased open the puckered entrance to delve inside and awaken all the nerve-endings there. He pressed back, squirmed a little against her face as though he wasn't quite sure if he ought to protest or beg for more.

'Easy now.' Kara steadied him by placing one hand firmly against his arse. 'Shall I tell you what I think of the plan, Zach? It's dodgy, but it'll work. But only if we believe that it'll work. We have to not hold back, but allow ourselves to be who we are. You have to relax and be accepting, not wary of what's going to happen next.

'For my part, I can't wait to see Ric fuck you. I want to watch him slide his cock between your cheeks and into this delicate little hole. I know how it feels, and I'll imagine it as I'm watching him sink into you right up to his balls. I think I might even suck you while he's doing it, or better still have you fuck me at the same time. There are so many wonderful possibilities. That's why it's going to work.'

She grasped hold of his cock again, and began to masturbate him as she continued to dab her tongue into his back entrance. Zach might claim to be in love with Ric, but he sure responded to her touch. Pre-come leaked over his glans and wetted his shaft, making the slide of her palm super smooth.

'I want you to understand why I'm doing this before we begin, so that there's no misunderstanding. I'm not really looking for commitment. What I want is a threesome with you and Ric. I want to know what it's like. I want to know how it feels. The idea of having you both, it turns me on. It's not that I don't care how it is between you and Ric, I want you both to be happy, but my motivation isn't security or love. It's experience. It's lust.'

'Uh-huh.'

'We can try and make him jealous. We can try to get him to admit to his feelings, but there are no guarantees, OK?' Well, not besides the obvious sexual gratification. 'Just remember I'm not in love with him like you are.'

The sound of the doorbell echoed through the house. Kara scooted between Zach's legs again, but she didn't head for the stairs to answer the door. Instead, she took Zach's cock in her mouth again. Ric would come up and he'd see them. It'd be the first test. She really wasn't sure how he'd react. If he did a Zach and about-turned, she'd have to have a serious rethink.

Zach whimpered again as she introduced a finger to the place where her tongue had so recently delved. His muscles quickly relaxed, sucking the digit deep. She added another, stroking him quickly and finally a third. His desperation soon began to show in the roll of his hips and the taut stiffness of his cock. If she didn't go easy on him, he might actually come just as Ric happened upon them, which might prove that she was good at giving head, but probably wouldn't benefit them in any other way. If Zach was spent, she suspected Ric would see that as an excuse to take advantage, and she didn't want them splitting off into couples; they needed to do this together.

As the chime of the doorbell faded from her ears, Kara caught the sound of the front door being opened. Anyone else would have called out. Not Ric. He made a quick sweep of the downstairs rooms then tramped up the stairs to find them.

If it was possible to hold her breath around the girth of Zach's cock, then she did it. Kara's nipples tightened in excitement, so that they strained against her thin nightshirt. Her clit nagged her for a touch as her anticipation built. She really, really wanted this to work. It had to work.

Finally, Ric stood in the doorway. She knew he'd arrived because every muscle in Zach's body tightened. His legs locked straight and the muscles in his arse squeezed her fingers. Despite that, his cock didn't flag a bit; if anything it stood a little more proud.

What surprised her was that Ric didn't make any remarks. She'd half expected to hear something scathing fall from his lips. Instead, as far as she could tell, he simply leaned against the doorway watching them.

Zach began to fuck her mouth with slower, steadier strokes, like he was almost there and determined not to lose it just yet. He was making a show of it, like he was performing for the camera.

Eventually, Ric stalked forward, treading quietly on the balls of his feet. He came right up to the bed, and stood just behind her.

Kara itched to turn around, but she didn't. She kept on sucking Zach and working her fingers in his now rather tight hole.

'Mind if I take a picture?' Ric asked. Before either she or Zach had a chance to respond, the flare of the camera flash lit up the dingy room. 'Very nice. Very nice.' He bent to whisper in her ear. 'I'll bet you'll want a visual record of this, won't you, Kara?'

Lord knows why the devil had his camera with him. She couldn't recall seeing it earlier, but it was possible that Ric had been carrying it with him. Maybe he did so on most occasions. That seemed the sanest explanation. She didn't want to think too hard about what it would mean if he'd gone home to collect it before coming here. He couldn't know that this was what he'd walk into. Then again, was it so very difficult to predict? They were all playing games with each other. He knew she was intrigued by the idea of them all getting it on together. What other conclusion would you reach?

'Where do you keep your stockings?' Ric asked.

Like she was in a position to answer with Zach filling her mouth! Not that it mattered. Ric found them quickly enough himself. He used two of them to tie Zach's wrists to the bed, but not without a fight. Zach squirmed, trying to fend Ric off, but unable to move very much without dislodging her hold too.

'Calm down, Zach,' Ric coaxed. He stroked his hand across the stubbly line of Zach's jaw. 'You'll upset the lady, and from what I can see you owe her a thank you, not a tantrum. Stand still and let her use you. Now, what's my intended part in this, official biographer? Or were you thinking of something more involved, Kara?'

He'd obviously decided the set-up was her doing. In part it was, but it was a mistake to believe that Zach had been cajoled into this, or forced into this position under duress. She hadn't coaxed him here so they could all play nice together and prove that there were no hard feelings about the fact that they were all fucking each other. Rather she'd agreed to help him shag Ric into a state of emotional vulnerability in the hopes that he'd open up and admit to feeling something a little more enduring than lust.

Ric climbed on to the bed. He knelt behind Zach and then reached around him to explore his tightly puckered nipples and the washboard planes of his stomach. He no longer held the camera, yet its flash still lit the room at regular intervals.

Ric's fingers scissored around the base of Zach's cock, so that her lips kissed the digits as she sucked him.

Kara sat back on her haunches for a moment to look at the two men together. She'd not yet seen them properly intimate, despite Ric having given Zach a blowjob in her presence. 'Either do him or me. I've no preference over which.' That was a lie. Right at the minute, she wanted to watch.

'What about you, Zach?' Ric tickled the shell of Zach's ear with his tongue. His words were husky and low. Kara felt their vibration through Zach's body. 'I'm guessing by your earlier reaction that you're not so keen on me getting my kicks with Kara. On the other hand, you wouldn't have invited me here to stumble upon this little rendezvous without anticipating me joining in.'

'You gave me your word,' Zach grumbled.

'What can I say? She's hard to resist. Almost as hard to resist as you are.' Ric pulled himself closer to Zach, so his chest aligned with Zach's spine. Although he unzipped his fly and exposed his cock, there was no way he could easily penetrate Zach, because of the position of the footboard to which his lover was tied. 'I guess this isn't going to work. Besides, we ought to establish certain things from the start. Like the fact that I'm going to fuck Kara and you're going to have to deal with it, same as I'm going to have to deal with her fucking you, if we're going to turn this into the threesome Kara so desperately craves.'

Ric returned to the floor. He left his fly undone and continued to stroke his rapidly thickening shaft as he looked around at the room. After a moment he smiled, picked up the dressing-table stool and moved it alongside Kara. She released Zach in order to lie on her stomach across the cushioned pad, from which position she could still reach Zach and did.

Zach's generous lips were pulled into a tight moue. He seemed trapped and slightly bewildered. 'Zach,' she coaxed. 'Relax, it'll be fine. Let him have his way – for now.'

He gave the briefest nod. Tension still ran through his muscles as she returned her fingers to his arse and applied her tongue to the task of relieving his frustration. She tried not to give Ric too much thought as he positioned himself between her spread legs. She couldn't help smiling, though. Hell, she was getting what she'd been fantasising about ever since he'd shown her those pictures her first evening on the island.

Ric didn't remove any of his clothes, though he made a great show of lifting her nightshirt, folding it back neatly, in order to expose her plump rear. His thumb quickly found her heat, dabbing into the thick pool of moisture there. 'Wow, you're really eager for this,' he purred.

'So do it.'

'For God's sake get on with it.' Zach bit his lip.

Ric teased her, rubbing his glans up against her pussy lips and pressing hard against her swollen clit, until she was jiggling in order to capture him. 'Aa-ah! I want to hear you both say please.'

'Fuck you!' gasped Zach.

Kara responded by lavishing even more attention on Zach. He was running really hot now; straining, it seemed, towards a release that wouldn't come. He screwed his eyes closed tight.

'Up and forward a little.' Ric advised her. 'It feels like a little swelling against the wall. You don't need to go too deep to hit it. He'll feel better once he's come. He's going to burst some blood vessels if he doesn't do so soon.'

Kara eased her fingers back a bit and concentrated on what she was feeling. She knew the moment she hit gold, because Zach bucked so hard he nearly knocked the stool over and her with it.

'Godammit!' he swore. There were tears in his eyes. Kara gently took him in her mouth again, before caressing the pleasurable spot. Simultaneously, Ric increased his stimulation of her own sweet spot. Her clit had grown impossibly tight and a knotted band of heat encircled her abdomen. He hooked a hand beneath her so that as he drove his cock inside her, filling her deeply, she rode against the heel of his hand. Kara started to come at once. The flare of her orgasm surprised her. It washed over her, so that her inner muscles clasped Ric tight. His pace remained constant. 'Finish him,' he insisted. 'And make sure you swallow his come. Spitting gives entirely the wrong impression.'

This was not how it was supposed to be. He was not supposed to be trapped like this. The aim was to push Ric into a position of emotional vulnerability. Zach would have cursed Kara roundly if not for the fact that she was doing such a magnificent job of sucking his cock. The woman had the mouth of a goddess. Dare he think it, but she had more talent in that department than Ric. As for the torture she was putting him through with her stroking ... He was so damn close to fucking exploding he thought he might damage himself. Only Ric's nearness and the fact that he was inside Kara held his orgasm at bay. He just didn't like seeing it. He appreciated the contradiction: he had no qualms about subjecting Ric to seeing him with Kara, but watching them together, no matter that he was involved, hurt, like someone was stabbing goddamned lancets into him. Curious, then, that he remained so hard. He'd never considered himself quite so masochistic.

Zach cautiously peeped beneath his eyelashes, bracing

himself for the vision of their bodies working in unison and praying his erection didn't nosedive. It didn't, but then maybe it couldn't. At least some of sex was mechanical, and rubbing his G-spot pretty much guaranteed a climax.

The vision wasn't nearly as bad as he'd anticipated. Kara lay spread between them like a sacrificial offering, or perhaps a conduit, and while Ric's cock was buried deep in her cunt, his attention was focused wholly upon Zach.

Ric beckoned him with a slight tilt of his head. This perhaps wasn't the time for deep apologies, but when their lips met, Zach knew that Ric cared. He knew it because even though the contact was brief, the resulting sizzle lit fireworks across his body.

'You know, you had me worried there,' Ric said.

'Good,' Zach murmured against Ric's lips. He goddamn ought to have been worried. He'd been ready to call a day on whatever it was they had, and go home to mourn it. Only the fact that his van had broken down had kept him here. Well, that and Kara's powers of persuasion.

'You know she doesn't have to come between us.' Hah! Kara was hardly the main issue. He'd realised that. If not Kara, Ric would be fucking someone else. At least Kara appreciated him too, and swore she wasn't trying to usurp him. She just wanted some fun.

'Unless you pull out, I think there's a very good chance she will,' Zach quipped. A tight smile stretched his cheeks, which Ric reciprocated. At least he understood that they'd called a truce on the subject. They both glanced down at Kara, but only for a second, and then they were kissing again as deeply as they could, given their awkward positions. Somehow it didn't matter that they weren't pressed tight against one another from lips to shins. Desire still rode

Zach hard, making him jerk and strain against his bondage. 'Let me go.'

'I will, once you've come. You accused me of being jealous of you being with her. I want to make it plain that I'm not. I think it's fabulous. You look fucking hot, Zach. Feel what she's doing to you.'

He already did, but Ric's words seemed to magnify the effects. Suddenly, it was all too much. He came hard into the warm willing cave of Kara's mouth. His knees threatened to buckle, so he locked them tight and clung to the bedstead.

When Kara released him, a trickle of his seed rolled down over her chin. She wiped it off slowly. Ric had stilled. He stepped away from her, his cock still potently erect. 'Unfasten him,' he said.

Kara leapt to the task of unknotting the nylon ties. 'What now?' she asked.

Zach ignored her. He crossed straight to Ric's side, bent and licked his shaft, which tasted strongly of Kara. He wasn't sure why that made it more erotic, but it did, enough that his spent cock perked up a little.

'Much as that's nice –' Ric said, his hands repeatedly mussing Zach's hair, '– I think we both know what we'd rather be doing, and I'd lay money on Kara being just as eager to see it.'

Zach sat back on his haunches and looked up at his lover. He glanced very briefly at Kara. Could he do it? Could he allow her to be part of what he had with Ric? Discussing it was one thing; doing it was another matter. Apprehension and something else, something that felt rather like excitement, rippled beneath his skin. It wasn't news to him that he had a bit of an exhibitionist streak. He'd learned that years ago when Ric had started taking photographs of him. But this took things further than that. This was about exposing himself at his most vulnerable. He couldn't hide what he felt when Ric was inside him. Then again, maybe if she witnessed that, Kara would finally understand what this whole endeavour was costing him.

He slowly rose to his feet. He didn't cross to the bed. Instead, his unsteady legs carried him to the broad squishy loveseat that occupied the corner of the room. Rather than sitting, he waited for Ric to catch up. 'Above or below?'

'Let's get you warmed up and then we can switch around.'

As if he needed much warming. His cock already jutted out from his loins, half-hard. Zach knelt facing the chair back, his arse pushed slightly up and out. He froze into position the minute Ric's large hand touched his cheek.

'Do you own any lube?' he asked Kara.

'Sure.'

Zach kept facing the wall, though he could hear her fumbling about, throwing open drawers looking for a bottle of Super Glide. She gave a small squeal of delight when she found it. Every muscle in Zach's body tensed as he waited for Ric to pop the lid and make use of the shiny gel. Excerpt, godammit, it sounded as though Kara had taken over the warm-up routine. Zach's teeth scraped back and forth across his lower lip. Too bad that he couldn't close his hearing off too, so that he didn't have to listen to the appreciative murmurs Ric was making and the slick slide of Kara's hand around his cock. A jet of relief punched through his guts when he heard them part ways. Kara shimmied into the corner, so that she appeared on the other side of the chair, facing him, her body wedged into the angle of the dingy walls. She'd stripped completely naked, leaving only a very thin gold chain that encircled her neck and ran into the valley of her breasts.

Ric patted him gently. 'Ready for this? Remember to breathe.'

Zach kept on holding his breath. He dipped his head so his brow rested against the back of his hand, unable to do this looking straight at Kara, for all that her nipples were pointed straight at him, and she was very cheekily wetting two fingers in her mouth to masturbate with.

Ric slid into him super smoothly, to nobody's surprise, given the warm-up routine. Still, that first moment bit at his nerve-endings and made his insides fizz. Only after a few strokes did he dare peep above the chair back to see how Kara was taking this.

By rubbing frantically at her clit and pinching her own nipples was how. He gave her a nervous grin that she returned threefold.

'Tell me how it feels,' she asked.

'You know how it feels. You told me he'd had you like this.'

'Yes, but I want to know how it makes you feel.'

'I don't suppose anyone is interested in how it feels to me,' Ric remarked.

Zach exchanged grins with Kara.

'We know you're in it for the thrills,' Kara said. 'Therefore I can figure out what you're feeling all by myself. Hot. Tight. His muscles squeezing against you, both drawing you in and threatening to push you out.' She leaned closer, dipping her head down to the level of Zach's, before gently brushing her lips against his. 'Tell me, Zach. I know you're feeling more than mechanics. How does he make you feel?'

He didn't normally wax poetic, but there simply wasn't any other way to describe it. 'Like a star about to turn supernova,' he confessed. 'There's so much energy that I can't control it, I can only cling on and hope I don't get too bumped about by the ride. He's inside me, as deep as he can go, and it's heaven and hell on so many levels. I want it. I want more of it, and yet part of me longs to hide and resist that need. God, Ric! I need you deeper.' He pushed back against Ric's thrusts, trying to satisfy that desperation. Instead, Ric withdrew. He stepped several paces back from the chair, with his hand clasped around the base of his cock. His expression settled into tense, nervous lines.

'Get off the chair,' he demanded.

Zach did as instructed. Kara too wriggled out from her corner. 'What's wrong?' she asked.

'Nothing.'

Ric sat on the empty chair with his thighs widely spread. 'Come here, Zach. If you want me deeper, you know this is the way to do it. Then you're in control. How much of me you take is entirely up to you.'

'Yes.' Zach wetted his lips. 'Yes, it is.' It was.

He lowered himself slowly, so that he took Ric's cock one glorious inch at a time until his body had swallowed the whole and Ric's balls tickled the smooth stretch of skin beneath his own. Zach braced his hands against the chair arms and used that leverage to rise and fall upon Ric's cock. Yes. Fuck, yes. That hit in all the right places. He started floating, his eyes wide open, but not seeing a goddamn thing. The head of his cock now slapped against his abdomen after every jerk, the shaft having grown fully hard and achy.

'Ease off.' Ric began pushing against his back, but Zach maintained his motion. Let Ric come. Let him lose control for once. 'Jeezus, I'm going to ... Fuck!' His words faltered, and were superseded by a string of ardent gasps. Zach felt his lover's release deep inside his body. It was almost but not quite enough to tip him over. He realised as Ric pushed him away that here was one good … no, very good reason to have two lovers, because Kara was already on the floor just where he fell, her legs spread wide, and her cunt completely welcoming. He entered her in one rough thrust, dragging her to him, so that their bodies were locked together with no spaces between. Her arms surrounded his neck, her legs crossed behind his back. Zach drove into her with every ounce of strength he'd got, until he was totally subsumed by the moment. When they came, it was both together, their cries drowning out one another. In the silence that followed, Kara rubbed her nose against his cheek.

'It's not so bad, is it, the three of us together,' she said.

'It's interesting,' he conceded. It'd take a while to sort out his true feelings from the jumble of emotions currently warring in his head. One thing he did know, his problems wouldn't be overcome by dawn or by making a fuss about sharing.

Zach raised his head to find Ric still in the chair. His grey-blue irises were no more than slivers of silver around his huge pupils. Although he was smiling, Zach could see the storm clouds roiling beneath the surface. They'd face some sort of reckoning after this. He just wasn't sure how that would play out. Ric felt something about this arrangement. What that was, Zach remained uncertain about, but they'd all had each other now. There was no going back. He had to believe in this arrangement in order for it to work.

Could it work?

Could he finally trap Ric in a triangular cage?

CHAPTER FOURTEEN

The thing about waking with someone was that it fostered closeness. Zach knew it because it was another of the intimacies Ric refused to indulge, yet here they were, nestled alongside one another in Kara's monstrously oversized bed. Ric lay on his side, facing away from Zach with a deep space between them, as though he'd consented to be here but couldn't tolerate the notion of being touched while sleeping.

Kara had no such problems. She lay on Zach's right, nestled into the crook of his arm, although, like Ric, she slept facing away from him. However, her back pressed against his side, binding them together, skin to skin. Her blonde hair fanned across the top of his arm. Her lips were slightly parted and shiny. He had more reasons that he could count to be grateful to her, but that wasn't the emotion he felt while watching her sleep. She'd come to his rescue last night, both in trying to manage his relationship with Ric and in getting him off the causeway. He didn't recall anyone ever rooting for him to such an extent before.

What he tried not to dwell on was what it might have cost her if he hadn't held on so tightly while they were in the water. If his grip had faltered, then she might very well have been swept out to sea.

Zach hadn't feared for himself. From an early age he'd been a strong swimmer. He surfed too, so he'd been battered by bigger waves than those they'd faced last night and still gone back for more another day, whereas his money was on Kara never having swum except in a heated indoor pool.

She murmured softly as he turned to spoon his body against her back. His hand slipped comfortably into the arch formed where her waist flared into the curve of her hip. More women ought to be built like Kara. Maybe they were; it was just that most of the models Ric worked with were stick-thin and not the least bit interested in him, only in getting his lover into the sack. To Kara he was another source of pleasure, not just someone to remove. He hadn't fully appreciated that until last night. Not that he was a hundred per cent sure her plan was working. It was too early to say. However, Ric was here, and he'd chosen to stay rather than fallen into a torpor.

Zach didn't know yet if Kara was the sort of woman who appreciated being woken to some tender loving, but he couldn't resist touching her. His palm stroked back and forth over her hip. The duvet covered most of her form, so he had to rely on his sense of touch to provide him with details. Her skin was delightfully warm, and the cheeks of her arse pleasingly soft, not at all like the muscular glutes Ric owned.

That thought prompted him to roll on to his back again, so that he might reach his other lover and trace a finger over that springy muscle.

Zach sucked his lower lip, his cheeks bunched into a grin

as he drew concentric circles over both his lovers' butts. Despite all the loving they'd done last night, his loins were growing heavy again. Soon enough, his erection would be making a tent out of the duvet.

Kara opened her eyes a moment later. She gave a sleepy yawn. 'Mm, is that for me?' Instead of clasping Zach, her hand bumped into Ric's reaching out to touch him from the other side.

'Oh!' They jerked away, rolled, and propped themselves up on their sides on one elbow. They stared at one another across Zach's chest before wordlessly, and in perfect sync, bowing down to fasten their lips around each of his nipples. Their fingers knit too, around his erection.

Zach revelled in the moment. Though it didn't stay quite so harmonious for long. Ric started getting a wee bit more demanding, his stroke dictating the rhythm. What's more, he coaxed Zach on to his side, so that he could nuzzle up tight against his back, and stroke his own erection between Zach's buttocks.

'What do you say, Zach, shall we make this a proper morning wake-up?'

Instead of immediately replying, Zach lifted his leg over Kara's body, which successfully tipped her on to her back, so that he lay above her, looking down into her pretty blue eyes. 'Absolutely.' He captured her wrists above her head, and lay against her so that the tips of her nipples brushed against his chest. His erection nuzzled up against her pubic curls. 'What do you say, Kara?'

'Come on in and let's party.' She smirked.

'I'd like that. I'd like that a lot.' He prayed she accepted his words on the many levels he intended, and that she realised he wasn't doing this purely to rile Ric. He wanted her. Maybe she had something with her crazy plan to form a triad. Maybe they could build a decent relationship as a threesome?

The only uncertainty was whether Ric would accept that. Really? Genuinely? Would opening himself to two lovers be any easier than accepting one? He seemed drawn in at the moment, but that didn't mean it would last.

Zach brushed his lips lightly over hers. Kara sighed into the kiss, her body relaxed beneath him, thighs parting. The lips of her slit were wet with fresh arousal. She opened up to him, guided the head of his cock into place so that one teeny push would see him seated perfectly between her thighs.

'Wait up.' Apparently Ric wasn't going to sit idly by and be left out. 'We can do this together.' He knelt up, straddled both sets of legs, and lined himself up with Zach's anus. 'Hold still now.'

Keeping still went against every instinct Zach possessed. The warmth of Kara's cunt beckoned him from the fore. He had only to slide forward a fraction in order to bury himself inside her and enjoy all the magic that union would bring. At the same time, if he just pushed back a little, then Ric's cock would stretch open his rear, lighting all the hungry nerve-endings in his arse.

He couldn't pick, so he stayed absolutely still, save that his prick kept twitching of its own accord.

Slowly, slowly, Ric began to exert more pressure. The wet and slippery head of his cock pressed persuasively against the puckered entrance of Zach's arse, and each time he pushed, Zach was nudged forward a fraction, so by the time Ric was fully sheathed inside him, Zach's own stiff cock was fully buried in Kara's cunt.

He was wedged between them, frighteningly, contentedly so.

Zach released a great sob of joy. Two sets of hands encompassed his hips, directing him, as he began to move, sliding swiftly forward into Kara, then slowly backwards so that he impaled himself upon Ric's cock.

'Are you convinced you won't be content with a mere single lover yet?' Ric drawled. 'This is absolutely why we should not be exclusive.'

Zach deliberately kept his mouth tightly closed. He refused to debate the pros and cons of forming a genuine relationship while wedged in this position. Instead, he concentrated on the strange, clinging tightness that filled his rear and the mirrored image of that when the walls of Kara's pussy hugged his cock. Forward and back, impaled and possessed, until everything became a red blur on the inside of his eyelids, and pleasure surged through him in a loop with no beginning or end. As his senses turned inwards, Zach's awareness of Kara writhing beneath him, crying out his name as her flesh spasmed around him, became distant and unconnected. Nor did he fully comprehend the increasing urgency of Ric's strokes, as he drove more deeply, snarling each time their bodies smacked together.

Zach trembled as his climax began to crawl across him. It trembled between his legs, not his arse or his cock. He clenched tight his fists and his bottom, wanting to slow the inevitable. If he just had a hand free to grasp his balls, or squeeze tight the base of his cock, then he might prolong this moment of delicious agony. Sadly, his balance wasn't good enough to attempt this one-handed.

His belly tensed. Beneath him Kara crooned, and her pussy began to milk him in pulsing strokes. He couldn't fight that. His seed forced its way up his shaft. His prick jerked, only for Ric to choose that exact moment to withdraw. His hot seed splashed against Zach's cheeks.

Zach groaned, bereft of the pleasurable intrusion into his rear. He cried out, releasing a hopeless moan, and then lolled against the pillows, his face buried in their cloudy softness, until Kara began to drum against his shoulder in order to get him to move.

'Never try to tell me we'd be better off as an exclusive couple when my way we can do things like this.' Ric rolled off the bed and landed on his feet.

His way, Zach thought derisively. Ric was acting like this was his idea. If he genuinely believed that then maybe it would work.

With an enormous effort, Zach lifted his head from the pillow. 'Only because Kara is special. I wouldn't want to do it with anyone else.'

'Hm!' Ric stalked towards the bedroom door. 'I'm going to avail myself of the facilities, and then you can explain to me what the hell happened last night. Kara, I believe, said something about your van having broken down.'

He'd certainly spoiled it now. Reality crashed over Zach like one of the waves that had claimed his ice-cream van. He pulled the duvet over his head.

Kara snuggled up to him. 'We ought to rise and find out what's happened. See if it can be salvaged.'

'I know,' he said, finding her lips and kissing her. 'And I will, in just a moment. Shit! You didn't tell him what happened, did you? He thinks the van is stuck in the bay.'

'Well, there wasn't anything he could do about it last night. I didn't want to spend all night reliving the experience of being half drowned. I thought fucking would be more fun, and I was right. I got repeatedly screwed by two gorgeous men and it was ace.'

'He's going to freak when he finds out.'

Her exuberance faded a little. 'Why would he?'

Zach crawled out from under the duvet scowling. 'Because his wife drowned, that's why. I'm going to talk to him.' He squared his shoulders and made his way to the bathroom. He took a deep breath. Time for a little reality check. What he was about to say wasn't going to go down well. He guessed it had been optimistic to think everything could be righted by one good shag or even three or four. If it could, the world would be a far happier place. He braced himself for a setback, then opened the door and waded into the steam-filled interior.

* * *

A small group had assembled on the shoreline by the time Kara caught up with Zach and Ric by the Bunker. They'd left her to get dressed, having drained the hot-water tank between them, forcing her to use the immersion heater to warm the water for a shower. They'd been in there a long time, and Ric had emerged grim and businesslike.

'How's it going?' she asked him. Ric stood off to one side in the shelter of the rocks, while Zach dealt with the salvage team.

His blond hair whipped about his face as he turned to acknowledge her. He'd pulled on a fisherman-style cable-knit jumper that he hadn't had on when he left the cottage. Zach was dressed in a similar assortment of cast-offs. 'The van's a total write-off. All the electrics are fried, the engine's full of seawater and there are barnacles stuck to the dashboard. They're going to have to winch the damn thing off there. Back two wheels are stuck in the sandbank. I think they're

215

about to start digging if you want to join in.'

'No, thanks.' She really didn't need to get any nearer to the water than she was currently standing. 'It's pretty quiet around here.' The normal flock of tourists weren't in evidence. There was only the work crew and a few curious seagulls.

'Nobody can get across. Well, I say nobody. Some people manage it.' He nodded towards the shoreline, where a lone figure was negotiating the causeway on foot. 'Not anyone welcome, mind.'

'Robin.' Kara recognised the figure after the wind claimed her hat. Her long mane of red curls was bound by a bun-net, but several corkscrew ringlets still framed her face. She spotted Kara and Ric and immediately waved.

'Why's she come across? Doesn't she have anything else to do?'

Ric's already weary expression became further drawn around his mouth. 'I'm going to help dig.'

Keep her away from me is how she translated that. She'd do her best, not that she wanted to talk to Robin either. She'd been hoping to find out what Zach had told Ric about last night

'This is all a bit exciting, isn't it?' Robin crunched across the shingle towards Kara. When they were side by side she turned to look back at the causeway. The front wheels of the ice-cream van were lifted at a forty-degree angle; the back two were buried in sand and mud at the side of the concrete path. 'What happened?'

'He broke down.' Kara said, without elaborating. She pushed her hands into her coat pockets.

'Oh! Coming across this morning?'

'No, last night.'

Robin dipped her chin in acknowledgement and then

mirrored Kara's stance, pushing her slender hands into the pockets of her dotted sou'wester. They stood in silence a moment, watching the men in their waders wielding their spades. 'I guess Zach's pretty miffed. I suppose the insurance will pay for it. Ric's looking good. I'm liking the chunky knitwear. It makes him look all masculine and brutish.'

Kara made a non-committal grunt. She actually thought the fisherman's jumper hid one of his better assets, which was a shame, because the waders kind of drew attention to his arse. For a moment she considered asking Ric to produce a naked fishermen's calendar, where various gorgeous blokes posed nude in waders with their rods and tackle.

Zach, meanwhile, paced up and down the stretch of causeway by the van with a borrowed mobile phone clamped to one ear. The wind blew an occasional four-letter expletive towards them from his direction. Evidently dealing with the insurance company wasn't going well.

Kara pulled her phone out of her pocket to check the time. Rather miraculously, a night in the airing cupboard had dried it out. Occasionally it made an odd screech, and the screen remained a bit dim, but mostly it was working.

'How have you been doing, Kara? We've not caught up since you moved in,' Robin asked, as if the fact they hadn't spoken was pure chance and not because Kara had actively avoided her.

'OK.' Kara started walking. Not because she had anywhere to go, but because she didn't want to have this conversation. She knew where it would lead, and didn't want to discuss her relationship with Ric. Unconsciously her feet took her nearer to the shore, though she stopped short of where the foam lapped at the pebbles.

'Just OK? I was hoping you'd have something a bit more

exciting to report. I know you've seen a fair bit of him. You're not telling me there've been no developments.'

Kara stopped pacing and turned to look Robin in the eye. 'Look, what happened before was a mistake. I don't get off on sharing my private life. Whatever I do with Ric is between me and him.' She started to move again, only for Robin to catch hold of her arm.

'Hang on. No. You don't get to just cancel the agreement like that. We agreed a deal.'

'No. No, we didn't.'

'I was prepared to give you the benefit of the doubt when you were rude last time, but you're mistaken if you think I'm going to let you fuck around with him if I'm not reaping the benefit.'

Kara remained sure that it was none of Robin's goddamned business. Implied threats weren't going to make her back away. Zach needed her to stick around in order for him to get Ric, and she'd enjoyed herself far too much not to want to help. If ultimately she happened to gain something long-term out of it too, well, there were worse commitments to make than being loved by two guys, like marrying her ex. 'I don't need your permission to do anything, and nor does Ric.'

She kept moving away from Robin.

'I know about you, Kara,' Robin called out. 'I found out. If you won't share, you're out of here, understand me. I've contacts.'

She understood the woman was stark raving crazy, so demented in fact that striding out on to the wet sand to help with the digging started to look appealing. Ric came up to her and ushered her back from the van, which, even supported by the crane, was starting to sway precariously.

'We don't need you out here. Stay on the shore and keep dry.'

Tears prickled the corners of her eyes. She shook her head and peered glumly at him, wishing he'd put his arms around her and give her a hug. Zach would have known to do so, but he was still on the phone. She hadn't realised what a fright their swim last night had given her, or how tense looking over their battleground would make her feel.

'All right.' Ric planted his spade in the sand between them and leaned on the hilt. 'What's going on? Did Robin just say something to you?'

The woman was watching the pair of them with all the zeal of a psychotic mediaeval sorceress. If she'd been standing at the top of the cliff instead of the bottom, Kara would have seriously feared for her life. Fuck! How had Ric's wife died? It wouldn't surprise her to learn at this point that Robin had pushed her off a ridge. Instead of pursuing that line of thought – he'd warned her off that subject once – she asked, 'What is it between you and her? Is she really as bat-shit crazy as she sounds?'

Ric raised both brows. Kara couldn't figure out whether he was surprised by the question or astounded that someone finally agreed with his opinion. 'I've told you how things are. I'm not interested in her. Do you want to tell me what she just said to you?'

Kara swallowed slowly. 'I've been given the "if you can't share, keep your hands off my property" speech.'

'Share?' he queried. His brows dropped, and a frown crumpled his forehead and the corners of his eyes instead. 'Share what, precisely? There's nothing between me and her. Never has been. What's she on about?'

'She wants me to share the details of our sex life,' Kara explained.

'Oh, for fuck's sake.' He slammed a fist down on the

handle of the spade, driving it deeper into the sand. When he looked at Kara, whatever other line of invective he'd intended to utter died on his lips. His eyes slowly narrowed. 'And have you done that?'

Fuck! She'd screwed up. She knew it even as she opened her mouth to make the confession. *God, I'm so sorry, Zach. I really hoped I could make this work for you.* 'Once. She caught me off guard the first time we met.'

'Jesus, Kara! I thought I could trust you. Have you told her all about Zach and me too?'

'No, of course not.'

He didn't seem to hear her. He hefted his spade and went back to his digging with renewed zeal.

Kara watched him go with her mouth hanging open. She'd always known that incident in the bathroom with Robin would come back to bite her on the arse and it just had. She didn't even have an excuse. She'd known at the time it was stupid but had allowed her libido to get the better of her. Drat! And just when the plan she had for getting him and Zach together had looked so promising.

Kara looked back at Robin with a snarl. No way was she going to allow that bitch to ruin it. It'd be difficult if Ric wasn't prepared to trust her, but she wasn't giving up. Having them both and then waking with them in her bed this morning had been an adventure worthy of endless repeats. She fully intended to make it happen again. Maybe if she explained to Zach what had happened he'd be able to get Ric to listen, except he had more important things to worry about, like his van and his livelihood.

She couldn't bring herself to go and apologise to Ric either. No way was she putting so much as a toe in the water ever again. Instead, she strolled further along the beach, following the line of shingle past the cut that led to the bowl of ferns at the back of the Bunker, and on to another old ammunition shelter. She didn't look back to see if Robin was gloating. An image of her triumphant mug had already lasered itself into Kara's brain.

Outside the decrepit ammunition store, Kara found a perch on a boulder. Damn it, she didn't want to be here looking out over all this water, but nor did she want to go home and allow the new wound in her relationship with Ric to fester. Surely he knew what Robin was like. She can't have been the first idiot to fall for her tricks.

Kara drummed her feet. The causeway was hidden from this position; only a broad stretch of the English Channel lay before her. A few seagulls squawked from up on the cliff face. An old rowboat lay nestled amongst the grass to the side of the store. It was chained to a stout wooden post, as though it still belonged to someone and hadn't simply been abandoned, though flecks of paint were missing from the planks and only one of the oars sat within its belly.

If she'd known about it last night, she could have rowed out to Zach instead of wading. Would it have made any difference to the outcome?

To her surprise, Ric appeared within a few minutes of her idling by the boat. He stormed right up to her, no hint of an apology on his face. Instead he growled, 'Don't you tell her anything. You don't mention me to her, understand?'

Kara glared back at him wide-eyed with shock. 'I won't. I didn't.' Thinking back, she hadn't really spilled anything. She hadn't answered Robin's questions. She'd just allowed her to make assumptions. It wasn't as though she'd spun a full yarn. Really, she'd made a few affirmative and pleading grunts, that's all. 'I didn't say anything about you and Zach.

I didn't even know about it at the time, and even if I had …
Fuck, you should have warned me about her.'

'And said what? Watch out for my stalker, she might
torture you for information?' He gestured wildly with his
arms as he spoke, and finished by clenching the front of his
long blond hair in his fist.

Kara stared at him bewildered. 'Did you really come to
just shout at me some more?' she asked quietly. 'Because I
don't need shouting at.'

'I'm not shouting.'

'Yes, you are.' She shoved him hard in the ribs. 'Back off.'

Ric didn't back up. Instead, he took a pace forward and
grabbed hold of her. He held her so tight that his fingertips
bit into her arms.

'What?' she asked. 'What?'

He shook his head, though his breathing still raced. 'Just
… just don't.' She wasn't sure what he was seeing, but it
didn't seem to be here and now.

'I won't … I never meant to. I had no notion at the time
that there were issues involved.' She sought his hand, tried
to unclench his fingers so that she could hold it.

'Good.' The emotion drained from his voice, though he
refused to unclench his fists. 'Don't give her ammunition like
that. She doesn't need to know anything about me.'

'I'm sorry,' Kara apologised. She pushed her face up against
his chest. Ric remained unyielding, his spine locked straight.
He didn't return her embrace, nor did he push her away. The
wool of his jumper tickled her cheek. Kara tilted her head to
look up at him. 'Have you thought … maybe you should get
a restraining order … keep her off Liddell Island for a bit.'

'I can't.' Finally, he wrapped his arms around her and
gave her a squeeze.

'But if she's bugging you to this extent … She told me, that first day, that you'd sent her. She implied that she worked for you. You shouldn't let her get away with that.'

Ric nodded, showing that he understood, but was unmoved. 'Kara, it's not that simple. There are layers to this you don't understand.'

No, but she wanted to. She really did. Something told her that this all tied in with why Ric had so staunchly avoided developing emotional relationships. Her thoughts immediately returned to their earlier darkness and the possibility that Robin had somehow been involved in the death of Ric's wife. It seemed unlikely, and, if it were the case, then why would Ric protect her? 'Who is she? What is she to you, really?'

'A prize nuisance, that's all.' He ran his tongue over his teeth, and then glanced down at the little rowing boat. 'Just like someone else I know.' In the space it took him to make the remark, his whole demeanour changed. Out went the anger; in came something less easily defined. 'What's more, I know just how to deal with a good nuisance.' 'Good' presumably opposed to 'bad', like Robin. 'Over you go.' He patted the side of the boat.

'What? No,' Kara protested. He couldn't make light of something so serious in this way, nor be allowed to divert his anger into sex play. Of course, Ric's expression said he was going to do exactly that. Maybe he did it all the time. From what she knew of his relationship with Zach, it seemed more than likely. 'Ric.'

'Forfeit,' he responded. Long strands of his blond hair danced around his face, and although his mouth remained hard a twinkle of amusement had returned to his eyes. 'You still owe me, remember. We agreed anytime, anyplace, anywhere.'

'Yes, but not like this.' Not to avoid confiding. Not to sidestep an issue he clearly wasn't comfortable with. And definitely not while Zach and a work crew were only a short way up the coast, not to mention the bitch responsible for this drama.

'Yes, now. I want you head down, arse up, over the side of this boat.'

'You're not even turned on,' she protested.

Finally a smile cracked his face. 'Oh, I will be,' he promised.

Hell, no wonder Zach got frustrated if this is what Ric did every time someone touched on a subject he didn't want to discuss. She liked sex, but this felt damn weird. Instead of moving into position, she continued to shake her head.

'Come on. Do it,' Ric cajoled. He gave her an encouraging nudge in the right direction. 'I guarantee, the minute your pants go down, my attention will be fully engaged. You know, if you don't, I'll have to punish you.' He picked up the little wooden oar as he spoke. 'I don't like girls who go back on their word.'

'You can't hit me with that,' Kara blurted, staring at the weathered paddle. If he did anything more than tap her with it, he'd batter her into next week.

Ric gave an explosive laugh, which drained the residual tension from his body. Suddenly he did look in the mood to be naughty. He gave the oar a test swing. 'You know that saying things like that is just planting ideas. Better brace yourself.'

'Seriously, no.' She held out her arms to ward him off, but Ric easily pushed inside her reach and tipped her over the side of the little boat.

Kara squealed and kicked her legs in protest. Her hair hung down around her face, masking at least some of her indignation. Ric's hands were cold as he wrenched down her knickers. He left them hanging around her knees.

He stepped back, and the breeze kissed the skin of her cheeks, chilling them, and then came the drum of the oar. 'It's the least you deserve, all things considered.'

'Ow,' she complained, although it didn't actually hurt. He'd put no power into the swing, so the sharp impact merely felt wet and cold. It actually seemed like a punishment, unlike the heat she knew he could raise with his palm. Maybe Ric realised it too, for he cast the oar aside after giving her a second swift pat, and instead started teasing a single finger back and forth along the split of her sex. 'I think you'd better tell me everything you told her, don't you?'

'Mmm-mmm, mmmm,' grunted Kara from her upended position, which finally earned her a proper smack. 'That's the truth,' she squeaked, once the sting in her cheeks started to dissipate. She wriggled her hips to try to ease the discomfort. If she wasn't so precariously balanced, she might have tried rubbing her skin, except he'd probably have rapped her knuckles if she did. 'I swear. She asked questions and I never gave a direct answer. I'm not sure I managed to utter more than a few syllables.'

Ric brought his palm down on her arse again, making a crack so loud it frightened the gulls perched all along the cliff face. The sound didn't tally with the blow, which left her skin mildly heated and pleasantly tingly. 'You fucked her?' Astonishment caused his voice to creak. His palm rested against the curve of Kara's cheek, warming the skin beneath, while the breeze continued to chill the rest of her skin.

'Not sex,' Kara insisted. She wasn't having him envisioning her doing anything two-way or overly involved. 'She rubbed me off while I was taking a bath. I was supposed to be describing what you and I had done, but mostly she talked and I didn't do a whole lot besides moan.'

Ric twitched one finger over her flesh. 'Fuck. I didn't ever think she'd go that far. I didn't think she'd ever had sex.'

'I don't think I was the first,' Kara blurted, although in some ways she agreed with him. She didn't think Robin had ever had penetrative sex with a man. A dildo, absolutely. She almost certainly got off regularly using a substitute dick while reliving other women's experiences with Ric, or Alaric, as she so loved to call him.

'Fuck.' He began to laugh in a slightly unbalanced way. 'Hellfire and fuck.'

Then he nudged his cock up against her labia. As promised he was at least partially hard. He rubbed himself in her wetness a moment, and then entered her, forcing her further into the boat, so that she was almost doing a handstand. 'You know that's twisted, Kara?'

'Only as twisted as this is.'

He grabbed hold of her shoulder to pull her more forcefully back on to his dick. 'Nah, it'd only be that if you weren't turned on, and you are. You really are.'

She was certainly wet. The sounds of their loving confirmed that, and she wasn't denying she was enjoying the thrust of his cock. There was even something to be said for the terror of discovery. It certainly lent a degree of urgency to the act. Any moment, Zach or one of the work crew could appear, and the shame would damn near kill her. If Robin appeared, things would be a whole lot worse.

Or would it? How would Zach react? He might get the wrong idea and take off again. 'We shouldn't do this here, without Zach.'

'Do you want me to whistle for him?'

'No.'

Ric steadied his motion into a slow, slow, quick, figure-of-eight roll of his hips. He certainly had a passion for doing things doggy-style. Perhaps it was just as well she intended to focus on maintaining two lovers, otherwise she'd have to instal lots of mirrors, just in order to get a glimpse of him. At least when all three of them were together, she'd be able to look at Zach.

Kara strained her neck, in order to satisfy her love of visuals. Ric looked fantastic in his oversized knitwear. His hair had completely escaped its binding now and danced against her shoulders as he filled her up.

'What are you looking at?'

'The man who's fucking me so good.'

'Yeah.' He began to lean forward, so that his front pressed against her back. His hands skimmed over her stomach, pushed inside her T-shirt and claimed possession of her breasts. Her nipples immediately hardened. Sparks of arousal shot between her nipples and her groin. 'I love that you have big tits. I love the way they feel and how they jiggle.' He thrust forward particularly hard, setting the boat rocking. It made their position even more precarious. One wrong jolt and they'd both fall head-first into the bottom of the boat, yet somehow that made it all the more wonderful. The downward tilted position meant Kara's heart raced and the head of his cock bumped the sensitive spot on the front wall of her pussy. She kept lifting her bottom to meet his strokes. It left her dancing on her toes as euphoria engulfed her. She clutched the sides of the boat tight. Time seemed to thin and stretch. For a while she danced entirely to Ric's tune. He possessed her breasts and her cunt, and somehow managed to get the angles right so that her clit got in on the action too.

This was living. This was real, in a way her life hadn't been before she'd set foot on Liddell Island. Hell, she needed this. She needed this man. Yes, fuck me. Fuck away the trauma of last night in exactly the same way Zach had done. What was wrong with sex to forget? It certainly beat stewing.

The ache in Kara's pussy soon spread. It washed through her synapses leaving every one of them alert.

She came hard, squealing out his name. It was so good that for a long while she dared not open her eyes, for something was sure to destroy the moment. Eventually, her muscles burned too much, and Ric's spent cock slipped from her cunt.

'You all right?' He offered her a hand so she could stand up. She did so rather unsteadily. Muscles ached that she didn't know she had. She pushed her cold hands inside his jumper, up into the warmth of his armpits. Ric grunted but he let her linger. He lowered his mouth and offered her a kiss.

'What are we doing, Ric?' It didn't feel light any more. At some point in the last few minutes they'd crossed an invisible boundary into uncharted waters. They weren't simply fuck buddies any more. This had developed into something else. She wanted him in the way Zach did. She wanted this to be personal, intimate. She wanted what she felt to be love and for them to explore it and grow together, only she wasn't sure Ric felt remotely the same way.

He scratched his throat beneath the roll-neck of his sweater. 'Better get back to it. They should have the van on the tow truck by now.'

'Is Robin still around?'

He shrugged. 'Forget about her.'

She couldn't. Not when he hadn't answered her questions.

Ric started back along the beach ahead of her. Kara caught up and grasped his hand. He paused, looked at their joined

228

palms a moment. 'You know Zach will freak out more about this –' he raised their clasped hands '– than he would if he'd seen us a moment ago.'

Kara squeezed Ric's fingers tight. 'Then you'll just have to hold his hand too, because I'm not letting go.'

CHAPTER FIFTEEN

Then ice-cream van stood on the back of the tow truck by the time Kara and Ric returned to the bay. Zach, as predicted, responded to their hand-holding by giving them both evil looks.

'I've made coffee,' he said, before handing over polystyrene cups filled with tar-like liquid.

Ric gave the sludge an uneasy glance before tentatively taking a sip. Kara swigged a mouthful of hers, but spat it straight out. 'Ew, gross!' She hoped it was down to bad coffee grounds and not Zach's seeking vengeance. He obviously had questions about where they'd been and what they'd been doing – she could see them dancing about in his eyes.

'Is the truck off to the garage?' she asked, hoping to avoid that issue.

Zach shrugged inside his jumper. 'It is, but I suspect the scrapyard would be more appropriate. It's not going to go after the swim it's just had. The bodywork is full of dents, the underside is probably going to rust to hell, and the engine and all the electrics are fried.'

'So, you're stuck here,' she said, determined to put a positive spin on things. If he wasn't tempted to leave the island

231

every night to run home, then there'd be more opportunities for them all to be together. 'Where are you going to stay?'

'With Ric,' Zach replied without hesitation.

The remark simply earned a shrug from Ric. 'We'll work something out. What's the going rate for a live-in sex slave?' he asked Kara.

'I don't know. I've never had one. Are you volunteering?' She placed her hands on her hips.

Zach made a low growl in the back of his throat that forced their attention back to him. Clearly the banter between them wasn't doing anything to alleviate his paranoia.

'Yes, you can shack up with me,' Ric said. He shoved his hands deep into his pockets, as if he was determined not to make a big issue out of the matter. He looked up at Zach from beneath his long eyelashes. 'Play your cards right, be a good boy and I might even let you sleep in my bed.' He tilted his head and smirked. 'But no twitching every time I look at Kara, please.'

Zach slowly swallowed, though his shoulders remained hunched. 'OK,' he replied breathlessly. He nervously rubbed his arms. 'Where've you both been?'

'Just along the beach,' Kara insisted. She wrapped an arm around his waist and snuggled close.

'Talking?' he asked in a way that suggested he knew they'd been doing something far more intimate.

'Arguing actually. I told Robin some things I shouldn't have. Ric was expressing his displeasure.' All of which was the absolute truth, without getting into details that would likely upset him. Evidently, jealousy was going to be an ongoing issue. One she guessed they were going to have to stamp out fast if things were going to progress between them. Mind you, it was early days yet, and poor Zach was hopelessly smitten, as well as being under tremendous stress because of the van.

'It had to be done, man.' Ric slapped his palm against Zach's shoulder. Clearly, Ric wasn't prepared to adopt any form of subterfuge, regardless of the consequences. 'I couldn't let her get away with that, but it's not something you need to worry over. Let's keep things in perspective, eh? You're coming to live with me, Kara's not.'

While that fact seemed to perk Zach up a little – the corners of his mouth even briefly turned upwards into a smile – it also reminded Kara that she was going to have to work at this if she didn't want to get left out of the fun. Maybe she wasn't feeling jealous in the way Zach was, but she certainly did feel prickly at the notion of them enjoying too much time together without her. 'Yes, but you're going to invite me over for dinner tonight, aren't you?' She smiled sweetly up at Ric, who remained unmoved.

'I am?'

'We are,' Zach interjected. He stopped rubbing his arms and curled them instead around Kara and Ric's waists. 'We're going to have dinner together. It'll be great. A first for all of us. I'll cook. You two just have to show up in some decent togs.'

'Right,' Ric drawled dubiously, but he didn't veto the plan. 'I'd better dig you out some more clothes then.'

That at least put a smile on Zach's face. 'No need,' he breezed.

'What about now?' Kara asked. The tide was beginning to roll up the beach again, a fact that was adding to her unease. She caught herself twitching each time the waves washed a little closer to where they stood. 'Are you planning on opening up?'

Given the grey weather and lack of tourists there seemed little point in opening the Bunker's doors. Zach hunched his shoulders up around his ears. 'I dunno, hardly anyone comes in at the best of times.'

'That's because it's full of crap,' Ric remarked, typically blunt.

Kara contemplated slapping him, except he had a point. Buckets and spades were all very well, but the other assorted seaside tat wasn't very appealing, especially given the Bunker's poor lighting. 'Have you ever thought about converting it for use as a café?' She turned Zach so that he was facing the front of the Bunker. It was by no means a visually stunning building. It'd been constructed for practicality, not aesthetics, but it did fit the landscape, and it was an interesting site. Inside, it had a wonderful cave-like quality, and there was something she found very appealing about the way the red-brick vaulting meshed with the natural rock. 'You could go for a proper continental feel, have lots of outside seating during the day.' The place definitely looked better without the ice-cream van parked outside. 'And offer intimate candlelit dinners inside during the evenings. I bet people would come for the novelty value and the location, especially if you hired a decent chef, maybe someone who knows the local delicacies or could make you a signature dish.'

'I can cook,' he grumbled.

'Since when?' asked Ric, sounding surprised.

'Since for ever. Which you'd know, if you weren't only interested in me for one thing. Wait and see. I'll prove it tonight.'

Wow, if Zach could cook, then the café idea definitely had currency, although Zach seemed less sure. He scratched at his sea-dampened hair. 'I supposed it might breathe some life into the place, and the insurance on the van might cover the set-up costs if I don't opt to replace it. A few extra visitors wouldn't hurt either. Course, it might be a bit seasonal.'

'It's still a fab idea,' Kara reassured him. 'Isn't it, Ric? People love unusual venues.'

Ric crushed his coffee cup in his hand and then flicked it into the nearby bin. 'I suppose,' he grunted.

The muscles in Zach's arm tensed beneath Kara's fingers. When Ric turned away and began to walk towards the cliff path, he brushed Kara off and trailed after him. 'Wait up. You know I'd be happier if you were on board the idea. It's your island. I know you like things quiet. I can just as easily keep things the way they are.'

Ric stopped abruptly to face him. 'I don't actually. I've never liked it quiet. I never deliberately set out to live like a hermit. As long as people don't pry into my personal life, I don't mind them being here.'

'Really?' Zach forehead rumpled into a confused frown. 'Then why aren't you leasing out all those empty properties you have and making some money on them, instead of having them stand empty?'

Exasperated, Ric tore a hand through his flaxen hair. 'Because I'm a photographer, not a flipping holiday rep. I don't want to be hassled with it. I don't do admin. It's a total soul suck.'

'But ...' Zach remained incredulous. Kara too couldn't quite grasp what she was hearing. Why would anyone sit on a gold-mine like that? Well, if they didn't need the money. She guessed Ric was even better off than she'd thought.

'That's mental,' Zach continued.

'I'll do it,' Kara piped up.

The two men turned to face her. 'You'll do what?' Ric asked.

'I'll organise your holiday lets. I've worked for a letting agency before. It won't be that much work once they're listed on the major websites. How many properties are there?' She was expecting him to say two or three.

'About six,' Zach replied. 'He has six empty cottages, and another handful of buildings that could be let if they had some work done to them first.'

'What? Seriously, you're sitting on that many?' Kara stared at Ric. He hadn't been joking about owning the whole island. Her brain started churning figures, likely income from a holiday home in this part of the country. He wouldn't need to take photos and more importantly, if he'd let her manage them, she'd have a job and a reason to stay on Liddell Island once her baby brother returned from New Zealand. 'Why are you holding on to them if you're not doing anything with them?'

Ric mooched about, kicking at the gravel. Obviously being put on the spot over money made him uncomfortable. 'I wasn't doing nothing with them. I was selling the leaseholds. That's how your brother got Beachcomber's. But I had to reconsider after I had some interest from certain undesirable elements.'

She knew without questioning him that he meant Robin. Still, that was no reason to leave them empty. Families would love to come here for a holiday. There were unspoiled beaches and rock pools, the mainland attractions were only a few minutes away and, if Zach opened his café, maybe even thought about an alcohol licence, then it would be pretty much what anyone wanted. 'Let me help.'

Ric shrugged. 'Whatever. Have a look at them, if you like. See if you think they're up to scratch.' He started back up the cliff path again. Kara watched him go for a couple of seconds before turning to Zach. 'Did he say what I think he said?' Had he just given her a job? 'Shouldn't we talk salaries and stuff?' she called after Ric. He just raised his hand in a wave.

'Is he serious? Will he actually pay me?' She danced around Zach, clinging to his hands, so that he was forced to turn with her.

'Probably some sort of commission,' Zach reassured her. He grinned at her exuberance. 'Anyone would think it was your birthday, not that you'd just been given a glorified cleaning job.'

'Yes, but it's a job. I didn't have one, in case you hadn't noticed.' She'd no longer have to live on her brother's kindness, and she could phone her family and tell them truthfully that she could look after herself. 'Where are these houses? Are the keys up at the fort?'

'Tomorrow,' Zach insisted. His mouth stretched wide into a yawn. 'I've done enough tramping about for one day.' He put his arm around her shoulder and guided her back towards the Bunker. 'You can start tomorrow. Most of them are up towards the eastern tip where the old lighthouse used to be.'

'I haven't been there.'

'No, I'm not surprised. Access is a bit of an issue. That'll have to be addressed, but, as I said, tomorrow. We'll persuade Ric to join us, and make sure he knows you're serious. Right now, though, come and toss some ideas with me for the Bunker, since you suggested converting this cave into a café.'

'Toss is an unfortunate turn-on phrase,' she joked, launching herself at him, so that he was forced to catch her. Kara wrapped her legs around his waist.

Zach held on to her tight. 'Yeah, well, maybe I'll let you do that to me too.'

'You know I'll do it good.'

'Mm-hm. That's why I love you so much.'

Kara stilled a moment. Had he realised what he'd said? Had he even meant anything by it? She shook her head. Nah, it was just a figure of speech, though her insides fluttered at the notion of him one day saying it and meaning it. She'd come to Liddell Island to escape, not seeking commitment or anything else. What she'd found, she suddenly realised she really wanted to keep. She squeezed him tight with her thighs, and clasped her hands round Zach's neck, then pulled him close until their noses brushed.

'What?' he asked.

Kara kissed him hard.

He was smiling even more bemusedly when she pulled back for breath. Kara kissed him again, this time teasing the seam of his lips with her tongue. She knew he still had reservations about how their triumvirate would work, but Kara was determined to ensure it did. No matter what, she was going to get Ric to open up about his past and confess how he felt about Zach. If one day both men managed to feel a little more than lust for her too, then that would be great. She'd look forward to it, knowing they'd already found a special place in her heart. It wasn't love yet, but little shoots were growing.

'I'll come into the Bunker, Zach,' Kara said, 'but to discuss us, not business. We can't let Ric take charge tonight, no matter how much we both enjoy it. We have to stand up to him, put him in a submissive position for a change.'

Zach's brows shot towards his floppy hairline. 'What are you suggesting?'

'Oh, you know.' She wriggled suggestively. 'That we reprise this morning's wake-up call only with him in the middle. I saw what that did to you, remember. I reckon it won't be any different for Ric. Once he's felt that, he's not going to want to set us loose.'

'I suppose.' Zach pressed a kiss to her smirk. 'You'd best play boss, though. I'm hopeless at it.'

That was true. Zach seemed to enjoy things best when he was being told what to do, rather than when he was in command of what was happening. That might have to change a little for tonight, at least to the extent that he'd have to work with her.

'Have you ever done him like that?' she asked, realising it might prove to be a major hurdle if he hadn't.

Zach squirmed against her. The skin across his cheeks turned pink. 'Um, not often.'

'But you have done it?'

'Yeah.' His husky affirmative sent a wash of arousal zipping through her womb. At the same time, she felt his shaft awakening. Kara snuggled closer still, rubbing herself against his thickening erection. Zach's breath tickled as he moulded his lips to hers. The tip of his tongue flicked briefly into her mouth. It tantalised her with the promise of more, drawing panty-dampening heat to her sex.

'Now come inside.' He produced the shop key and fitted it to the lock. Kara's back rested against the stout door.

'Come where?' she asked mimicking his flirtatious tone. 'I'm not sure I ought to go anywhere with you. I suspect you've dirty things in mind.'

'Filthy,' he assured her. 'I think we need to rehearse some of the physical techniques we'll be using later.' His loins continued to nudge against her pussy, making her wet. Wet, eager and as impatient to feel his cock as Zach apparently was to sample her cunt.

She leaned close to his ear. 'You mean you want to put your long, hard dick in me?'

'Precisely.'

'While we hash out our plan to do dirty, naughty and x-rated things with your male lover?'

He pecked her cheek and then her eyelashes.

'You sure know how to persuade a girl.' Despite her precarious balance and the fact that they were still outside the Bunker, Kara reached for Zach's fly. He wanted to be inside her and she wanted that too. But first she craved the feel of his cock in her hand. Its steel and suppleness sliding against her curled palm until he was so rigid he wept real tears. This was how things had begun between them – desperate, immediate and risky – maybe it was how they should endeavour to make it stay. It worked for her and Ric, why not for her and Zach too?

Zach's trouser button popped and the metal teeth of his zip slid apart, giving her access to where the head of his cock already peeped above the line of his underwear.

'Christ!' Zach squealed at the contact. He slowly ground his hips, so his cock rubbed back and forth in her palm. He'd just snuck a hand beneath her skirt to reciprocate the pleasure when the growl of a car engine drifted across the bay. A line of cars were slowly trundling across the causeway before the tide cut the island off again. Zach made an immediate grab for the key and wiggled it in the lock, a feat made difficult by the fact that Kara had no intention of letting go. Stuff the tourists. They'd have to avert their gazes a moment. She wondered, if she slipped him inside her, would he still be able to walk them far enough to get inside the shop and out of sight?

'Stoopid lock,' he moaned.

The first car, a silver BMW, pulled on to the cobblestone car park and drove straight towards them. Zach continued his fight with the key, while Kara cautiously watched the car's approach over his shoulder. By the time the vehicle stopped before them, her enrapture had died. Instead, her fingers had curled into clawed fists.

'Someone you know?' Zach asked when she struggled from his arms. Her clothing fell back into place.

This couldn't be. No way, not here and now, when everything had taken such a turn for the better. Her past life had no place on Liddell Island. This was her sanctuary.

'Kara?'

She leapt forward away from Zach's touch, and brought her fist down hard on the bonnet of the now parked BMW. 'No fucking way,' she growled. First the van, then Robin, and now this – they said trouble came in threes.

The driver's side window rolled down and Gavin stuck his head out. He was exactly as she remembered him, designer sunglasses and studiously coiffed hair. 'Kara,' he said politely. 'We need to talk, honey.'

Just the sound of his voice made her want to curl up and cry. Gavin emerged from the vehicle with his arms spread, not in a pleading fashion that might at least have placated her, but in a way that said, 'Come here, I'll give you a big hug and all will be right.'

How many times had she fallen for that trick? What he really meant was 'We'll have this out later.' He wouldn't raise his voice or harm her in a physical way, he'd just see that he knew exactly what she was doing and when. He'd make sure she was wearing his approved choice of clothing and seeing his approved selection of friends.

'Fuck off!' she spat. How dare he come here and do this

to her? She'd freed herself of him, and it had cost her. Now she'd moved on. She had Zach, she had Ric and, as of ten minutes ago, she had a job that wasn't just house-sitting for her jet-setting baby brother. She didn't need rescuing and she absolutely didn't need Gavin Covey in her life any more. How had he managed to find her for that matter? She thought she could trust Christopher not to blab.

'Why are you even here? Did you miss the fact that we're over? What's the matter – did the novelty of Gemma's comfort wear off?'

'Babe,' he drawled. Hell, even his voice annoyed her. It was whiny and high-pitched for a man, a tone that lent itself to delivering wheedling endearments. 'There was never anything between Gemma and I, you know that. She's been worried sick about you, Kara. Look, I get it. I know the wedding plans were stressing you out, but that's not a reason to call it off. We can postpone. Let's talk, like adults.' He said the latter as though he was talking to someone with severe brain damage and not capable of communicating on an adult level. 'Darling, we just had a minor falling out. Things don't need to end between us.'

Except they already had, and she knew without thinking about it that dumping Gavin had been the wisest choice she'd ever made. Stuff what her family thought, or whatever Gavin thought. She wasn't interested in being anybody's pet. Here on Liddell Island she didn't have to pretend. She'd been herself in the way that back home she'd only been when she was drunk. She'd done all the things she'd wanted to do without worrying about what anyone thought, or whether it would hurt Gavin's career. She'd had sex out of doors, for a camera, been spanked and had a ménage à trois. Why would she ever consider giving that up for a boring life in suburbia as part of his mind-control experiment?

'It's already over. I moved on. You ought to do the same.' She turned her back on him, wearied by his very presence. 'Go home, Gavin. Find someone else.' Not that she wished him upon anyone.

'Not without you. You know I love you.'

She knew he was a manipulative jerk, and that he didn't sound remotely sincere. Zach's profession of love two minutes earlier had sounded more convincing, and she knew he hadn't meant it in that way. 'Go home, Gavin. I've found someone else.'

Really she ought to have kept that part to herself. Gavin always had to be number one. Sure enough, spurred by the thought that he'd been usurped, he strode forwards and caught hold of her arm. He looked at her, eyes cold behind the bronze of his glasses. 'Don't be ridiculous. Whatever you think you've found, it's just rebound stuff. It's not real, like what we have. It won't last.'

She shook her arm, determined to throw him off.

'For God's sake, Kara, you ran away, just like you always do when you can't deal with stuff. Are you really so selfish and stupid that you're going to throw your whole life away because of the stress caused by a few floral bouquets?'

The wedding fixtures had never been the issue. The problem had been that she'd known she was marrying the wrong man. She'd known it the moment he grinned when she lost her job.

Zach came bounding over the rough-hewn wall that separated the edge of the car park proper from the space outside the bunker. 'Hey, mate. I think you need to leave the lady alone. And she's not stupid.'

Gavin sneered at Zach's shapeless pullover, which was a

joke in itself considering he had on a pimpy grey suit, and Zach normally dressed beautifully. Only last night's events had caused his current dishabille. 'Yeah, and who are you?'

'He'd be *one* of the guy's who satisfying me,' Kara said, placing particular emphasis on the number. Yeah, she thought as Gavin's eyes narrowed to slits, you just think on that. Contrary to what you'd like me to believe, other guys do appreciate me and don't require me to be completely under their thumbs. Why she'd ever put up with him confounded her. He was an out-and-out jerk. They'd never suited one another. He'd always tried to make her feel bad about what she'd wanted in bed too. That was why she'd never quite managed to be entirely faithful to him.

'If you need more than one guy, clearly neither is any good at satisfying you,' Gavin scoffed.

Kara couldn't help it. She laughed. It was a choice between that or spluttering and choking on her own pent-up rage. 'Oh, they satisfy me all right. I tell you what. I'll send you some pictures so you can see for yourself just how well they manage it. Get lost, Gavin, before I consider posting them to your boss too.'

She grasped hold of Zach's wrist and dragged him inside the Bunker, slamming the door shut behind them. 'Kiss me,' she insisted. 'Just do it.'

* * *

That slimy git was Kara's ex!

Zach held her. He accepted her savage kisses and returned them with equally ardent ones of his own. He only stopped her when she started pushing her hands inside his clothes. Until this moment, Zach figured he knew Kara. She was

244

everything he admired in a woman: strong, independent, adventurous and capable of reducing him to a quivering puddle of bliss. Hell, she was prepared to take on Ric for him. But from that one small meeting he could see her life hadn't been like that with Gavin. She was trembling now, even as she tried to wriggle her hands inside his jeans.

What the hell had the guy done to her?

'Kara, stop it. Ric uses me like this. Talk to me instead. What's going on?'

She edged slowly back from him, her hands raised so that they covered her mouth to mask her sobs.

'Hug?' Zach offered.

Immediately, Kara returned to him. She buried her face in the wool of his jumper. 'I'm sorry,' she apologised a moment later. 'He drains all the life out of me. I can't believe he's shown up. How did he know I was here?'

Zach cradled her, and stroked the back of hair. 'I don't know. Someone must have told him. Hold out, eh? Eventually he'll go.'

Tears glazed the surface of her eyes when she tilted her head so that her chin rested against his breastbone. 'This stuff between you, me and Ric, it's not rebound stuff,' she said.

Zach nodded, then changed his mind and shook his head. Better that they were both honest about this. 'Sure it is,' he said, as if it didn't matter. 'You're cutting loose. It's allowed. It doesn't mean what we have can't develop into something special. Seriously, don't worry about it. I'm Ric's rebound too. So we can all bounce around nicely together.'

A picture briefly formed in his head of them all in Ric's bed enjoying vigorous sex. Kara was going to squeal the place down when she saw the restraints on Ric's bed.

Too late Zach realised he'd said the wrong thing.

'From what – his wife?' Kara gasped, Gavin instantly forgotten. Her eyes continued to shine, but with interest now, rather than unfallen tears. She wiped her face with her palms. 'That's one hell of a torch he's burning if he's still not over her yet.' She pressed their palms together, and hooked her fingers over the top of his. 'Is she why he refuses to commit?'

In a sense, he supposed. Ric had said time and again that he'd done the life commitment thing once and had no intention of repeating the process. He wasn't clinging to the memory of her, though, rather he seemed afraid of repeating past mistakes. Not that he knew a lot about Ric's past. The guy rarely if ever opened up, but now and then titbits escaped. Zach remembered those moments because they were so rare.

Kara thoughtfully pressed her lips to the back of his clenched hand. 'Robin said they were pretty wild. That he used to chase her about, and that they'd have wild sex outdoors.'

'How would she know?' he asked. 'She was only a kid at the time.'

'Hardly. It wasn't that long ago. She's well into her twenties.'

Zach shook his head. He didn't want to discuss Robin. Mentioning anything to do with her or Ric's private life were both fast exit routes out of his life. Zach had seen Ric cut ties with countless lovers over similar issues. It didn't matter how much fun Ric shared with any of them, the moment they started digging, they were out the door. It was a mistake he had no intention of making. He didn't want Kara making it either. 'We were talking about your ex,' he said, hoping to draw her away from the subject. 'How belligerent is he exactly? Is he likely to stand out there all day?'

Kara didn't seem to hear him. 'Long, long crush,' she observed of Robin. 'She's been mooning over Ric a heck of a long time. I mean, I knew that, but I never really considered it. Why doesn't he do something about it?'

'Like what? She's not doing any harm.'

Kara gave him a look that made plain she didn't agree on that point. 'They're connected somehow, aren't they? I mean they have to be or else he'd have told her to eff off.'

'Not that I'm aware of. Kara, can we get back to the present?' Just speculating on this topic was making Zach's skin crawl. 'Much as I love this place, I don't want to spend the day in here if I'm not open for customers, so tell me what the plan is regarding your ex.'

'Fuck him,' she said. Zach assumed she didn't mean in a literal sense. 'I'm through with him. You, Ric and I are going to party tonight.'

Thank God, he thought. They were back on ground he was comfortable with.

CHAPTER SIXTEEN

At seven o' clock Kara sat on the edge of the sofa in her living room with the laptop perched beside her on the cushions, flicking through the images Ric had left behind, and a few extra ones he'd emailed her of them all together last night. Though it appeared Gavin had left the island, she didn't trust him not to return, which meant she was arming herself. Any funny business from him, anything at all, and she'd send a selection of these beauties straight to his colleagues at the town hall. The resulting uproar would definitely keep him busy, and to hell with the fact that it'd get her labelled as a slut. Everything came with a price, and that was one she was prepared to accept.

Five filthy images now sat on her phone in addition to the ones she and Ric had taken of one another on the beach. Her favourite amongst them wasn't arty at all. It was crude, blatant, showed too much skin and a whole lot of cock stuffed into her pussy. Looking at it made her muscles quiver and prompted her to squeeze her thighs tight in anticipation of living such moments over again. She wasn't even sure which of Zach and Ric it was that was fucking her. It didn't really matter. What mattered this evening was that they'd all be together again. Her senses kicked into action every time she thought about it, so that a huge grin stretched her cheeks.

Damn, anticipation of her two men meant she could hardly sit still.

Ten minutes and she'd set off. Zach was preparing dinner for eight o' clock. Kara flicked through more of the slide-show, until it was impossible not to lift her skirt and touch herself. Maybe she could send them a little aperitif to whet their appetites for the main course.

It took seconds to angle the web-camera lens, and then she was staring at her own pixelated image on the computer screen. Kara coyly ran her hand up her inner thigh so that her skirt lifted, revealing the fact that she wore no panties. Ric was forever accusing her of leaving them behind, so tonight she was ensuring there was no possibility of that. She was going to walk over to the fort bare, the wind tickling her pubic curls and helping to maintain the simmer she was already rousing in her cunt.

OK, enough with the tease. Now for the action.

Legs spread wide apart, Kara held open her slit with one hand, while she rubbed her exposed clit with two wetted fingers from the other. *Look at me, boys*, she was saying. *Look what I have to offer.* She knew Zach had his doubts. He seemed to fluctuate between enjoying her company, and the prospect of the two of them winning Ric over, and being convinced it would all end horribly. She just wished he'd have a little faith in her; ever since she'd stopped listening to those around her and started acting on her own instincts, her life had drastically improved. That method could work for Zach too, she knew it. Plus, she refused to give up. She intended to hang on to Zach and Ric for a good long time. Where else was she going to find two men who understood her so well, and who were willing to accept her for who she was?

Within seconds Kara's clit grew tight and engorged, so that it peeped out from its protective hood. Of course this wasn't the same as having the boys do it for her, but it wasn't difficult to imagine Ric and Zach here lending a hand each, or her returning the favour, so that she held and masturbated both their cocks at once.

She was going to do that – that and every other delicious thing that entered her head. There'd be no coyness or restrictions between them. They'd all express themselves, and get what they needed, especially poor Zach. He especially needed to know that he was loved.

Kara closed her eyes as she sank into the rhythm of her daydream. She lifted her top and squeezed her nipples, imagining the pinch of Ric's hands while Zach attended to her clit with his mouth.

What would they think of her little display? Would it get them all hard and ready for her? Would it prompt them to a little warm-up action of their own? Maybe they'd strip off right there in the kitchen where Zach was preparing food, and Ric would go down on Zach even as he stirred the cooking pot. She could picture them so clearly, their lean bodies straining against one another, Ric blond and smooth, Zach dark and covered in all those masculine hairs. God, she loved the fact that he was so rugged and manly, and that his scent clung to his chest hair. In her mind, too, she could smell the food bubbling on the stove, tomatoes and basil and a hint of garlic.

Tonight she was going to make sure that Ric was the centre of things, but come morning she was also determined that she was going to have had them both at once; one in her cunt, one in her rear. She knew it was possible. Ric had those photographs. She couldn't wait to be filled by two men.

Kara's orgasm broke sharp and swift. It trembled down her thighs and in her belly – satisfying, but only enough to slake her need until the main act. She attached the recording to an email and pressed send. With any luck, they'd view it just before she arrived.

It was dark out, cloudy, but relatively still. Only an occasional gust caused the nearby grasses to rustle and sway as she made the trek across Liddell Island.

The fort formed a dark blot against the twilit sky as she approached, and from it two bright spots of warmth glowed like lighthouse beacons. Kara's heart rate accelerated as she trudged up the slope towards the rope bridge. She'd worn flats to walk over in, but a pair of stiletto-heeled sandals swung from her fingertip ready to slip on once she got inside. The slender heels emphasised the length of her legs. She'd also worn her favourite party skirt, an itty-bitty little thing that resembled a gymslip, and that Gavin had refused to let her wear. It was black with silver pinstripes, and only just skimmed her upper thighs. Below it, she'd remained bare. Her naughtiness in doing so added an extra spring to her step.

She sped up when she reached the bridge. The bottom of the gorge was all too clear tonight – a long, long way down. Its sides were covered with nettles and moss. At the bottom a small brook tumbled over craggy rocks.

Kara was three-quarters of the way across the bridge when a shadowy figure appeared between the two gargoyles on the bank nearest the fort. She stopped. Only for a second did she think it was Zach, come to meet her and light her way up the steep steps. Then she recognised the boxy silhouette.

'Kara,' Gavin said, stepping fully into the moonlight. He

wore the same clothes he'd had on earlier. 'You know we need to talk.'

She'd known in her heart that he wouldn't give up so easily, but she'd thought he'd approach her again in daylight. Kara glanced back to the start of the bridge, wondering if there was another route into the fort, or whether she could get far enough away to call Rich and Zach and have them come out and meet her.

Gavin stepped forward on to the bridge, and began walking towards her. This wasn't the place to engage in a struggle. It was too narrow, the fall too far. Immediately, she backed up.

'What do you want?'

'To talk, that's all. Just discuss things with me sensibly. Why are you here on this rock playing perverted games? What are you trying to prove? This isn't you, Kara.' He reached out to her beseechingly. 'It's not the woman I intend to marry. She has more sense. Can't you see that what you're doing is dangerous?'

What was dangerous was the way the bridge swung after he made each step. Couldn't he learn to walk on the balls of his feet instead of stomping everywhere? He was right that she was no longer the woman he'd asked to marry him, as she was no longer prepared to put up with his shit. Matter of fact she'd decided to stick with giving orders rather than taking them, both in and out of the bedroom.

'Kara, I can't let you ruin things like this.'

'What exactly do you mean by "can't"? You don't own me, Gavin. I'm a grown woman; I can make my own decisions. And this is who I am. The only thing that's changed is that I'm no longer being cowed into silence. I'll thank you to get off the bridge and let me pass.'

'So that you can go in there and behave disgracefully?

253

No, I don't think I will. Think of your mum, your family, do you think they'd approve of this?'

'I don't need their approval, and I don't need yours. It's my life. I intend to live it.'

'For heaven's sake, Kara, they're dangerous. Alaric Liddell probably killed his wife. Yes, I know that's who you're seeing,' he hissed. 'Think about this. Is that the sort of man you want to be with? He and his wife were both notorious users and deviants. Her death was almost certainly a result of a drug-fuelled sex game gone wrong. Is that what I'm supposed to leave you to walk into? What if you're his next victim?'

'That's bullshit,' she yelled. Admittedly Ric had commitment issues, but she didn't believe for a minute they were caused by murdering his wife. Yet again Gavin was resorting to mind games in order to control her.

'Is it? Are you so sure?' he wheedled, still moving towards her with his arms outstretched. 'What do you really know about either of them? What sort of life are you going to have with an ice-cream seller? Come home with me, Kara. Stop behaving like a child.'

Kara stepped back again. The minute she had solid ground beneath her feet she was going to run. It didn't matter what she said any more. The concept of listening bypassed Gavin entirely. And, if he caught her, there'd be no fighting him off. While his brawn was of the gym-built variety, he was still double her weight, and he'd thrown her over his shoulder before now to stop her going somewhere.

Kara's hand reached the end of the rope. She stepped back, limbs taut and ready to spring, only for two slender arms to wrap around her waist.

'Got you,' Robin squealed in delight. Her corkscrew curls blew in front of Kara's face. 'I warned you that if you didn't co-operate I'd see you off the island, bitch.'

Kara twisted and turned, but couldn't quite shake off Robin's tenacious hold. 'You contacted Gavin?' she questioned.

Robin's delight ran through her voice. 'Your mother actually,' she boasted. 'It wasn't difficult to dig up the details of the Beachcomber sale, or to get through to his next of kin. Your mum was really interested to learn where you were and all the sluttish things you were doing to demean yourself. You can't blame her for sending him here to haul you home. As she said, he's the best person to sort you out. He's the only one who has any control over your wilfulness.'

Gavin sprinted over the last few yards of the bridge. 'I'm sorry, Kara, but you have to see reason.' He grabbed hold of her legs, so that he and Robin lifted her between them. They lowered her on to the ground, only to pin her and wind gaffer tape around her wrists and calves.

'Get off me,' she squealed, lashing out with her elbows as best she could and attempting to roll.

Gavin went through her pockets, turning her house keys, a couple of mints and her mobile out on to the grass. Robin immediately claimed the latter. A taut grin stretched across her heart-shaped face as she raced through the list of contacts.

'Give me that back.'

Robin laughed and tucked the phone into the pocket of her sou'wester. Then she slapped a piece of tape over Kara's mouth.

'I've done my bit,' she said to Gavin. 'May you have great joy of her. I'll send you a wedding card.' She stood and saluted him, before darting on to the bridge. 'Oh, and Kara, don't worry about Ric. I'll make sure he has a good time. I've lots of plans for him. Really wild plans. I know he's going to enjoy them all.'

'Let's go.' Gavin hoisted Kara upright, and then set her across his shoulder. He gave her bottom a friendly pat. 'It's time we went home, babe. I'm sure you'll admit this was all a mistake once we're back to civilisation.'

Her mother! Her mother was as bat-shit crazy as Robin, and so was Gavin if they thought for one minute that abducting her was going to mean the wedding was back on. The minute Gavin put her down, she was going to knee him in the balls and then call the cops with his phone.

* * *

Zach stood hunched over a chopping board in the fort's basement kitchen. He glanced up from the selection of peppers when he heard the patter of Ric's feet on the tiled floor. His lover had discarded his woollens since he'd arrived home, returning to his usual black jeans and bohemian range of T-shirts. The curves of his biceps bulged from beneath the short sleeves as he sauntered into the fort's converted basement towel-drying his long hair. His feet were bare and left damp imprints behind on the tiles.

Ric chucked the towel he'd been using on to the countertop and hopped up alongside it so that he sat directly behind where Zach stood at the island counter. 'How's it going?' he enquired cheerfully.

'Fine.'

'Kara sent us a video message. She's not wearing any panties tonight. I thought, maybe we could surprise her with a similar look.'

Zach cut into another fruit. 'Maybe.' He didn't demand to see the recording. He was trying hard not to think about anything but the cooking. Thinking only got him worked up.

256

'What's up?' Ric enquired. He began drumming his feet against the cupboard. 'You seem a little tense. Is all this prep too much of a pain?'

'It's fine.' Zach dug his teeth into his lower lip. Cooking wasn't the problem. His issues were with what happened after the meal. He couldn't deny last night had been fun, and as Kara had promised it had brought them together into some semblance of a relationship. Maybe, just maybe, it had also chipped a few chunks off the glacier-like walls around Ric's heart. However, that didn't mean he didn't have reservations about tonight. Everything could still fall apart.

To Ric and Kara this was a game; neither of them had as much invested in the outcome as he. If it collapsed, they'd simply move on, whereas he'd be devastated. The niggling doubts he'd had about Ric loving Kara more hadn't gone away either. What if, once the novelty of their ménage à trois wore off, Ric and Kara coupled up and decided they no longer wanted him around?

He paused to reach for another tomato. He enjoyed everything Kara had done, he really had, especially her sense of adventure, but he still felt threatened by her. She was lovely, but ... damn it, but he'd wanted Ric to be his for eternity. Sharing him with someone had never figured as part of his plan, and how could that possibly make things any easier?

Just thinking it over made his back teeth ache.

Why would three of them being involved sweep away the restrictions and barriers that time had failed to erode?

He wished he could wholly believe in it. But he didn't. He just didn't. Instead his initially small doubts kept spinning into larger ones.

'What have you been doing?' he asked. 'Did you make up the bed in the spare room?' Night after night, year upon

257

year, that's where he ended up staying. There was no reason to suppose tonight would end differently just because they'd all slept together at Kara's place.

'Nope. Should I have done?' Ric asked. He bumped down off the bench and pattered across to Zach's side. 'I kind of thought ... We discussed this earlier, remember?'

'What, that you're making an exception because of Kara?'

'No. Look, how long are you planning on staying?'

Hurt splintered in his soul. Zach slammed the knife down on the chopping board before turning to Ric. 'I won't get in your way, if that's what you're asking. Christ, if you don't want me around just say. I'll go.' Tears sprang fully formed into Zach's eyes. He raised his hand to wipe them away and brush the mop of hair away from his eyes.

Ric's brows scrunched into an unfathomable frown. 'Hey, that's not what I was saying. I do want you around. That's never been in question. I was going to say that you could stay in my bed whatever number of nights you mentioned.'

Was he supposed to believe that?

'I can't do this,' he confessed. 'This, whatever it is we're doing. I don't want sex with no strings, whether it's with you, Kara or both of you together. I want some emotional warmth.'

'Hell, give me a chance.' Ric folded his arms across his chest so that one set of knuckles pressed against his chin. 'Isn't that the point of this dinner? You're cooking so we can chat and enjoy one another's company without it being all about the sex. Oh, and then you both fuck me silly so I never want to be parted from either of you ever again.'

So much for subterfuge; Ric had seen right through the plan. Well then, there was no chance of it working. Zach's eyes began to sting again. He immediately snatched up the tea towel to hide their fall. 'Onions,' he blubbered. God, now he looked like a complete fool. Zach wiped his face with the cloth, which only worsened the problem as he genuinely got onion residue in his eyes. He rubbed at his eyes as tears coursed across his face.

'Put your face under the tap.' Ric's fingers curled around his shoulder and guided him to the sink. Zach ducked his head and Ric turned on the water. He let his anger grow cold as the cold spray cascaded over his face and ran into the collar of his borrowed jumper.

When Ric turned the tap off, Zach slowly straightened.

'I wasn't hinting that I wanted you to leave,' Ric explained. His fingers briefly brushed Zach's as he passed over the towel he'd previously used to dry his hair. 'I was just thinking about the fact that you don't have any of your stuff with you. I mean, you're welcome to my pants, but you …' He tugged at the fisherman's sweater that Zach wore. 'You look better in your own stuff. I figured maybe we could go and pick some bits up.'

Zach shook his head slowly, refusing to accept the implied meaning behind Ric's words. Ric would say anything in order to ensure he got his fun. The fact was this notion of the three of them having sex together turned him on, so he was just making sure Zach was around to play his part. 'Tell me why I should go ahead with this,' he said. What was the point if Ric already knew their plan? He wasn't about to fall for it. 'Aren't I just going to end up hurt?' No amount of fun would cushion the heartbreak afterwards, when it became apparent he was still in the same place he'd always been; only now he was sharing Ric on a permanent basis with a female lover. 'You're not actually going to open up. You can't really trap someone with sex.'

'You can if it's good enough.'

Zach continued to shake his head. His fringe flopped over his eyes, hopefully masking his pain. 'You don't actually give a damn,' he complained. 'Would you even have cared if I'd drowned last night?'

'What the fuck!' Ric growled. He held his hands out wide. 'I'm trying to give you what you want. And yes, I'd care. Fuck it, I always did. Why do you think I put up with your whining?' Frown lines carved roads into the glacial smoothness of Ric's freshly shaven skin. He rubbed his hand hard across his face. 'When did you nearly drown? You weren't in the water.'

Zach forced a laugh. 'Of course I was in the friggin' water. Both Kara and I were. Why'd you think I have no fucking clothes? I got wet. The tide was coming in. Do you think I'd have left the van there otherwise?'

The colour entirely drained from Ric's face, leaving him ashen except for the red of his lips. His back stiffened, so that he stood ramrod straight. 'Why didn't you tell me? Why did neither of you say anything? Jesus, you invited me over last night for a threesome when you should have been at the hospital getting checked out.' He looked ready to say more, but lapsed into silence.

Zach scoffed at the mention of hospital. The nearest one with an A&E department was forty minutes' drive. He refused to believe in Ric's concern, as genuine as it actually seemed. 'I was fine. We both were. A few bruises, nothing else. I've been more battered surfing.' He refused to go into the details of how he'd nearly lost his grip on Kara, or her subsequent reluctance to go near the water's edge. What was the point?

Ric turned his back on Zach and began to pace. He completed two circuits of the kitchen island before he stopped abruptly and sank to the floor on the far side of it.

Zach waited a moment, but when Ric didn't re-emerge, he began to realise that maybe he had actually made a mistake. Perhaps Ric really had meant what he said, that he was trying to open up and give things a try the way Zach wanted them.

Ric sat with his knees hunched up and his face hidden by his hands.

Slowly, Zach bent down by his side. 'Do you mean it? You're actually prepared to make this a proper relationship?'

Ric turned his head so that one eye was visible behind the wall of his arms. 'I guess so.' He held out his hand, and grasped Zach's tight when he offered it in return.

'Why now? Because of Kara?'

Ric slid his free hand across his face. 'I guess I can see the three of us working together in a way I couldn't when it was just the two of us. I don't want anything that claustrophobic … or gay,' he added quietly. 'Now, tell me the truth about what happened last night. How much risk were you really in?'

'We got buffeted about a bit. It was no big deal. Kara got a bit scared though.'

'Well, I'm glad you're both safe.' Ric squeezed tight Zach's hand. 'Seriously though, if I'd had any inkling, last night wouldn't have happened. I wouldn't have done that stuff.'

'That'd be why we omitted the details. I know your wife drowned, so mentioning our dipping would have dampened the mood. We wanted you eager, not maudlin.'

'You do know what happened, then?'

'Only the local gossip.' Zach had always wondered what had happened, but he'd never directed his questions at Ric for fear of the consequences. This time, however, he did ask. 'What actually happened, Ric?'

Ric glanced up at him with sad eyes the colour of the

English Channel. 'I wondered if you'd ever ask. You kept demanding more from me, but you've never seemed to want to know about me. Most people pry too much; our interactions were always on the surface.'

Only because he'd seen what had happened to those who did ask questions. Zach curled his fingers into Ric's shoulders, realising his whole plan of attack had been wrong from day one. 'I've always wanted to ask. I just didn't want to upset you. I thought you'd end things completely if I asked questions like that. Please. What did happen?'

'She committed suicide.' Zach's eyes widened and Ric gave a juddering little nod. 'I managed to keep that part out of the press. The rest I'm sure you know. We hired a yacht in order to have a party to celebrate my first big magazine cover. There were lots of foolish people there doing extremely foolish things. I don't miss those days, Zach, nor do I remember much about them.' He sniffed hard and then rubbed his nose against his arm. 'At some point during the night, Scarlett jumped overboard and drowned. She was pumped full of coke and alcohol. Some walkers found her washed up on the shore. I didn't even know she was missing.' He looked up then. 'Horrid, isn't it? It should tell you what sort of person I was. The woman I loved above all else took her own life and I didn't even notice. I was passed out on deck in a drug-fuelled haze. The police found her note.'

Zach cuddled up to Ric's side and put his arm around his lover's shoulder. 'Do you miss her?'

Ric shook his head. 'No. I don't miss any of that world. There was never any space to breathe. It's why I decided to move here permanently instead of staying in London.'

The strands of their hair meshed together as Zach tilted

his head to rest against Ric's. 'I'll give you whatever space you need, you know that?'

'You'll try.' Ric nodded. 'I know that Kara's the right solution for us too. I don't want to be part of a couple, but I think I can stomach the idea of a triad. That's if you're happy with it too.'

'Just as long as no one gets left out.'

'Is that what your greatest fear is?' Ric got to his feet. He held out his hand and helped Zach up. 'As long as we're prepared to trust each other, that shouldn't be a problem. Besides, you can't have a threesome with only two people, and Kara's far too sold on the idea of having us both.'

'Then we'd better not disappoint her.'

'We won't.'

Zach returned to his chopping board, a smile stretching his lips and a fluttery feeling in his stomach. He finally had a chance of what he wanted, despite all his doubts and worries. He kept glancing across at Ric, desperate to reach out and touch him. However, Kara would be arriving soon, and he hadn't even turned on the cooking pot.

Ric slammed into the bench beside him, occupying the space between the chopping board and the cooker. 'What do you think Kara's expecting from us tonight?' He teased a piece of cut pepper off the chopping board and popped it into his mouth.

Zach waggled a warning finger at him. 'From what she said earlier, she wants to see me fuck you in the arse.'

'She said that?' For a moment, Ric's mouth hung open. Then he chuckled, and reached for a second slice of pepper, only for Zach to bat his hand away. A strange sort of hand jive occupied the next minute or so, as Zach protected his vegetables and Ric tried to steal them. Eventually, Ric settled for a slice of tomato.

'Course, I said I didn't know if you'd be up for that. I wasn't sure being in the middle would rock your boat.'

Ric pinched his lips between his forefingers. He watched Zach scoop up the ingredients and throw them into a saucepan. 'Reckon you can satisfy me like that?' he asked.

'You know I can. Remember the shower that time. The real question is: can you satisfy her like that, or are you going to come after forty seconds?' Zach glanced up in order to watch Ric's reaction. His lover's expression grew serious a moment, lips pursed, jaw emphasised.

'I think … I think,' he said slowly, 'I'd better have some practice, hadn't I?'

Zach blinked. He dropped the spoon he'd been holding. 'Now?'

Ric gave a nod.

Oh, God! It was aeons, absolutely aeons since they'd done this. Prickles of tension rode Zach's skin so strongly that he had to move. He lurched forward unsteadily, caught Ric and forced him backwards until they hit the wall. Then Zach kissed him. He kissed Ric in the way he'd always wanted to, holding nothing back, taking everything he needed. It was raw and brutal, and at the same time left him exposed, but it no longer mattered. He clenched his fist in Ric's long hair and bent him backwards, exposing his throat, then wrenched up his cotton T-shirt, uncovering first his abs and then his chest. Skin, muscles, the ridiculously intricate tattoo inked across Ric's back, Zach was going to claim it all. For a moment or two at least Ric was his, and he was going to prove it.

'Hands flat against the wall,' Zach growled. He actually pushed Ric's hands into place where he wanted them, out wide either side of his hips, palms flat against the whitewashed brickwork, fingertips slightly curled. 'Don't move.'

He wrenched Ric's jeans down to his ankles, and then set to work lavishing attention on the jutting spire that was Ric's cock. His lover's taste flooded his tongue and infused his senses with greater need.

Hungry ...

Yes, he was hungry for this. Images of what he would do and how he would do it already flicked through his brain like snapshots. He imagined pushing Ric face first against the wall and fucking him hard in the arse. Zach saw them sprawled over the kitchen counter too, and then up in the studio, entwined with exposed 35mm film, him holding the camera and calling the shots, while Ric was forced to pose.

Predominantly, as he sucked on Ric's cock, a sense of relief and power surged through Zach. He knew the taste of Ric's body, and kept on sucking him, dragging him closer and closer to release, though he stopped short of actually making Ric come. Instead, he fell back on his haunches, a smug smile plastered across his face.

'Now?' he asked.

Ric didn't answer, he just stared.

'Answer me. I want to hear you say it.' Zach stroked a finger along the length of Ric's erection from base to tip. He finished with a swirl around the top. 'OK, if you're not talking, let's see how you respond to a bit of incentive.' Zach rose, reached out with his free hand and fished a plastic spatula off a hook above Ric's head. He tried a test strike against his thigh. The implement made a nice whippy sound through the air and a thwack on impact. The burn was nice too, and no worse than being hit with an open palm. 'Game?'

'What if I like the prospect of punishment more than pleasure?'

Zach shrugged. 'Then you'll end up with a very red

backside and I'll wear my hard-on out on Kara when she gets here.'

Ric twitched beneath his touch.

'Ah, you don't like that idea, do you? The thought of me fucking Kara irks you something chronic, doesn't it? Why is that, Ric?'

'If you're fucking her, then you're not available for me.'

Zach slapped him across his bare thigh with the spatula. 'Nnnn. Incorrect. We both know that's not true. It worked out pretty OK this morning. The truth now, and be specific?'

'Because I want you to put your cock in me,' Ric hissed, though his voice bore a hint of uncertainty.

'Do you? Do you really?' This time Zach aimed for the chest. The impact left a pink, forked impression on Ric's skin, which faded even as he watched. Ric didn't seem remotely impressed. Then again it was hard to tell considering the show of petulance he was putting on. Not that it stopped him shuffling away from the wall, turning slightly so as to make his arse a target and raising a brow in a provocative fashion.

Zach cracked the spatula across both cheeks.

'Fuck!' Ric cursed. He braced his hands against the wall, assuming a position that just invited another smack, and then two more. That apparently was the limit of it though, for Ric turned around and wrestled the spatula from Zach's hand. He chucked it to the far side of the kitchen. 'Enough. Let's do this.' He cupped the bulge of Zach's cock through his fly. 'Let's take this upstairs, and I don't want you to go easy on me.'

CHAPTER SEVENTEEN

Zach stood at the foot of Ric's sleigh-shaped bed as his lover climbed on to its surface, wondering if he could maintain the belief that this was real. It had been mere fantasy for far too long.

Naked, Ric stared back at him archly. He knelt in the centre of the bed, with his thighs spread apart, a pose that gave his erection plenty of room to jut out hard from his body. It wasn't a submissive pose. Rather it seemed a position from which one might suddenly spring into action. 'I'm all yours. Come and claim me. That won't be too hard for you, will it?' he teased.

Zach edged along the side of the bed, aware that Ric's gaze followed his every step. This wasn't how things were between them. There was always tension in their relationship, but not like this. Not this unsettling wariness that came from venturing into new pastures. Zach kicked off his shoes. Then he tugged his borrowed jumper over his head. His flat nipples were so tight they stood proud. Ric shuffled over to him. He grabbed hold of Zach's belt and loosened the buckle.

'What would you like me to do, O master?'

'Be yourself. Be straight with me over what you want.'

Ric responded with a dry chuckle. 'You want me to play at being straight? That might be difficult.' He knelt up, grinning, His torso pressed tight to Zach's as they shared a kiss. Then Ric threw himself backwards as if scalded. He scampered up towards the headboard and cowered in a protective huddle. 'I don't know if I can do this. I'm not like this. I don't have sex with other men.'

He couldn't. He couldn't keep this pretence up. Zach dissolved into laughter. He put a knee on the mattress and then stalked up the bed towards Ric on his hands and knees, until he crouched over the lower part of Ric's body. 'That's right,' he agreed, capturing one of Ric's wrists and lifting it to that he could fasten it in position with one of the silk cords knotted around the bedposts. 'You only have sex with me.'

A few loops, a few quick knots and Ric lay wantonly spread out for him. Excitement drove Zach. He wasn't a natural dominant. He knew he wasn't. In truth he'd have been much happier strapped to the bed alongside Ric, both of them blindfolded and waiting to see what delights Kara had in store for them. He suddenly longed for her presence in a way he hadn't before. Kara's desires overlapped theirs and complemented them. Kara wanted to share Ric with him. Which meant ensuring his man could take the pace.

'We're going to do this facing,' Zach told Ric, looking him straight in the eye, before stealing a few slow kisses. 'Not that you're going to be able to see any better than if I were behind you, because I want you to concentrate on the feel of this. When I push into you, I want you to experience the full, undiluted sensation of my cock filling you. I don't want your attention wandering off to the corner of the room. I don't want you thinking about angles and lenses or how good a shot something would make, and I don't want you ogling Kara when she turns up. You have to focus on me, and just me.'

'Yeah – then hurry up and give me something to focus on.'

Zach closed his fist around Ric's erection. He took his time exploring his lover's length, making sure he knew every contour – the thickness at the base, the flare of his glans and the collar of his foreskin. The tiny slitted eye seeped tears as he tickled it with his tongue. Ric remained stoically poised at first. Not for long. Slowly his breathing deepened. Then the odd whimper or groan escaped his lips.

'You're going to stay hard for me, aren't you?' Zach asked, as he coaxed Ric on to his back and came to kneel between his parted thighs. 'I don't want you going all floppy on me while I'm in you.' It happened. It had happened to him once or twice, particularly in the early days of their relationship. Ric seemed startled by the idea, as if the eventuality had entirely passed him by until that point. 'You can't fuck us both together if you can't keep it up,' Zach teased. 'It's a good job we're having this practice.'

He knew where Ric kept his toys. Hell, he'd been on the receiving end of most of the items in that drawer. Revenge was going to be sweet. A long black silk scarf he used on Ric as blindfold came out first, followed by a bottle of lube, a pair of nipple clamps and a handily hinged cock ring. 'That should help keep you frisky.' He gave Ric a pat of encouragement having fastened the metal ring in place around the base of his lover's cock. 'I think we're all set now.' He pushed his trousers down to his knees, then squeezed out a healthy dollop of lube and worked it over his own erection, before going on to explore Ric's hole with his fingertips.

'Man, you're tight.' Ric bucked at the first hint of intrusion. 'And a bit jumpy. Calm it down there.' Zach stroked his finger in and out of the grasping little hole, loving the way Ric's muscles tried to hold on to him and draw him in. He loved anal sex, adored everything about being taken like that; Ric holding him down, the feel of his lover's cock sliding between his cheeks and pushing right inside his body. The way the world stopped for a moment each time something nudged his prostate.

He liked fucking too, and prior to meeting Kara he hadn't got to do nearly enough of that. He could count on one hand how many times he'd had Ric in this way.

Zach withdrew his fingers from Ric's arse. He squirted another blob of lube, and then lifted Ric's legs so that his feet rested against Zach's shoulders. He knew exactly what he'd be feeling. Indeed the flutter of nerves in his stomach even showed in the way Ric's abdominal muscles pulled tight. 'Relax,' Zach reassured him. 'Open up for me.' Zach thrust forward, felt Ric push back against him, and then his muscles relaxed, granting him admittance. He sank deep into his lover's embrace, groaning as he did.

Perilous heat surrounded Zach's cock, which sent wild fire racing through his body to the top of his scalp. He'd anticipated heat, but not such an inferno coupled with a squeezing grip. It felt … it felt incredible, and he was only inside Ric an inch. Zach wasted no time in sinking deeper, so that his balls nestled against Ric's body and he lay above his lover's supine form.

He might not be a dominant, but he was loving this. He ought to have insisted that they switched things up more often.

Ric's fists clasped tight the silken cord that bound his wrists to the bedposts. A red blush swept across his cheekbones, and then down across his neck and upper torso. His head thrashed from side to side but the blindfold remained in place.

'How does it feel, Ric?' Zach couldn't help teasing a little, especially as Ric kept his lips pressed tightly together. The blindfold half hid his face but didn't entirely mask his expression. Ric was caught on the edge of rapture, powerless to stop what was happening, his body hungry for more and desperate to escape the intrusion and shame of it. 'I never knew you blushed so prettily.' He wrapped his hand around Ric's erection and gave him some extra help. Soon their rhythm became a smooth rolling motion. Zach lost himself in the moment. He hadn't realised how much he'd longed for this, or how lopsided their relationship had been.

Nor was he done yet. The crescendo was still building, no more than a tingling ache at the moment, slowing, building in intensity. He'd do this again tonight, once Kara was here with them. This was only the practice run.

When his phone began to bleat, Zach hardly noticed it at first. He stayed inside Ric as he answered and read the text message. 'Kara's here. She's downstairs.' He didn't want t to keep her waiting, even though he didn't want to part from Ric's body.

Ric made his first really expressive groan as Zach pulled out of his body. 'No,' he pleaded.

'I'll only be a tick. You can hold on that long to finish this off, can't you?' Ric's cock remained rock hard, and probably would have even without its silver adornment.

'Finish it now,' Ric growled.

'Think of this as an exercise in stamina.' He bent and gave Ric's cock a quick kiss. 'I'll be right back.'

Zach hitched his trousers in order to jog down the stairs. He fastened the zip but left the waist button undone. Ric's two Dalmatians were barking in the hallway. 'Hey, quieten down, will you? It's only Kara.' He grabbed them both by the collars and dragged them into the study before answering the door.

The doorstep was empty. 'Kara?' A woman's shadow clung to the stone at the far end of the tunnel. 'Hey, are you coming in? I've got Ric waiting.'

He frowned when he received no reply, and glanced down at the text message on his phone again. It definitely said she was at the door.

Zach pattered forward, the stone icy against his bare feet, wondering what it was that had captured her interest. He turned the corner only for something to hit him hard across his midriff. Pain exploded in his stomach and ricocheted along his nerves to pulse in his ears and drive bile up his throat. Bent double on his knees, he coughed up the phlegm, aware only of a pair of black stiletto-heeled shoes positioned before him.

'So kind of you to let me in.' Robin chuckled as she swept past him into the fort. Zach snatched at the back of her sou'wester but failed to grab the fabric. He crawled after her, finally gaining his feet inside the entrance tunnel. The fort door slammed in his face, and seconds later the portcullis smashed down, trapping him beneath the archway. 'Fuck. Fuck. Fuck!' he yelled. He had his phone and nothing more, and it didn't matter how many times he tried to call Ric, there was no way he'd be able to answer it. 'Kara?' That text had definitely come from her phone, so where the hell was she now? What had Robin done to her?

* * *

Ric lay against the sheets panting, his nerves frayed beyond reason and his body desperate for more of Zach's savagery. Not that his lover had been rough. In truth he'd been quite gentle. It was simply that Ric hadn't anticipated how intense the sensations involved would be. He knew the thrill of a dildo in his arse, though he considered that a solitary pleasure, and had even had genuine anal sex a time or two. He knew also the thrill of denial, both from the restraints and from building scenarios in his head, but he had not planned for the deprivation of his eyesight too. Taking away his vision had caused his other senses to work overtime. A simple stirring of air in the room felt like a caress against his skin, and actual touch made his pulse race.

The bang of the front door below echoed through the building.

'Zach, is that you?' he asked a moment later, his need bordering on desperate.

Ric waited, his muscles tensed, as footsteps echoed along the corridor. Hell knows what response this was going to get from Kara.

A pair of high heels marched towards him. Zach was hanging back, sending Kara in first. God, he'd probably done it intentionally so as to have Kara see him this exposed.

Well, he could still handle her, even from this position.

His cock gave a little welcoming jerk as the bedroom door swished open. He expected some sort of chuckle or remark at his expense from Kara and frowned beneath the blindfold when it didn't come. 'Who is that?' He struggled into a more upright position, sensing something was wrong. The scent that whispered towards his nostrils was neither Zach's nor Kara's, though it was familiar. It caused the hairs on the back of his neck to stand. Some things time erased, like the exact composition of a person's face or the sound of their voice. Others remained embedded in the brain like a primitive warning system.

'Who is that?' he demanded.

Ric's already heightened senses kicked into a state of red alert. He tugged upon the bonds around his wrists, but the knots held fast. The scent strengthened until he sat in the midst of a fragrant cloud. Jasmine and begonia – he'd never forget the scent of his wife's perfume. But this was no ghost come home to haunt him; this was a solid, living presence.

'What do you want?'

'Oh, Alaric.' The sound of her voice caused his heart to pound. Then dainty fingertips stroked the line of his jaw. 'After all this time, is that any way to greet me?' Dry lips brushed lightly against his mouth leaving behind the waxy taste of lipstick. Then a finger tapped his bare thigh, reminding him more sharply of his vulnerability. 'Although it's a delight to see that you're so pleased to see me. The body never lies, does it?'

Her palm wrapped around his erection, kept hard by the metal cuff snugly fitted around its base.

'No!' he gasped. He didn't want to react positively to the stimulation, but his already tightly wound body leapt to the promise of relief.

'No? You're always so contradictory. Why ever not, Alaric? It's been such a long time for us, and you clearly need the relief. Who did this to you? Who left you so wanting? Let me make it right for you.'

The mattress dipped as she climbed on to the bed.

No! Oh, hell no. 'What are you doing?'

The hem of her dress swished against his thighs as she straddled his legs. Even without seeing her, Ric knew the dress she wore. The navy ensemble had been one of Scarlett's favourites.

The soft wool clove to her hourglass figure, emphasising her narrow waist and abundant hips – hips that her niece simply didn't possess. 'Robin, get off me.'

'It's OK. Relax, my love. Let me give you what you need.' The kiss of her pudenda against his most intimate flesh caused Ric's toes to curl. Every muscle he possessed pulled tight, but there was no escaping the inevitable slide of his cock into her pussy, or the damn sense of relief he gleaned from it. The metal cock ring kept him trapped in purgatory. But, while his mind rebelled at the choice of cavern in which he was likely to find relief, his dick remained untroubled.

'Robin, please. Don't do this.'

She struck him hard across the cheek, causing his head to bounce back against the headboard, which left his flesh tingling in two places.

'Scarlett,' she hissed, holding his chin so that she could smear kisses all across his mouth. 'I'm Scarlett. Surely you recognise the feel of your own wife?'

Her hands sought purchase on his chest, so that she held him down and caused his breathing to become shallow. Once she had him panting, her fingers closed tight upon his nipples. The sharp pain sent a delightful feeling of warmth zapping down to his loins. 'You like that, don't you? You always did like it rough. And so nice of you to leave these out.' She'd found the nipple clamps Zach had tipped upon the bed. The bite of the metal built on the need within his balls. Zach had already driven him close to the edge. Now he was teetering there.

'Robin. Untie me.'

'It's Scarlett. And no, I won't. You're supposed to be mine. Everything she had was supposed to be mine, but what do I want with furniture and jewels? You were the only thing she had that was worth possessing.' She fell upon him swift and hard then, pushing down, so that his cock drove deep into her moist pussy. 'Oh, yes. That's so good. I've waited so long for this.'

Her inner muscles fluttered around his shaft. 'Oh, Alaric. Darling. You're fucking me exactly like you used to fuck her. Do you remember? She always preferred to climb astride you.'

'I remember she talked less and got me off faster.'

'Then just tell me what to do. You know I'll do it.'

Given a choice, Ric wouldn't have had things this way, but from his current position he wielded little power, which meant he had to make his decisions wisely.

'Tell me.'

She did so want to please him. Poor Robin, she'd finally got the sex she'd always craved from him, but he was damned if she'd find fulfilment. 'You need to turn around,' he said. 'Scarlett always loved the reverse cowgirl. She loved the way it made my dick rub against her sweet spot.'

Predictably, Robin rose up so that he was free of her. Alas, only for a moment before she settled upon his cock again, this time facing away from him. Her broad bottom rubbed against his abs. 'Oh, yes. That is good,' she agreed. The catch in her voice certainly seemed to confirm her words.

'You need to touch me,' Ric instructed, knowing that his body wouldn't let him down. 'Stroke along my inner thighs. Now my balls.' Her fingers were immediately doing his bidding, dancing lightly over all his most sensitive flesh. A heavy, pulsing sort of fever tore at his senses, while his body embraced the contradiction of what he was pushing her towards. 'Wet your fingers. I think you know what to do.' He heard her suck. 'No – use the toy instead. Push it in slow, and then turn on the vibrations.'

'God, you're so kinky,' she giggled.

He was also done for. The dildo filled his arse to perfection, and gave his muscles something to clamp down upon when the vibrations worked their instant magic. His synapses screamed. Ric plunged fully into the fantasy scenario in his head of doing this with Kara and having Zach watch. 'Oh, yes, my love. Kara,' he cried, 'that's it, make me come.'

CHAPTER EIGHTEEN

'Wanker!' Kara cursed when Gavin removed the tape from her mouth. He'd dumped her unceremoniously in the back of a white van. She'd taken the absence of his car earlier to mean he'd gone, not that he'd swapped the BMW for a hired vehicle more suited to a kidnapping. 'Fuck!' She drummed her heels against the metal floor. She knew he wouldn't give up that easily. How stupid had she been not to take more care?

The skin around her mouth itched horribly. Kara tried to rub it with her bound hands. The tape had taken off her lipstick – the red smear of which remained on the tape back – along with what felt like a few layers of skin. Kara struggled into a sitting position, with her back to the van wall. How on earth had their relationship come to this? She knew he had control issues but really, she'd never have imagined he'd push things this far.

Gavin leaned over her, looking down not at her face, but her outfit. It was not something he'd ever have approved. He liked her flesh covered, her assets hidden, unless he wanted to look at them, and then he stripped her naked. Kara's top had ridden up leaving her midriff exposed, while her gymslip skirt had barely covered anything to begin with. That didn't stop him flipping back the pleats to peek at what she wore beneath it. His eyes rounded when he glimpsed her bare flesh. 'Hussy,' he muttered disappointedly, before leaning over to a plastic supermarket bag, from which he produced a clean pair of cotton briefs. 'You'll need to put these on before you see your mother.'

Her mother! So that was it. He was dancing to her mother's tune now, was he? Well, she didn't intend to see mummy dearest. She had a hot date with Ric and Zach to attend.

She smiled sweetly at him, though it proved hard not to make it more of a rictus grin. 'That'll be difficult with tape around my legs.' Kara let her cheeks rest the moment Gavin glanced down at the restraints.

'It'll wait till later. Once we're nearer home.' He shuffled backwards on his knees, and then rose. 'Once we're off the island you can get dressed properly.' He half turned as if to leave.

'Gavin,' she barked, determined to stop him before he got behind the wheel. 'Gavin.' He stopped at her second call, so that he stood silhouetted against the backdrop of the cliff face. 'I thought you wanted to talk. You're right. We ought to. You must realise that we're wrong for one another. You're a councillor. You can't have a wife who screws around and poses for naughty pictures. And I will do both those things. I already have. It won't take a minute to get those images out to the press.'

'No!' Immediately, Gavin took a swift pace back towards her. His normally placid face was screwed up into a puckered knot: mouth tightly pinched, his nostrils thinned. Kara's breath caught in her throat. For a moment, she thought he would strike her. Instead, he crouched beside her. 'Robin told me that you'd been prancing around half naked. She made no mention of photographs. I told her I knew my fiancée and that she wouldn't do that.'

'I have done it, and worse.' Kara couldn't help smiling inwardly at his consternation.

Gavin's mouth opened and snapped closed a few times as he chewed over that detail. However, the question over what could be worse remained unspoken. He patted her leg.

'I've let a guy screw me in the arse in public and I've masturbated another one for the camera. There's also a whole sequence of footage showing me entertaining two guys together.'

Instantly, his fingers snapped back from her thigh as though the contact burned. Gavin's face paled except for two red spots on his cheeks and another where his pulse showed in his temple. 'Why? Why in God's name would you do that?' He hugged his singed fingers to his chest.

'Because I can, Gavin. Because I enjoy it.'

'I don't believe you. You're bluffing.' His whole body quivered as he repeatedly shook his head. 'You're not that insane.'

Neither sanity or lack of it had anything to do with it. 'They are real, and make no mistake; I will go public if you attempt to coerce me into anything. And while we're on the subject of insanity, take note of your own actions. Kidnapping?' She raised her still bound hands. 'Unlawful imprisonment? I don't think either of those things will look good on your re-election material. And what's the purpose in it? Dragging me home isn't going to change my mind about anything. That happily-ever-after my mum has planned for us, it's not going to happen.'

She was talking in language he understood now. Scandal, even the slightest whiff of it, would destroy his political power

281

base like nothing else. Gavin seemed to sink into a stupor.

'Let me go, Gavin.' She held her bound wrists out towards him.

'I ...' Trance-like, moving as though wading through molasses, he produced a pair of scissors from the same plastic carrier bag as the underwear. Two snips freed her of the tape binding her legs. Another two and she'd be out of here. But he paused before making those cuts. Instead, his fingers worked over the small bones in her wrist in an unlikely caress. Kara stared straight at him.

'What?'

'You do know that he's been in rehab, don't you? And that he probably ought to have done time too.'

'You alluded to it earlier.' Clearly he referred to Ric. Zach simply didn't strike one as the sort to land himself in trouble. 'I've no reason to fear him.' Admittedly, the subject of Ric's wife was a touchy one, but not, she thought, because Ric had hurt her in any way. Rather the experience had emotionally scarred him. 'I'd be more worried about what nonsense Robin is likely to inflict. You let her take my phone. She'll use it to get to Ric.'

'Why would she need to do that?

Had he somehow overlooked Robin's manic glee over having her bound? Didn't he find it a little strange that a woman he barely knew would help him orchestrate her capture? 'She's his stalker, that's why. And you just gave her a way to get to him. Now will you free me, please?'

'Are you sure it can't happen between us?' he asked as he severed the remaining tape.

'Positive.' Kara rubbed the life back into her cramped wrists. She refused Gavin's outstretched hand to help her stand, and shuffled over to the doors on her bottom instead.

'How come you're here anyway?' she asked as her feet hit the gravel. 'Why aren't you in Hawaii with Gemma?'

Gavin smoothed a hand across his brow. 'I never went. She took her sister. I figured someone should benefit from the break. Where did it go wrong, Kara?'

She hopped out of the van into the night air. The sea breeze ruffled her clothing, and a fleeting smile crossed her face. 'It didn't go wrong. It'd never been right. I just let myself be swayed by the judgements of those around me instead of listening to myself. I've never wanted any of it – the politics, suburbia, a nice middle-class wholesome life.' She shook her head. 'That's what my mum wanted for me. She vetoed anything I did to try and escape that. The occasional night on the tiles was the limit of what she'd allow. She liked you because you have the same goals as her, but I don't want that respectability.'

'So you're shacking up with an ice-cream salesman and a sleazy photographer.' He clapped his hands. 'You're a goddamn fool, Kara. But thanks for setting me straight.'

She wasn't a fool. She was free.

Kara watched him drive off from the top of the cliff path.

Free, and hot for some kinky loving to wipe away the memories of the last hour of her life.

* * *

Zach sat hunched on the fort doorstep trying to preserve body heat. Goosebumps covered eighty per cent of his body and his toes were so cold that he no longer wanted to place them in contact with the ground. He'd rung the local police station, but they were on the mainland, and he wasn't anticipating a rapid response unit, having been rather scant on the details. Hence the edited version he'd given – 'I'm locked out. My friend's inside and I think this woman has him tied up' – rather than the truth.

It was a wonder they hadn't laughed at him.

Still, he leapt into action at the sound of approaching footsteps, and ran along the tunnel to the fallen portcullis.

'Hey,' he called through the iron latticework, his voice hoarse from all the shouting he'd done earlier. 'Hey! Over here.'

Profound relief surged though Zach's body when he recognised the slim figure jogging towards him as Kara. Ever since he'd realised Robin had her phone he'd worried over what had happened. After the way Robin had swung at him, all manner of crazy scenarios had entered his head. He hadn't entirely dismissed any of them.

Kara seemed well, if a little dishevelled. Her outfit was certainly one he and Ric would have appreciated, and would look ace with a pair of patent leather heels. Instead she wore sturdy flats.

She ran straight up to the portcullis and pushed her hands through the gaps to clasp his forearms.

'Are you all right?' they asked simultaneously.

'Fine,' Zach replied, though a residual ache remained in his stomach muscles from the impact. Robin had caught him off-guard more than anything. 'We need to get inside. Robin has Ric trapped.'

'Seriously? Shit!' The warmth of her hands left his skin, to curl instead around the bars of the portcullis. She gave it a test shake. 'How do we get you out?'

Zach scrubbed his hand through the long front of his hair so that it hung over his eyes instead of lying swept back. 'It's more an issue of getting in. Maybe if you could reach the study window?'

'I'll try it,' she said before he'd properly finished the sentence, and disappeared at once, leaving Zach pressed against the iron latticework straining for sounds for her ascent.

'Be careful.' No matter how hard he strained his hearing, the wind drowned out everything but the bleats of the nearby wildlife. He was almost ready to tear his hair out when light bled across the cobblestones beneath his feet. Two dogs bounded into the space beneath the archway, forcing him to fend off friendly licks in order to reach the door. The overhead light cast a radiant glow over Kara's smiling face. Zach wrapped her in a crushing embrace, lifting her clean off her feet in order to spin her around. 'Thank God! I don't know how you did it but huzzah.' He smacked a generous kiss across her beautiful lips.

'Lay off the smoochy stuff a moment.' Kara wriggled until he deposited her feet back on the floor. 'Which room's he in?'

'Master bedroom.' Zach paused long enough to sweep his tongue across his lips. 'Just so you're aware, I had him tied to the bed.'

'You tied him up?' Kara's eyes opened so wide that Zach was forced to look over his shoulder to make sure that nothing else had startled her. '*You* tied Ric up?'

'I blindfolded him too,' he added rather proudly, only for his conceit to immediately crumble into dejection. 'This is my fault. I let her in. Do you think he's realised it's Robin and not either of us with him?' Spurred by that uncertainty, Zach attacked the stairs with extra zeal, driving Kara ahead of him with some encouraging shoves.

An ominous quiet filled the first-floor corridor. Zach steered Kara towards the master bedroom, where they burst into the room together.

285

Zach realised two things immediately: one, his worst fears evidently hadn't been realised; and two, Ric had a camera in his hand. Where it had come from, he hadn't a clue. Maybe Ric kept a spare under his pillow. He certainly didn't go far without some form of recording device. The camera whined and spat out a ghastly white light. Once Zach had stopped seeing disorientating spots, he recognised a few other details.

Ric's blindfold lay on the pillow. Only one of his hands remained tied to the bed, the knot of which Ric sat working with his teeth.

Robin, whom Zach had expected to come at him like a banshee having a temper tantrum, lay on the floor in a semi-foetal position, her breathing disjointed and irregularly punctuated by pitiful sobs.

'What happened?' he asked, frozen to the spot. His gaze slipped back and forth between Ric and Robin, until the pressure of Kara's palm on his back urged him fully into the room.

'Did someone spill some perfume?' Kara enquired.

'Never mind that,' Ric barked. He beckoned Zach over. 'Help me with this.'

The knot was released with minimal effort. Zach immediately captured Ric's hands. His lover looked every bit as perfect as when Zach left him; no cuts or bruises, no deeply engraved lines worn into his face, in fact no evidence of any physical harm except the red impressions around his wrists caused by the cords. He traced each line with his fingertips. 'Are you – are you –?'

'Fine.' Ric shook off his hold to unclasp the cock-ring from his flaccid prick.

'What happened? What did she do?'

'Shush.' Ric knelt up on the mattress. 'Don't beat yourself

up. Come here instead.' His hands slid comfortingly into the fine hairs at the back of Zach's neck, so that he was pulled down into Ric's embrace. 'It was nothing I couldn't handle.' The pressure of Ric's mouth, hot and loving, seemed to confirm that. His passion didn't seem much dimmed since earlier, or maybe he craved company. Either way, the trace of his tongue against Zach's stirred memories of what they'd been enjoying prior to him answering the door. As Ric claimed he was fine, then Zach was obliged to believe him. But even the tingle of arousal stirring in his loins couldn't entirely quell his doubts.

Robin gave a horrified squeal, and curled herself tighter.

Kara crossed over to the bed. Rather than joining them, she crouched by Robin's side and gave her shoulder a prod. The girl gave a loud hiccough, but refused to look up. 'You didn't hit her, did you?' she asked Ric.

A tremor ran through Ric's limbs. He pulled away from Zach and crossed to the wardrobe, where he began rummaging for clothes. 'No, I bloody didn't. You don't need to feel sympathetic for her. She got what she asked for.' He pulled on a pair of jeans with torn-out knees and an equally tatty chrome-coloured jumper.

'Which was?'

Ric shook his head in reply, while Robin let out a teary burp. 'Stay away from me,' she said to Kara. She got to her feet and backed away from the bed. Ugly smears of mascara marred her heart-shaped face, while her usual red lipstick had been rubbed from her lips, leaving them seemingly bleached. 'Wanker,' she accused Ric. 'You did it on purpose.'

'I came. That's what you were trying to achieve, wasn't it? Proving you had me under control.'

'You were ready for me.'

287

'No. You disrupted Zach fucking me. Just because he laid me out like a banquet didn't mean you were invited to take a nibble. You ought to learn some manners.'

'Nibble?' Zach interjected, unsure if he actually wanted to know. He followed the line of Robin's gaze to where the discarded camera lay. The last picture on the slideshow showed Kara and him bursting into the room like a pair of comic-book heroes, complete with the requisite dumb expressions. Before that there were dozens of wildlife shots, pics of kitchen worktops and, much further back, some of him occupying the spare bed. Ric had to have sneaked in while he lay sleeping to have taken them. He'd have remembered posing in that position.

'Would you mind not going through that?' Ric insisted. 'She's already deleted all the relevant stuff. Not that doing so changes anything. The memories remain. May as well face the truth, Robin.' As if to emphasise whatever point he was making, Ric wrapped his arms around Kara, and nuzzled up against her neck.

Zach dropped the camera back on to the bed and then tilted his head questioningly, only for Ric to continue lavishing affection upon Kara, a display that caused pangs of jealousy to cramp his innards, and which turned Robin an unfortunate shade of puce. Her blotchy cheeks clashed hideously with her red hair.

'Robin objects to the fact that I love Kara and that her sexy body really turns me on. Hard photographic evidence of that proved a little too much for her. Luckily, the pictures are easily replaceable.' Ric pushed a hand inside Kara's top, so his fingers splayed across one of her breasts. Within seconds her nipples were hard, and poking against the fabric of her top.

Zach did his best not to wince. Ric loved Kara. Not him. He breathed deeply through his nose, determined to let the issue ride until he could address it properly.

'It was still my actions that made you come,' Robin snarled defiantly, though her voice wobbled a little and lapsed into a croak. She stared at Ric, tears trickling over her cheeks, though her eyes continued to track his movements. Her lips pursed tightly.

Ric gave her a cold smile that made his blue-grey eyes seem like splinters of ice. 'I guarantee that if you shove a vibrator up any man's arse he'll come. It's basic sexual mechanics. It doesn't mean a thing. It certainly doesn't prove that I want you. We both know who I was thinking about and, lady, it wasn't you.' Ric gave Kara another tight squeeze. 'Doesn't matter how many photographs you delete, the truth is right in front of you. Stick around and I'll give you a demonstration if you like.'

'No!' Robin shuddered.

'Best not,' Zach advised. 'I called the police. She stole Kara's phone –'

'– and colluded with my ex,' Kara interjected.

Zach paused a moment, surprised by the revelation. 'Colluded with Kara's ex, damn near knocked me out, broke in –' He stopped short of saying any more, still horrified by the idea of Robin putting her dirty, nasty fingers anywhere near any part of Ric's anatomy.

'And failed to make off with anything of value,' Ric concluded. 'I'm still here, and there wasn't any point where I wasn't in control of the situation.'

'That's no reason to let her get away with it,' Zach finished dubiously. 'Anyway, they're already coming out.'

Robin gave a dismayed screech, echoed in a less ear-splitting grumble from Ric a moment later. 'I'm not sure that was entirely necessary.'

'It totally was. Robin had been a pest for years; it was time to put an end to her sulking about. I had no idea what she was going to do. And what you've described doesn't convince me I acted wrongly.' Christ! He'd genuinely feared for Ric's life.

'Better go.' Ric gestured towards the door, staring pointedly at Robin. 'I said scat!' he added when she didn't move. 'And stay off the island, or I'll be sure to send the police round to pay you a home visit.' He snatched up his camera and snapped a mug shot of Robin's face, which provoked another horrid scream. 'I trust we can call it a day on this stupid obsession.'

Robin spat at him. Her gaze tracked across the three of them, and then, as requested, she fled.

'You shouldn't have done that either,' Zach complained. 'Ric, she's dangerous. When has she ever listened before?'

'This time is different.'

'Yeah? How is it?'

Ric closed his eyes and gave a weary sigh. 'It just is.'

Kara turned to wrap her arms around his waist. 'Maybe if you actually told us what happened, rather than just the edited highlights.'

'There isn't much more to tell.' He glanced up at Kara from under his eyelashes. 'Robin objected to the fact that I screamed your name not hers when I came. That always tends to piss off a woman.' His lips twisted into a smirk.

Zach embraced him too, so that Ric stood cocooned by his and Kara's bodies.

'Hey!' Ric pushed them both away a little. 'Chill the fuck out over the angst. I told you, it's no big deal. I put her up to it.'

'What?' Zach asked.

Ric simply nodded.

'Why the fuck would you do that?' Not that long ago Ric had promised to make a go of them having a proper relationship, involving fidelity and all the other stuff that defined commitment. This felt like a kick in the teeth. Zach slumped on to the end of the bed. 'I thought she'd just taken advantage.'

'She did.' Ric came to stand by Zach's knees. 'I just directed things a bit.' He clasped Zach's shoulders and pulled him close, so that Zach's brow pressed against Ric's abs. 'It wasn't like I had much choice. You left me bound. It's not as if I could fend her off. I used the situation to my advantage, rather than simply letting her have her victory. And while you might not agree with my methods, I think this way will be more effective than a restraining order at keeping her at bay.'

'Hm.' Zach shook his head. He didn't agree. What Robin had done deserved a stiff sentence rather than a rap on the knuckles, but he knew Ric, and squabbling over the issue wasn't going to get their new relationship off to a good start. 'Just promise me if she sets foot on Liddell Island again you'll call the cops, OK?'

'You got it, boss,' Ric said, giving him a salute.

'So what's the issue with the photographs?' Kara picked up the camera, which Ric immediately took off her.

'Confirmation that my cry wasn't just a slip of the tongue. It made her pretty irate. I have ... had a few shots of us looking pretty blissful together. Both Kara and me, and the three of us together. I think anyone looking at them would have had a hard time disputing the emotions depicted.'

Zach gave a barely perceptible nod of understanding, an action Kara duplicated.

'There were a few shots like that on my phone.'

'Yeah, I did point that out,' Ric said. 'I'm afraid your phone bit the dust. She seemed to like your pictures even less. It's over there.' He nodded his head towards the right-hand side of the bed.

Kara scooped it up to survey the damage. She turned the phone to show them. The screen had split right across. That, coupled with the sea-damage it'd sustained, made it a write-off. Kara took the sim card out of the back and dropped the rest into Ric's wastebasket. 'I'll have to get another one.'

A moment or two of uncomfortable silence followed, none of them knowing quite what to do. Eventually, Kara extended her hand towards the bed, where an assortment of bindings and toys still lay scattered across the rumpled duvet. 'So, what was it you had her use to make you come?' she enquired, seemingly innocently.

'Kara,' Zach barked. 'Not now. I think we'd all better go downstairs and chill out.'

Ric's gaze flicked towards an object half hidden by a pillow.

'This thing?' Kara lifted the dildo by its base, and flicked the switch that set it humming and performing a writhing dance. 'This little thing makes you come super hard?' She cocked an eyebrow.

Ric pursed his lips.

'It's hardly got any juice.'

'Yeah. I'd like to see you stave off coming if similarly tormented.'

Kara's grin immediately broadened. An impish light gleamed in her eyes. 'Bring it on, babe.' She placed a hand on her hip. 'Any time you want to test me out.'

'No,' Zach said firmly. 'Guys, this isn't the time.' His words fell on deaf ears. Ric's posture had already changed.

He looked predatory, while Kara's gaze kept flicking back and forth between Ric's face and the stubby vibrating cock.

'Five minutes,' Ric insisted, holding up that number of fingers to Kara. 'I'll be right back as soon as I've made this phone call. Then you'd better be ready to rumba.' He lifted the phone from its cradle and padded out of the room carrying it.

'You're kidding, right?' Zach shoved the front of his messy hair back into a quiff. 'We can't go about tonight as if nothing just happened. Robin's just – she's just –'

Kara shuffled along the edge of the bed until she sat beside him. She gave him a tight hug. 'Have you considered that maybe Ric wants to, because it'll help him forget? That, and why should Robin be allowed to wreck what we've planned?'

She did have a point. If it helped Ric, then he'd definitely do it. There was the matter of what had been discussed earlier to take into consideration too. He didn't want Ric changing his mind about giving a proper a relationship a go. Although maybe it was more accurate to say an improper relationship, as a threesome was hardly most people's definition of normal. 'Very well,' Zach tentatively agreed, which earned him another hug from Kara. 'But not in here.' The cloying scent of Robin's perfume still permeated the air.

'Where then?'

'Let's go upstairs instead. She's never been up there.'

They wound their way up the spiral staircase to Ric's studio, where he stood thoughtfully holding the phone to his chest. He smiled on seeing them. 'Couldn't you wait?' He placed the phone down on the computer desk. 'The station didn't seem too concerned. I think they thought you were drunk, Zach. Apparently it's well known that things get a bit kinky up here. They were going to stop by at the next low tide and check it out.'

So that was it.

'What sort of kinky stuff?' Kara enquired.

Zach considered poking her, until he saw Ric hit the dimmer switch, which reduced the light level to an ambient orange glow.

'Well, on this occasion, I think it mostly involves two guys and one girl, and all the permutations of sex that could possibly involve.' Ric flipped the lens cap off a tripod-mounted camera. 'You don't mind if I take a few pictures, do you?'

* * *

Kara stood under the glare of the spotlight pointed straight towards her, not sure what Ric expected or desired, only that she could feel her cheeks going red. In the end, she found herself walking towards him, ignoring the cameras' regular whirrs and belches of light. Judging by Ric's smile, that's what he'd wanted. The camera was just his record of events. It wasn't really anything to do with them. Once she stood right before him, Kara reached a hand out. Ric had never stood still and given her a proper chance to explore him. There'd been that one time on the beach, but it hadn't been nearly enough to satisfy her curiosity. She intended to remedy that now, and wasted no time in removing the baggy jumper that masked his shape. Ric's body was ripped with long lean muscles, the curves of which bulged beneath his skin, making a swooping road across which she could slide her palm.

Unlike Zach he was smooth and lacked significant amounts

of body hair, though his skin was slightly raised in the areas of his tattoo. In some ways his smoothness made him more tactile. It also seemed to make his skin more sensitive to her touch, judging by the way his breathing stuttered and the throb of his heartbeat sped when she circled certain spots.

'You're not eager for this, are you?' she teased.

Ric kept his expression neutral, but heat filled his eyes. Well, let him practise his restraint for whatever reason he chose. She knew how to undo him. Certain tricks never failed.

'You're not forgetting me?' Zach nuzzled up to her back. He rained gentle kissess on to the nape of her neck.

'Of course not.' She was just pacing herself.

Kara remained facing Ric. She held his gaze as she swept her hands upwards to encompass his shoulders, then down traversing his back until she reached the waistband of his jeans. His pale nipples she teased with her lips and tongue until the little peaks were proudly erect and he gasped each time she sucked hard.

In turn, Zach cupped her breasts, slipping his hands inside her top to free them from the confines of her bra. He pinched and rolled her nipples, sending sizzling darts of pleasure hurtling down towards her womb.

At no point did Ric reciprocate her touch, until her fingers found his fly, and then it was only to stay her hand. 'Not yet. Zach first.'

For a moment, Kara was tempted to disobey. Behind the shield of denim, Ric's erection formed a diagonal bulge that she itched to squeeze and suck. She wanted him naked for her, as she'd briefly glimpsed him upstairs. She wanted to undress him slowly, peeling away the items of his clothing one at a time, so she had time to savour each phase.

There had always been something very appealing to her

about an erect man with his fly undone, and his trousers still hugging his thighs. Perhaps because it hinted at urgency. What then would be the effect of two such men, side by side? She glanced backwards at Zach, knowing immediately what she wanted to do.

She turned her attention to him, teasing him in the way she had Ric. They were alike, but different. Both tall and wiry, but Zach was broader and more compact, and slightly heavier too. The only ink on his skin was a small pentacle over his right hip. What Zach did have was that tantalising line of hair that ran down his body like an arrow pointing to his groin. Zach's pure manliness had been the thing that attracted her to him in the first place. He possessed a kind of visceral pull that no amount of man-sculpting could ever compete with. More importantly, Zach knew how to give, and did so without reservation.

He lifted her skirt in order to dip a hand between her parted thighs. 'No panties, Kara?' His touch there made her vocalise a sigh.

'Ric kept accusing me of being lax regarding their whereabouts, so I thought I'd keep things simple.'

'You left them in your underwear drawer.'

Ric chuckled. 'That is probably the best place for them. Is she turned on, Zach?'

'What do you think?'

Kara turned so that she stood side-on to both men. This way she could partially see them both.

'Show me,' Ric insisted. Rather than flipping up the front of her skirt, Zach withdrew his wetted fingers and offered them up for Ric's inspection. To her astonishment, Ric's pink tongue flicked out and tasted her dew. He then sucked Zach's fingers clean. Seeing him do so sent a shiver of anticipation racing through her innards. 'So, about this kinky stuff?' she asked.

Ric's fingers slipped into her cunt, briefly filling her, before he withdrew them to offer Zach the same pleasure he'd just enjoyed.

Zach sucked Ric's fingers clean with noisy relish. He seized hold of Kara's hand and pressed it to his covered cock, urging her with a silent roll of his hips to play with him, to stroke and squeeze.

This time when Kara reached for Ric's fly he didn't object, because simultaneously she unfastened Zach's zip too. She encompassed Zach's cock with her hand while she knelt to take Ric in her mouth.

Perfect. She'd always loved using fellatio as a tease. Ric couldn't remain aloof as she sucked. She drew him to her, so that his fingers soon meshed within her hair. Only then did she leave him momentarily bereft in order to give Zach the same pleasure. If she could have sucked them both at once, she would have. As it was, she contented herself by alternating. Above her, she was thrilled when the two men began to kiss. Watching them together tumbled her heart inside her chest. It made everything fizz, and infused her actions with additional energy.

It came almost as a surprise when as one they lifted her into a standing position. Ric claimed her top, Zach her skirt, so that she stood between them naked.

Ric walked her backwards to his little rest area of leather pouffes. He remained standing while Zach sank into the squishy cushions. He pulled Kara down into his arms, and their mouths and bodies met. One hand remained on Kara's breast, while Zach used the other to aid her in removing his trousers. His cock stood beautifully proud, surrounded by its thick nest of curls. She loved that the two men were so different, and yet so into one another and her. That they understood her needs made this special too. Zach didn't waste time. He filled her, pushing deep into her hot wet hole. They'd had sex many times now, but she recalled the time when Ric had thwarted them just shy of this point. Today he allowed them their fun, though he flitted between them, stealing kisses first from her and then from Zach.

When he kissed Zach, she felt the effects of it ripple through Zach's body, warming him, firing him up, so that he demanded more, and became more aggressive about getting it. He pumped into her hard, bucking with all his might so that she jigged up and down and her breasts bounced within the cage he'd made with his hands.

Ric wasn't content to remain left out for long. He let his jeans fall, so that they puddled around his ankles. Nude, he was every bit as magnificent as she remembered; something made all the more exciting by his lack of modesty.

'Switch around,' Ric urged. He smacked her arse for emphasis.

When Zach persuaded her to lift up off his cock, Kara expected Ric to take his place in her pussy. Instead Zach simply adjusted his position, to a more upright one, with his back supported, before welcoming her back on to his lap. She understood a little better when Ric knelt down behind her. His fingers stroked around the whorl of her anus, tickling, teasing, only dipping inside long enough to make her crow, before he withdrew again. She'd loved when he'd taken her in the arse, but this felt different – sharper, more intense, because Zach already possessed her cunt.

Ric nuzzled her neck. 'You might not be ready for this,' he whispered close to her ear. 'I'll understand if you say no.

298

I realise you're not that experienced, but if you trust me, if you relax, I think we might manage it.'

'Manage what?' she forced herself to ask, though she already knew. It was pretty obvious from the way he was now exploring her hole with two wetted fingers. She just wanted to hear him say it.

She desperately wanted him to do it too.

'Oh, you know.' He added a third finger into the mix, so that it felt almost like a stubby little cock was shifting in and out of her arse. 'A little DP.' He switched back to two fingers, this time pushing them deeper and scissoring them apart. 'What do you say, Kara? We both know it's what you've been angling for ever since you first walked into this studio.'

The picture she'd so admired lay just across the room. With only a slight turn of her head, she could make out its crisp lines and the absolute joy on the woman's face.

'Won't it be too tight for you?'

Ric nibbled the base of her earlobe. 'That'll be half the fun. I'll be able to feel Zach. He'll be able to feel me. It'll be like I'm fucking him as well as you.' He blew a kiss at his lover. 'So, what do you say? Shall I put my cock in you?'

Really, there was no persuasion involved. They all knew it was going to happen. This was simply the drum roll announcing the moment. It was also Ric's method of saying, 'Hey, I'm still in charge here.' His cock nuzzled between her butt cheeks: warm, solid, slippery with lube. He pressed against her hole, but didn't delve inside. 'I need to hear you say it, Kara. I need to know this is what you want. Think carefully now, before we get a taste for it.'

Kara wriggled back against him as best she could without dislodging Zach from her cunt. 'Yes, please,' she whispered.

'Don't just do it to prove you can hold out when I couldn't.'

'I want this. I've wanted it from the moment we met.' She glanced again at the image that had seeded the thought in her brain.

'Yeah.' He squeezed her tight. 'Hold still, then.'

Kara's fingers clawed at Zach's biceps as Ric slowly entered her. It was a lesson in balance and endurance, both in waiting for something and trying to dampen down her reaction to it. Having both of them fill her rode the line between pleasure and pain. It was sweet and sinful, but overwhelming too. The intensity of it dazzled her, so that she moaned and sobbed aloud, unaware of what she was saying.

She wanted both less and more. Less fullness, more pleasure, yet the two were inescapably combined. Kara could barely tell the men apart. She knew only that they filled her, and that every part of her that could possibly experience pleasure did. It roiled inside her, building pressure, until her body jerked hopelessly.

Ric strained against her back, holding himself rigid, while Zach raced, dictating their pace.

She had a job here on the island; a future with these two men. This might be the first time they did this, but it surely wouldn't be the last.

Slowly, slowly, as their movements synchronised, Kara knew true bliss.

This was surely what her body was made for. They soared, holding tight to one another and then finally collapsed, satisfied and exhausted.

Zach rained gentle kisses upon her face. Ric's head rested between her shoulder blades. They held her close, even when they were no longer inside her, proving that it had been every bit as intense for them. After a while, they lay side by side on their backs. Kara left the men cuddling and padded over to the tripod-mounted camera.

'I think that's enough, don't you?' She hit the off switch, whereupon the background hum of the battery fell silent.

Zach sat up. 'What happened with your ex?' he asked. 'You said that Robin colluded.'

Kara unconsciously tapped the camera. 'He saw sense. He won't make trouble again or come anywhere near Liddell Island. I'm not worth his career.' She smiled. 'But just in case, I've a few things that'll help to convince him. You know, maybe we're not quite finished with this after all.' She dismounted the camera from its stand and trotted back to the men. 'Smile, please.'

Ric glared. 'That's an expensive piece of kit, you know.'

'Excellent! Then I might manage to not chop your head off.' The flash blinked into life as she took a shot from the hip. 'I'm going to call this collection "Two Adorable Wankers". Now, masturbate each other. I want to watch you both ejaculate.'

Ric looked ready to tear her head off, but Zach snorted with laughter. 'I love it.'

He immediately reached for Ric's cock. 'I love you both.'

Lightning Source UK Ltd.
Milton Keynes UK
UKHW01n1434090718
325444UK00008B/451/P